to Jona!

COMMISSARIO STANCATO'S
BLIND DATE

A Commissario Beppe Stancato Novel (6)

By Richard Walmsley

Buona lettura!

Richard Walmsley

22/4/24

Other titles by this author

The Puglia series
Dancing to the Pizzica (2012)
The Demise of Judge Grassi (2013)
Leonardo's Trouble with Molecules (2014)

Short Stories
Long Shorts (2015 – new version)

The Commissario Beppe Stancato novels – set in Abruzzo
The Case of the Sleeping Beauty (2015)
A Close Encounter with Mushrooms (2016)
The Vanishing Physicist (2017)
Death is Buried (2020)
The Vendetta Tree (2022)
Commissario Stancato's Blind Date (2024)

The Curse of Collemaga (2019)
A tale of modern-day witchcraft set in Abruzzo

Puglia with the Gloves Off (2019)
A travelogue

© Copyright 2024

Richard Walmsley

Email: author@richardwalmsley.com
Web: www.richardwalmsley.com
nonno-riccardo-publications

Front cover design

Antonio Matteo Adamo

(...who was fourteen years old when he created this design)

Jonathan Wright

(...who put the whole book cover together)
Computer services
fixit@jonwright.com

(South Bucks area)

This novel is dedicated to all those men and women who tirelessly combat the mafia in Italy - by any means at their disposal.

1:	Commissario Stancato's dilemma	1
2:	The Commissario miscalculates…	11
3:	The Commissario becomes involved in other matters…	19
4:	The sightless witness…	26
5:	Astonishing insights…	38
6:	Life-changing revelations…	44
7:	In a safer place…?	55
8:	On the darker side of Italy…	66
9:	Pippo Cafarelli takes over…	70
10:	The Commissario's volta face…	78
11:	Annamaria's love of water…	85
12:	Annamaria Intimo's sense of smell…	96
13:	How to interrogate a suspect…	108
14:	Cat out of the bag…	118
15:	How it's done in Italy…	124
16:	A glimpse behind the scenes…	133
17:	Into the lion's den…	136
18:	Not such a good night…	146
19:	Small talk…?	162
20:	The quick-step…?	171
21:	The grieving 'widow'	179
22:	The end of the road…?	193
23:	A 'date' with destiny…?	201
24:	Unforeseen consequences…	213
25:	Close encounters with an archbishop – et al…	220
26:	As one Questore to another…	228
27:	The youngest marriage counsellor in Italy	237

28: How not to be bored in church..249

29: The new Questore leaves his mark...............................260

30: Plus ça change…?..273

1: *Commissario Stancato's dilemma...*

His mobile phone was ringing on his bedside table whilst he and Sonia were still asleep. It looked as if it was still dark outside. But maybe that was simply because the curtains were still drawn. Sonia and he had been out to dinner with friends in Atri the previous evening and had not got back until well after midnight. He let it go on ringing, reluctant for once to interrupt his slumber prematurely.

The bedroom door opened. That was odd, thought Beppe. Sonia was lying asleep beside him, so it could not have been her entering the room. Sonia simply turned away from the intrusive version of a Chopin tune which Beppe had recently installed on the device. A mistake, he was now thinking. Then he became aware of his daughter, Veronica, standing by the bed. Chopin had become deafening. This, he realised on opening his eyes a bit wider, was because Veronica was holding the phone right up to his left ear.

'*Rispondi papà! Per favore!* [1] I was woken up by that silly tune. But I'm glad you're both safely home – when I heard your phone ringing and ringing, I thought you must have forgotten to take it with you.'

Beppe smiled sleepily at his daughter. Veronica had grown increasingly aware of life's uncertainties as she grew older. She had used the excuse of the ringing phone to reassure herself that her *mamma* and *papà* were safely back in the fold, Beppe realised. She had also become ever more assertive these days. She had a pretty face and a charming smile coupled with an appealing sparkle in a pair of bright brown eyes. She had inherited her father's dark southern Italian skin, unlike her younger brother who had taken after his Abruzzese-born mother. It was difficult not to react positively towards her – and

---

[1] Answer it please, papà.

she knew it. Veronica even pressed the green icon before handing the phone over to her father.

'Another woman in your life who has learnt how to get her own way with you, *amore!*' mumbled a sleepy voice next to him in the bed. Veronica gave an engaging giggle.

'Buongiorno, mamma!' she said as she made her retreat out of the bedroom before the positive effect of her dramatic entrance risked wearing off. She wondered if her *papà* had secretly understood her real motive for barging into her parents' bedroom. He always seemed to understand what was going on in her mind. She felt a warm glow spread through her body at this thought.

'Go back to bed, Lori,' [2] she said to her little brother, who had emerged from their bedroom. 'It's just *papà's* phone going off. It's only half past seven.'

'But school,' he muttered. 'It's getting late, isn't it?'

Lorenzo had only recently begun to observe the passing of time, but his stomach was telling him it was breakfast time.

'We've got another twenty minutes in bed, Lori – if we get dressed quickly.'

Lorenzo, very different to his sister, returned to the bedroom, got dressed without help – apart from doing up his shoe laces - and shuffled his way into the kitchen to read his favourite *vignetta* [3] - significantly, about a seven-year-old boy whose father was a cop. He had helped himself to his morning fruit yoghurt from the family-sized fridge.

Back in their parents' bedroom, Beppe had managed to force himself to utter the word *'pronto'* to whoever was phoning him, praying that it was not an emergency, but a wrong number.

---

[2] Lori – an affectionate contraction of 'Lorenzo'
[3] Cartoon book

The clock on his screen informed him that it was much later than he had imagined.

A young man's voice spoke timidly.

'*Mi dispiace disturbarla, Commissario.*' [4]

Beppe remained silent. He did not recognise the voice.

'I'm sorry to phone at this hour, *Commissario*. But my superiors asked me to call you early this morning. They haven't had a reply to their invitation yet...'

'*Ma Lei, chi è, signore?* [5]

'*Agente* Mario Acrina – from the *Questura* in Terramonti. The mayor and our *Questore* [6] are very anxious to meet you today...'

'TODAY!?' snapped Beppe, aware that he was unjustifiably taking it out on this junior officer. He had quite deliberately declined to think about this potential career move ever since it had been mooted by his own *Questore,* Mariastella Martellini, some three weeks previously.[7]

Sonia was no longer drowsy. She was sitting up in bed looking alert. But she had a mischievous smile on her face. She was well aware that Beppe had 'shelved' any decision about taking the next step up the ladder of promotion. His name had been put forward by some invisible network of high-ranking officials with a view to him being promoted to the rank of *Questore* in the province of Terramonti, due to the pending retirement of the present incumbent.

'Yes, *Commissario* - I am charged with the responsibility of reminding you that you are expected here at

---

[4] I'm sorry to disturb you, chief inspector.

[5] But who are you?

[6] Chief of police in charge of a whole province. He or she is described as a 'director' – the 'Questore' is technically not a police officer.

[7] See 'The Vendetta Tree'

10.30 this morning. Shall I confirm that you are available to attend at that time?'

It was on Beppe's lips to refuse the invitation. But one look at the intense expression on his wife's face was sufficient to check the impulse. He simultaneously had an image of his own *capo* shaking her head in utter disbelief at his total lack of ambition.

'Tell your superiors I shall be there by eleven, *Agente Acrina,*' he stated defiantly.

'*Sì Signor Commissario,*' said the young officer, obviously greatly relieved. '*Grazie mille, Commissario.*'

The line went dead. Officer Acrina had been instructed to exact a response from the *Commissario* and bring the call to a close before the man he was addressing could change his mind. The die was cast.

'It won't do you any harm to attend this preliminary meeting, *amore.* You'll be in a much better position to say 'yes' or 'no' to this post if you go there in person. You might even be favourably impressed.'

Sonia had uttered these words in a gently persuasive voice. He knew Sonia was right. They had never discussed the financial aspect of a promotion to this high-level job. It was irrelevant to the moral issues involved – even if the move would triple his salary.

'When I first told you about the offer, just as we were leaving Mariastella Martellini's [8] country house, all I said to you, *amore,* was: 'I have an important decision to make'. You simply replied: '*Oh no you don't*'. You remember saying that, don't you, Sonia?'

She merely smiled and nodded by way of reply. She knew what was coming next.

---

[8] She is the young Questore at the Pescara police headquarters.

'So, I am presuming that Mariastella had already spoken to you beforehand.'

Sonia merely nodded again. She suspected that Beppe would accuse the two women in his life of collusion.

'Mariastella only wanted to give you the opportunity of applying for this post, Beppe. I had the impression that she did not want to be responsible for your missing out, even though she patently does not wish to lose you.'

Beppe brushed aside her words.

'I understand that, *amore*. But I was struck by what you said to me in answer to what I hadn't yet told you. What were you implying when you said that I did *not* have a difficult decision to make?'

Sonia sighed. She might have guessed that Beppe had been analysing the words she had uttered without thinking, on that memorable occasion as they drove away from Mariastella's country house.

'I am sure I simply meant that whatever you decide, I shall still love you just the way you are.'

Those simply expressed words were sufficient to conquer his resistance. He kissed Sonia on the mouth and then proceeded to get himself ready for the day ahead – presenting himself at the breakfast table dressed in a suit and tie. Veronica giggled. Lorenzo stared with his mouth open.

'But the last thing you said to me as we drove away from Mariastella's house was: 'And *I* have some news to tell *you!*' said Beppe. 'So far, you haven't been all that forthcoming...'

'I remember that!' piped up Lorenzo. '*Mamma* was about to tell us she's going to have a baby. *È vero, mamma?*'[9]

Beppe looked self-satisfied. His premonition at the time had been accurate. He really was developing some of the

---

[9] It's true, isn't it?

Archbishop of Pescara's ability to foresee future events. So, apparently, was his thoughtful, seven-year-old son.

'We might even know for sure by the time you get back from Terramonti this evening, Beppe,' said Sonia.

Both parents walked their children to school. There were smiles on all their faces. Veronica was devising in her head what story she should come up with to explain why her *papà* was dressed up to the nines in civilian garb. She decided not to bother – nobody would even recognise her father, dressed in a suit. She would just mumble something about an uncle, in the unlikely event of anyone asking. Far more important was the discussion as to whether the unconfirmed new-born would be a boy or a girl.

'*Amore mio,* would you be the one who phones Mariastella to tell her I shall be a bit late today?'

Sonia grinned mischievously.

'Scared she might forbid you to go to Terramonti?' she taunted.

* * *

Thirty minutes later, the *Commissario* was driving serenely along the road to Terramonti. In point of fact, the distance between Atri - where Beppe and family shared a very tall house with her parents - and Terramonti was about 35 kilometres; a mere three kilometres more than his daily trip to Pescara, but along country roads rather than the hectic main road down to Pescara. The distinct likelihood that a third son or daughter would arrive, suddenly made the notion of a higher salary quite attractive. But no! He would not allow himself to become attached to the idea of promotion as a *fait accompli*. His rise to the rank of *Questore* was far from certain, given his chequered career as a maverick *Commissario*. He would go out of his way to enlighten his interviewers as to his regular departures from standard police procedures. Beppe wondered whether Mariastella Martellini, his very own *Questore*, had already outlined to his potential future employers, details of his all-too-often unconventional approach to policing. He found himself very much at ease as he alighted from his car in front of the modern-looking *Questura* in Terramonti. The town of Terramonti, which he had never visited, had looked picturesquely traditional. Quite the opposite of Pescara, which had had to be largely rebuilt in modern style after the Americans had almost managed to bomb it out of existence during the Second World War – when the majority of bombs, destined to destroy the railway station, had landed in the city.

It was a few minutes before 10.30 when he announced his arrival at the reception desk to the officer on duty.

The smart-looking officer with a pair of knowing blue eyes greeted him with a smile.

'I apologise for waking you up so early, *Commissario*. Those in charge here thought fit to relegate the important task of contacting you to a very junior officer such as me.'

Beppe looked at the young man with his famous unblinking stare – for all of five seconds - before breaking into a radiant smile. He even held out his right hand to *Agente* Mario Acrina. Even if it had not been intentional, this low-ranking officer had succeeded in compressing into one short innocent-sounding sentence, a multitude of implications about the underlying set-up in this police headquarters.

It was as if the young officer was begging him not to pass judgement on him for his intrusive act of that morning. Officer Mario Acrina was looking apologetically at Beppe.

'You are entirely forgiven, *Agente* Acrina!'

Beppe walked off in the direction that the officer had indicated. Mario Acrina followed Beppe with his eyes. He was wondering if things might begin to change if this unusual *Commissario* was appointed as their next *Questore.*
'*In bocca al lupo, Commissario!*' [10] he murmured to himself.

* * *

Beppe felt the tension in the air as soon as he was shown into the upstairs meeting room by an unsmiling uniformed police woman. She had not made any attempt to introduce him formally, but had simply left him by the open doorway.

Two men were sitting behind a table facing the door through which he had entered. One of the men was wearing a mayoral red, white and green sash attached round his neck – despite being dressed smartly, but very informally. The second man was much older than the one who Beppe assumed really was the mayor. This man looked as if he had got up in a hurry that morning and had not had time to have a decent shave. He was dressed in an old brown corduroy suit with a faded purple tie whose knot did not quite reach his open shirt collar. He looked vaguely harassed and ill-at-ease. Neither man had stood up, so Beppe simply sat down on the chair facing the two men. Beppe had the distinct impression that he had interrupted a not-very-cordial *discussione.* [11] Beppe assumed that the man in the corduroy suit must be the out-going *Questore.*

'Excuse me, *signore,*' began the mayor with a note of irritation in his voice. 'How can we help you? We are expecting an important visitor here very soon...'

---

[10] 'In the mouth of the wolf' = Best of luck!
[11] Can also mean an angry verbal exchange in Italian.

It struck Beppe that his 'early' arrival had thrown them. The couple assumed that he was some sort of uninvited intruder.

'Oh,' he said. 'I do beg your pardon, *signori*. I am sorry to be a nuisance. I am merely here for an interview. I understood you were looking for a new *Questore?*'

There must really be some serious lack of communication in this establishment, thought Beppe.

The look of horror on the mayor's face was comical. He leapt to his feet and walked round the table with his right hand outstretched.

'I am so sorry, *Commissario*. I didn't realise it was you. You look very different to the sort of person I was expecting. Please forgive us. My name is Di Domenico, Benedetto. Welcome to our beautiful town, *Commissario*. We are very proud of it.'

'It does indeed look very inspiring,' conceded Beppe with the appearance of a friendly smile. 'And I am sorry not to comply with the image of me which you had conceived.'

The mayor looked flustered and babbled some apologetic excuse about a fuzzy portrait photo as he sat down again behind the table.

'And this is our current *Questore, Dottore* [12] Elmo Ferretti, who is looking forward to passing on his responsibilities to…a suitable successor,' added the mayor in a tone of voice that made it sound as if he would like to have chosen harsher words. Beppe turned and smiled at Elmo Ferretti, thinking the man's surname sounded too much like *furetto* for comfort's sake. The epithet 'ferret' seemed vaguely apt to describe the sly look conveyed by the man's eyes.

The *Questore* merely reached across the table to shake Beppe's hand. Beppe was endeavouring to interpret the

---

[12] A title of respect – not necessarily to a medical man.

expression on the man's face; a cunning look of sadistic anticipation that this newcomer would soon be suffering in his place, maybe?

The 'ferret' managed to utter a few surly words.

'We were expecting you at eleven o'clock, *Commissario.*'

'I understood the interview was at 10.30, *Signor Questore.* I apologise for being a few minutes late.'

Beppe was beginning to enjoy himself – for reasons he did not bother to analyse.

'Some junior officer informed me that you would be arriving at 11 o'clock. I shall reprimand him as soon as we have finished here, *Commissario,* I can assure you!'

'Not on my account, please, *Signor Questore.* I have already spoken to *Agente* Mario Acrina – a very bright young man, I thought. I have apologised for treating him with a lack of due courtesy when he informed me that he had been ordered to phone me at 7.30. I was still asleep at the time.'

Beppe was gratified to see a look of fleeting bewilderment on the *Questore's* face that this outsider had registered not just the young officer's full name, but had also passed an opinion as to his worthiness to be a policeman.

'Now, should we not begin this interview, *signori?'* said Beppe, as if he was already in charge. 'I'm sure we all have many other matters to attend to today.'

It had all panned out very well, thought Beppe. He felt he had set up a situation in which he would be rejected for this post out-of-hand. He would not have to make the decision which would overturn his life completely. So far, he was feeling moderately self-satisfied with the image of himself which he presumed he had established.

2:   *The Commissario miscalculates...*

'I am sure you are aware, *Commissario,* that as a mere mayor, I am not in a position to appoint you as the future *Questore* of Terramonti. That is the sole prerogative of the *Ministero degli Interni* [13] in Rome. But I understand that those individuals involved in this particular appointment have been approached by a number of high-ranking police officers – and even a scientist and some archbishop, I am told – all of whom have vouched for your suitability for such a position. Your reputation, so it would seem, precedes you, *Commissario.*'

Beppe was temporarily at a loss for words after Benedetto Di Domenico's revelations. Could it really be the case that his friend Don Emanuele, the Archbishop of Pescara, had been dragooned into plotting his demise as a maverick but contented *Commissario* in Pescara? He wondered if the 'number of high-ranking police officers' amounted to just one - his own *capo,* Mariastella Martellini. Maybe she really *did* want to be shot of him, just to ensure the rest of her career would be spent in relative calm. And a scientist, the mayor of Terramonti, had said? Who on earth...? Despite his bewilderment, the *Commissario* felt that a reaction to the mayoral utterance was called for.

'I am, of course, flattered by their appraisal of my capabilities, *Signor Sindaco.* But I fear they may have exaggerated. I have often displayed an alarming tendency to ignore correct procedure or even fail to notify my superiors as to certain actions that I have taken on my own initiative. It has, on occasions, got me into all sorts of trouble.'

'Well, *Commissario,* a number of your acquaintances, quite obviously, have a higher opinion of your achievements than you yourself do. Or perhaps you possess the very qualities

---

[13] The Home Office

of character and a willingness to be innovative which are just the attributes that we are looking for. I gather from *Questore* Martellini that your team worship the ground you walk on,' concluded the mayor with an artful smile on his face.

Was there nothing that he, Beppe, could say to stem this tide of adulation which totally ignored his past misdeeds? He cast a hopeful glance in Elmo Ferretti's direction. Maybe Beppe was expecting to intercept a look of cynical disbelief at the mayor's eulogistic pronouncements. No joy from *that* quarter - the *Questore* was impatiently tapping out some message on his mobile phone.

The man sent his message and looked up to find himself under scrutiny from this newcomer.

'I ordered refreshments to be sent up before this interview began, *Commissario*. I was just reminding someone of their duty,' stated the ferret.

The mayor could be heard tutting quietly in disapproval.

'It is possible that *Commissario* Stancato has more pressing matters on his mind than coffee and biscuits at the moment, don't you think, *Signor Questore?*' stated the mayor with ill-concealed impatience.

'*Everybody* requires a cup of coffee at this time of the morning, *Signor Sindaco!*' replied the *Questore* brusquely, in an attempt to conceal his discomfort at being snubbed so openly.

'I wouldn't mind a cup of coffee, *signori,*' Beppe interjected calmly. He had been accurate in his earlier assessment; there was absolutely no love lost between the mayor and the *Questore*. But, whilst addressing both men, Beppe had cast an apologetic glance in the mayor's direction. The mayor nodded, as if to himself, in covert approval; their candidate was a diplomat, he realised. Another good point in his favour!

After five minutes had elapsed and no refreshments had appeared, the *Questore* stood up and, without a glance at Beppe – or the mayor – left the room with an impatient intake of breath.

Beppe looked expectantly at the mayor, who was trying to maintain a neutral expression on his face.

'I would like to invite you for an early lunch, *Commissario*. Just the two of us. I know the perfect *trattoria* where we shall be undisturbed.'

Beppe hesitated for a minute, his usual indecisiveness when it came to making decisions about his own personal life had come into play.

'I really ought to be heading back to Pescara, *Signor Sindaco*. We are all engaged in a rather complex murder case...'

It was a blatant untruth, in point of fact. Beppe had just invented this excuse so as to extricate himself from the dilemma he was reluctant to face up to.

The mayor did not react in the way Beppe was expecting. He was smiling in a manner which it was difficult to decipher. His subsequent quietly spoken words came as a shock.

'I think you will find yourself to be in a much better position to resolve your justifiably conflicting feelings over this appointment, *Commissario,* if you would graciously consent to spend just one more hour in my company. I too have a number of pressing engagements looming this afternoon...but the food at *La Buona Forchetta* [14] is quite exceptional.'

The return of Elmo Ferretti, looking very cross, did not give Beppe time to invent a further excuse, He merely nodded curtly at the mayor – who, despite himself, Beppe was beginning to like.

---

[14] Literally: The Good Fork. Meaning 'A lover of good food'

'Have to forego the coffee, *signori*. The whole police force apart from *Agente* Acrina on front desk duty suddenly seem to have discovered the need to leave the police station on various vital missions in town...' concluded the *Questore*, in a voice which registered fake surprise at such an event.

'Never mind, *Signor Questore*. The *Commissario* needs to go away and consider whether he is interested in the position here and to discuss it with his wife and his own *Questore* in Pescara. Is there anything you would like to ask the *Commissario* before he takes his leave?'

'When can you start, *Commissario?*' said Elmo Ferretti abruptly. 'I have the impression you are eminently suited to fulfil the role of *Questore* here in Terramonti.'

Elmo Ferretti shook Beppe's hand in a perfunctory manner, turned round and headed for the door without so much as a glance in the mayor's direction.

Benedetto Di Domenico merely shrugged his shoulders in Beppe's direction without a word. There was nothing to be said apart from the all too obvious – and the mayor was not the kind of person to waste his breath on idle words.

* * *

The trattoria *La Buona Forchetta* lived up to its name. Beppe loved restaurants which clung on to a traditional ambience rather than eating places where the owners had decided to install clinically clean white walls and stainless-steel accoutrements all over the place with modern art pictures of garish geometrical designs attached permanently to the walls – whose identical copies could be found anywhere in the world.

He chose to eat a simple pasta dish of fresh tuna fish in a sauce of black olives and baby tomatoes flavoured with parsley.

'The best tuna dish I've ever tasted,' confessed the *Commissario* reluctantly to his lunch companion.

Over a simple *macedonia di frutta,* the mayor of Terramonti began to talk.

'You must have worked out for yourself, *Commissario,* that relationships in the police headquarters are somewhat strained. On bad days, it is totally dysfunctional. I cannot altogether blame the gentleman concerned. He lost his wife to cancer about one year ago.

'I gained a negative impression hinted at by *Agente* Acrina this morning on my arrival. But surely, the situation should become manageable again with the appointment of any new *Questore?*' asked Beppe hopefully.

'Still trying to find wriggle room, are we, *Commissario?*'

The mayor had spoken the words with genuine amusement. It was impossible to be offended.

'I fear that morale throughout the *Questura* has deteriorated almost to the point of collapse,' continued the mayor. 'Let me give you an example, *Commissario...*'

The *'Commissario'* in question had to stop himself saying to this amiable mayor, who had dropped the pretence of sounding officious during their brief lunch, 'Just call me Beppe – or even Giuseppe.' Before he committed this major breach of *le regole del galateo,* [15] he was caught up with the incredible story of corruption which the mayor had begun to relate. It struck Beppe, after only a minute or so, that this state official was putting total trust in his – Beppe's – discretion. It was a sobering moment.

---

[15] The rules of etiquette – far more rigid than they are in the Anglo-Saxon culture.

'As far as I can gather from various sources, there are two police officers involved. I won't name them until an official investigation has been initiated – which will probably be never under the present incumbent. I'll just call them *Agente G* and *Agente L.* They are relatively new recruits – with an eye out for ways they can profit from being officers of the law.

They have relatives – cousins or uncles – and even close 'buddies' who are plumbers or electricians by trade. They pick on the gullible or the vulnerable by getting themselves invited into their homes under some pretext. *'We understand there has been a break-in in one of your neighbours' apartments a few nights ago'* is their favourite ploy to gain admittance. They will find fault with their plumbing or their electrics – all too often in old houses or flats where the meters date back a few years and genuinely don't comply with modern regulations. *'We'll be obliged to report you to the proper authorities,'* they threaten. And then they offer the occupants a way out – all smiles and sympathy. *'We know somebody who can solve the problem for you at a reasonable price,'* they claim.

If any of their victims suggest they too know someone who is an electrician, the two officers begin to issue veiled threats – all with a smile on their faces. Most people just give way and take the easy way out. The net result is a lucrative little side line activity – difficult to nail down. This kind of corruption is spreading. It is creating a spirit of indifference and apathy throughout the whole station…'

The mayor had paused in his narrative. Beppe must have had a look on his face which suggested there must be an 'easy solution' to the problem. The mayor did not want to let his companion find any excuse to weaken his case, so he continued to forestall any comment from his 'special' guest.

'And that, *Commissario,* is only scratching the surface.

There are rumours – unsubstantiated so far – that our two bad cops paid a visit to one family who had stood its ground and roughed up the father in front of his wife and kids. It really is as bad as that.

Our present *Questore* was told confidentially what was happening by one of our more honest officers – yes, there are still some left – *Agente* Acrina to name but one. It is reported that officers L and G have some moral hold over our present *Questore*. Something to do with his handling of the one young female officer who has been recruited recently. Elmo Ferretti appeared to sweep the whole matter under the carpet. This couple of officers have a number of similar scams going on with shopkeepers too, I learnt only a couple of days ago – via the grape-vine as usual. Come on, *Commissario,* let's get back to the *Questura.* That's enough for one day!'

The mayor obviously had a tab arrangement with the *trattoria.* They left the restaurant without money changing hands. They walked back towards the *Questura* with Beppe by his side, looking very thoughtful.

'I understand you have a beautiful wife and two delightful kids, *Commissario!* That must be a source of great comfort to you.'

Beppe grinned broadly at the mayor but said nothing in reply. The look on Beppe's face told the mayor clearly that his not very subtle change of tactics had been duly noted.

'Alright, *Commissario,'* said the mayor suddenly giving his 'adversary' a radiant smile. 'I have done all I can to convert you. I am sure you will make the right decision in the end. But please indulge me a little – just to satisfy my curiosity. Do you feel more or less inclined to accept the post of *Questore* after spending some time here?'

Beppe chose his parting words carefully – looking the mayor straight in the eyes.

'I would say that I am more inclined to accept the post than I was when I was woken up at 7.30 this morning, *Signor Sindaco*. And I thank you for introducing me to the *Trattoria La Buona Forchetta.*'

The mayor shook Beppe's hand warmly in both of his, turned round and walked back into the *Questura* without another word. A secret smile played across his face, which was observed by nobody else except possibly *Agente* Mario Acrina, who was being replaced by another officer at the reception desk.

The mayor retrieved his briefcase from behind the reception desk and walked back towards the town hall. He spotted Elmo Ferretti briefly haranguing another junior officer.

Now, he could only hope and pray that *Commissario* Stancato would accept the offer once it was formally made. He would call the *Questore,* Mariastella Martellini later on that day…since she had sweetly requested to be told how the interview had panned out.

3: The Commissario becomes involved in other matters…

On his arrival back home, Beppe was met with three pairs of eyes looking at him. He managed to retain a neutral expression on his face, determined not to be bombarded with questions. To his surprise, nobody asked him a single question – not even his normally inquisitive daughter, Veronica.

It was Sonia who spoke first.

'You will be happy to know that you have a free evening ahead of you, *amore*. Mariastella phoned about thirty minutes ago. She said she was not expecting you to come in until tomorrow. She assured me that nothing out of the ordinary has occurred today. She even forestalled your tendency to ignore her advice on these occasions, saying she would be out of the *Questura* on unspecified business.'

Beppe was secretly relieved but did his best to look indifferent.

'So, you'll be able to come and watch our swimming lessons, *papà*,' stated Veronica with a radiant smile on her face.

Beppe had a mild aversion to swimming-pools. He preferred swimming in the sea – despite the fact that Atri had a magnificent, almost Olympic sized pool. Sonia looked at him appealingly and nodded encouragingly. A swim in their local pool with his family was just what he needed to relax.

'*Andiamo, ragazzi!*' [16] he declared. 'Now I shall be able to see for myself just how much progress you two have made.'

It was Lorenzo who could outswim his older sister. Beppe and Sonia had to be careful about showering their son with compliments in Veronica's presence. She hated it when anyone could outperform her – in any field.

---

[16] Let's go, boys and girls.

'Just like me when I was her age,' Sonia had once confessed.

'And, this evening, we're going to eat out at that *agriturismo* just outside Atri where we all went last year,' Sonia informed Beppe. 'You remember, don't you? It's called *La Quercia.'* [17] My parents have offered to pay for the meal.'

'*Geniale!'* [18] was the verdict of both children excitedly. The matter was settled, it appeared. Beppe had no say in the matter – it felt as if some conspiracy was afoot.

* * *

Beppe's family, accompanied by Sonia's parents sat round the table devouring the seemingly endless dishes of fish, meat and vegetable antipasti which arrived non-stop on their table. Carafes of local red and white wine stood on the table, but only Beppe and Sonia were responsible for the slowly diminishing levels of liquid in each carafe. The grandparents and children drank still mineral water. Hardly a word was spoken that was not praise for the food.

While they were waiting for the next course to arrive, Beppe finally broke the speaking truce by commenting:

'This meal feels as if we ought to be celebrating something – but I'm not sure what…'

Sonia attempted to look as if she was far away on a mountain top. Her parents appeared not to have heard what Beppe had said. Lorenzo kept his eyes lowered, concentrating on his empty plate. Only Veronica decided it was time to come up with some imaginative answer.

---

[17] The Oak Tree
[18] Brilliant! Cf L'amica geniale – My brilliant friend.

'Because it's your birthday, *papà*. Don't tell me you'd forgotten about it!'

Beppe had to laugh at her inventiveness. Only Lorenzo's face remained solemn. He tended not to find his sister's regular flights of fantasy amusing.

'But my birthday is in October, Vero. It's only the month of May...'

'Ahh, but how do you know that it's not today, *papà*? You've only got your mother's word for when you were born. And she has a very muddled brain.'

She got her collective laugh from everyone – even her little brother. Roberto, Sonia's father, somewhat pedantically explained to his grand-daughter what a birth certificate was, for which he received a scornful glare.

'Have *I* got one of those *'cerfiticata, papà?'* asked Lorenzo.

'Everybody gets one as soon as they're born,' explained Sonia. 'I'll show you yours when we get home, *tesoro*.'

Beppe was looking lovingly at his children, but selected Lorenzo as the one who might be relied upon to give him a straight answer. His son had a reputation for being incapable of telling lies. His schoolmates had often been overheard saying; 'If Lori says it's true, then you have to believe him.'

'Maybe I should ask *you* what we are celebrating today, Lori?'

'Mamma told us we mustn't ask you questions about where you went today, because you might not want to talk about your new job...' muttered Lorenzo.

'That's after *mamma* had a phone call from Mariastella,' blurted out Veronica. The cat was out of the bag.

'Ah, now I understand *everything! Grazie,* Lori – and you too, Vero!'

Veronica spotted the mild sarcasm and grinned cheekily.

Beppe's sense of humour easily won the day, at the same moment as it dawned on him that even his children understood what was at stake – and were equally involved in his future choices.

'Well, *ragazzi,* I haven't been officially offered the job yet. So, our wonderful celebration this evening is a bit premature...'

'But Mariastella told *mamma* that...' began Veronica, only silenced by a severe warning frown from her mother.

The rest of the meal was more relaxed as Beppe kept them entertained by his account of the events of that long day – leaving nothing out.

'So, you did your very best to portray yourself in a poor light just to put the mayor off, *amore.* Is that about the size of it?' asked Sonia.

'Yes, but my attempts at denigrating myself seem to have backfired.'

'You should take this job, Beppe.'

It was the normally taciturn Roberto – Sonia's father – who had uttered these words between mouthfuls of food. He, apparently, had not been forewarned about the ban on talking about Beppe's day in Terramonti.

Beppe merely smiled enigmatically at his father-in-law.

Sonia kept her true thoughts to herself. She would continue to tell her husband that she would support him in whatever decision he made. Mariastella had clearly inferred that the offer of this important post was a *fait accompli.* But she knew Beppe was stubborn enough to refuse the post of *Questore* if he felt he was being pressured into accepting it.

'Please just let's enjoy the rest of our meal,' pleaded Veronica. Beppe ruffled her hair affectionately. This time, she did not react by pulling her head away.

'*Ti vogliamo bene, papà,*' [19] she said on the family's behalf.

* * *

By nine o'clock the following morning, Beppe was facing his *capo* from the opposite side of her desk. He was attempting to treat her to his notorious unwavering stare. She simply smiled indulgently.

'*Commissario*... Beppe... Don't look at me like that! The truth is, more than half of me hopes you will turn this job down. In general, you make my life so much easier – you may be surprised to learn. But I could not live with my own conscience if I thought I had hindered your promotion in any way. So, I am ostensibly helping you get there.'

Beppe gave way with a good grace.

'Thank you, Mariastella. As you put it that way, I appreciate your help.'

'Do you want to tell me about your initial reactions to your interview, Beppe?'

'They need to appoint *someone* urgently. But I do not envy the person whose lot it is to fill the role of the *Questore*. The present *Questore* is dysfunctional and there are at least two bent cops on the payroll. I did like the mayor, however. He was intelligent and he coped with me very well! I could work with him easily...'

---

[19] We love you, dad. (Not 'ti amiamo' – which has physical connotations.)

'He took a liking to you too, *Commissario!* He told me he could never live with any appointee who did not appreciate good food and wine.'

'Yes, he was an honest and good-humoured man – who treated me with respect, despite the fact that I tried my best to put him off me.'

Mariastella smiled at her second-in-command.

'Yes, I regret to have to tell you, *Commissario,* that your approach had the opposite effect on him!'

'But he mentioned the Archbishop and a scientist who had apparently had a go at sealing my fate. But I can't for the life of me think who it could be,' said Beppe seeking enlightenment.

'Oh, come on, Beppe! You remember the physicist, Donato Pisano, whom you rescued from being abducted and sent to the United States…'

'Of course. It's obvious now I think about it. But how did he know…? Ah, I see. It was *you* who…'

To Mariastella's relief, her desk phone rang at that opportune moment.

The smile on her face vanished as soon as the duty officer downstairs began speaking.

'O mio Dio!' she said. 'I'll let the *Commissario* know at once. He's up here with me right now…'

The *Questore* turned to Beppe.

'Officers Cristina Cardinale and Emma Campione were called out to a block of apartments in *Via Giuseppe Verdi.* It's that *palazzo* [20] in the supposedly affluent district of Pescara. It's only four or five storeys high. The girls were called out because one of the residents had grown suspicious, since they had not seen their neighbour for three days. Our two ladies got the

---

[20] Block of apartments

janitor to open the door to the apartment with his master-key. Apparently *Agente* Cardinale had to rush to the bathroom to be sick. *Agente* Campione phoned in quite distraught. She said she had never seen such a bizarre and horrendous killing in her two years as a police officer. It was like some ritualistic sacrifice, she claimed, with the Blessed Virgin Mary thrown in for good measure. And the victim is a young woman in her early thirties...'

'I'll get the exact address from Giacomo D'Amico downstairs and drive over there immediately, Mariastella.'

'Come back and see me as soon as you return, *Commissario*...' said the *Questore* to Beppe's departing back.

Beppe waved a hand without turning round.

'Ci mancherebbe altro, Signora Questore! [21] he called out over his shoulder.

Beppe ran downstairs. He was thinking of the white lie he had told the Mayor of Terramonti about having a particularly difficult case to solve, simply to buy himself time before he was forced to make a decision. It looked as if his words had generated yet another self-fulfilling prophecy. *'Merda!'* he muttered to himself - although he failed to quash the sensation of relief that he would be involved in a real investigation rather than a fictitious one.

The address - *Appartamento 34, I Tulipani Gialli,* Via Giuseppe Verdi, would remain in his memory for many years to come.

---

[21] Of course, I will! (Lit: I would be failing if I did anything less)

4: *The sightless witness…*

Their youngest and newest recruit in Via Pesaro, [22] whose name was Donato Pavone, was hanging around the reception desk looking lost. It was only his third week in his very new and uncreased uniform. He reminded Beppe a bit of his former colleague, Remo Mastrodicasa, who had left the police force to run an *agriturismo* just outside L'Aquila. Remo had fired only one shot in his career as a policeman – killing a man who was about to inject a lethal dose of curare into the body of a young policewomen called Oriana Salvati. *Agente* Donato Pavone looked as unlikely a candidate for the police force as had Remo Mastrodicasa.

But there was something about this young officer which led Beppe to believe he might be more resilient than he appeared on the surface - as well as his being particularly savvy when put in front of a police computer. He seemed to know his way around most aspects of modern technology and could come up with information that left Beppe agape with admiration for the way youngsters managed to put modern technology to practical use.

'Come on *Agente* Pavone. It's time you had a taste of the seamier side of police work. You're coming with me to the scene of a murder.'

Agente Pavone looked gratefully at his chief.

Armed with the details handed to him by his longest serving officer, Giacomo D'Amico, Beppe told the new recruit to drive them as fast as possible to Via Giuseppe Verdi – with the siren switched on. The lad drove well, thought Beppe and did not need to ask where the street was. He evidently knew his way round Pescara better than Beppe himself did.

---

[22] Via Pesaro – where the *Questura* is situated.

* * *

Beppe and Officer Pavone arrived outside flat 34 by dint of working out that the apartment was number four on the third floor.

'Logical, I suppose,' said Beppe to his junior colleague after they had taken the lift up to the top floor – level 5 – and then walked downstairs one storey at a time until they spotted Officers Campione and Cardinale standing on guard outside the half-open door of the victim's apartment.

Officer Cristina Campione was looking deathly pale, her expression still looking bemused by what she had witnessed. She had obviously been crying, judging by the redness of her eyes.

'I'm so sorry, *capo,*' she stammered pitifully to Beppe. 'I'm not as tough as I thought...'

Beppe put a reassuring arm round her shoulder.

'Why don't you two girls make a start by going round the other flats and see if anyone has noticed anything unusual going on over the last two or three days...you know, strangers spotted in the lifts or in the corridors. There's no need to alarm anyone that there's been a gruesome killing. Stay together and see if you can glean anything useful. Why don't you concentrate on the apartments immediately above and below this one?' he suggested.

They nodded and looked gratefully at their *capo*. He had understood that they needed something to do to take their minds off the murder scene, but did not want them to simply give up by sending them home or back to Via Pesaro.

'Are you ready for this, *Agente* Pavone?'

The young man shrugged his shoulders, but said nothing. After a second or two, he nodded at Beppe. He stepped into the apartment close on Beppe's heels.

Both men stared in horrified disbelief at the dead woman lying propped up against the living room wall. Her legs were splayed out across the parquet flooring. The look of horror on her face was too awful to behold. It clearly told the tale of her dying minutes on earth. It looked as if her cheeks had been crudely embalmed in an attempt to emphasize her suffering. Her lips had been hurriedly rouged. By her side stood a cheap, eighty-centimetre-tall plaster statue of the Virgin Mary – her hands held out in hopeless supplication.

Beppe was having complex, emotionally charged visions of a topsy-turvy universe. He had, without thinking, conjured up images of himself playing with his two children and hugging Sonia tightly in affirmation of their love of being alive and together. There must exist multiple dimensions – even just on Planet Earth. What they were looking at was a travesty of everything he held dear. It revealed the deranged mind of some horrendous being who had set out to overturn every decent aspect of human existence.

'It's satanic, *capo,*' a shaky voice was saying from some other alien space impinging on his.

Beppe shook his head to clear it of the dark images that had been called into existence. He looked at his young colleague wondering if he too would be rushing to the bathroom.

Strangely, *Agente* Pavone seemed to have mastered his nausea.

'Someone wanted to stage this horror show as an act of revenge… or punishment,' added the young officer.

'I agree with you, *agente.* I have never witnessed anything quite like it…'

His voice tailed off, simply because he knew what he had just said was untrue. It conjured up some childhood nightmare from a time of his life when the habit of having memories had barely become a natural element of growing up.

'I'm going to get the forensic team over here,' he told Donato Pavone. 'We dare not touch anything in this room.'

The Commissario made his call.

'They'll be here in about twenty minutes,' Beppe informed his colleague.

They both looked at the pink plastic shoe-covers on their feet and the pink gloves on their hands. They plodded towards the door and pulled it to behind them without closing it fully – as if to expunge the memories of what was on the other side of the heavy, metal reinforced door.

Once in the corridor, Beppe made a second phone call to his friend, Bruno Esposito, whose expertise seemed to cover the whole range of criminology – even though his official role was simply that of chief toxicologist.

'I'll come over with the forensics team, Beppe,' he promised.

'I'm sorry to take advantage of you, *Agente* Pavone. Could you please stand guard here until the forensics team arrive? I'll get the girls to take me back to the station. That way, you can drive back under your own steam later on. You might like to make sure that the janitor gives you safe-keeping of the key to the apartment before you leave...'

'Yes, *Commissario* – the fact that it was the janitor who let Officers Campione and Cardinale into the apartment just using a single master-key was a bit strange.'

'And what do you conclude from that, might I ask, *Agente* Pavone?' said Beppe sharply.

'That the killers must have rung the doorbell and the victim – whatever the poor girl's name was – opened the door to them. When they left, they just pulled the apartment door closed behind them, *capo.*'

'In other words, *agente...?*'

'She might have known her killers, *Commissario,* or am I just being...?'

Beppe stared disconcertingly at the young officer, who was waiting for a reprimand for the audacity of his wild surmise. He had not been in the Pescara police force long enough to know that his chief always mulled over what people told him before reacting.

'I'm glad we appointed you, Donato,' said Beppe and walked off down the corridor leaving the young officer open-mouthed in shock.

* * *

Beppe, walking downstairs in search of his two young ladies, found them saying goodbye to someone in apartment 24 – the one immediately below the victim's.

'Thank you so much for talking to us, *signorina,*' Officer Campione was saying to the occupant, who Beppe could not see because she was standing just inside her doorway.

'Please get in touch with us if ever you need help, won't you, *signorina?*' Officer Cardinale was saying as the door was shut by a young woman thanking them in a beautiful, melodious voice.

The two 'girls' turned, smiling, to greet their chief as he walked along the corridor towards them.

'Well, did the young lady have anything to say?' asked Beppe. 'Why would she need help? I ask out of sheer curiosity.'

'She was a beautiful, articulate young woman, *capo*...'

'But she was blind, *capo*,' added Officer Cardinale.

Beppe was looking intensely at his two *protégées*.

'Did you glean anything at all from her?' Beppe asked.

'She apologised and told us why she had not seen anything,' said Emma.

'We didn't want to insist...' began Cristina.

'Just for a moment, we thought she was going to tell us something, *capo*. But she seemed reluctant to put it into words, so we...' began Emma.

Beppe stopped himself from saying anything even vaguely sarcastic. His two young officers had both been traumatised by the sight of the dead woman upstairs.

'I hope she is not deaf as well as blind,' stated Beppe in all innocence.

'*O Dio*,' said Cristina. Beppe was pleased to see her blush slightly. It was good to see colour returning to her cheeks.

'We're not thinking straight, are we?' said Emma. '*Ci dispiace, capo!*' [23]

'I'll have a quick word with her, ladies. Just in case she has something to add,' said Beppe. 'You two do the rounds of the other apartments. I'll catch up with you in a minute. Did you get her name?'

'Annamaria Intimo,' [24] the two officers said speaking in unison.

Beppe raised a quizzical eyebrow at the unusual surname.

'It's a not uncommon surname in Abruzzo, *capo*,' explained Emma to her Calabrian chief.

---

[23] We are sorry : we apologise
[24] 'Intimate'

Beppe rang on the doorbell as his two officers walked down the corridor to the next apartment. They were giggling, Beppe noticed, whilst he was straining to hear what they were saying to each other. He thought he could make out the words:

'Our *Commissario* may be in for a bit of a surprise,' said one of them.

(Giggles)

'Maybe we shouldn't have let him go on his own,' joked the other.

Nearly two hours would elapse before Beppe would be taking his leave of Annamaria Intimo. His opinion about blind people – indeed about the ways in which the human mind works – would undergo a profound reassessment during the course of the seven-thousand-five-hundred seconds of 'space-time' spent in her presence.

The door to apartment 23 was opened a split second after Beppe had rung on the doorbell. It took the usually-in-control *Commissario* a lengthy five seconds of silence before he thought he ought to introduce himself. He was staring at the sight of one of the most beautiful women he had ever seen. She had a dark, southern Italian complexion with a mass of jet-black curly hair cascading round a perfectly formed face. Her eyes were black jewels in contrast to the perfect whiteness of her teeth as she broke into a smile.

'Oh, did you forget something, girls? Ah, no, I'm mistaken, aren't I? You must be *Commissario* Beppe Stancato. Your girls told me you might want to talk to me, but I did not expect you quite so soon. Won't you come in?'

Making a supreme effort, Beppe rediscovered the powers of speech only seconds before his silence would have become embarrassing.

'Do you usually ask strange men into your home, *signorina?* How did you know it was a man standing here in the corridor and not officers Cristina and Emma?'

Annamaria Intimo laughed – delightedly.

'It was a bit of a guess, I admit, *Commissario.* But I could tell the person standing there was a man – and I realised that your two officers were further down the corridor. I could hear them giggling. But you give off a comforting aura. I knew I was not in any danger. Now please come in,' she said closing the door behind her.

'But how did you know I was a man? May I call you Annamaria? Do we smell different, or something?'

'Yes, men smell different. But you give off a powerful masculine aura, *Commissario.* Does that answer your question?' Annamaria asked with an engaging giggle.

'My two colleagues had the impression you might be able to help us,' said Beppe – whilst still trying to digest the words he had heard.

'I might be able to help you – but only if you tell me more precisely what is happening. Your two girls kind of gave up as soon as I told them I was blind, so I didn't want to say too much in case it was totally irrelevant.'

'They were – still are – in a state of shock, Annamaria. I can't blame them for their reaction towards you. They had just witnessed a very shocking scene. It was a terrible experience – even for a hardened policeman such as myself...'

'So, someone has been murdered, I would guess – someone who lives in one of these apartments. *Vero, Commissario?'*

Without thinking, Beppe nodded.

'I see you are nodding, *Commissario.* May I call you by your first name?'

Beppe stopped himself from asking how she knew he had nodded. He was just beginning to realise that he was dealing with an exceptional human being.

'Yes, call me Beppe, if you want. But not in front of my officers. People might talk,' he said without thinking.

He was treated to a burst of trilling laughter as he saw this beautiful body walking towards him. He managed to stay on the spot where he was standing. Before he realised what was happening, Annamaria Intimo was touching his face with her firm but soft fingers.

'Ah, Beppe, now I understand what your officers were whispering in the corridor. You are a very good-looking man. Your features are so perfectly balanced. Even your ears are like identical twins.'

Beppe sighed deeply.

'Alright, I see I shall have to take you into my confidence, *signorina...*'

'Annamaria, please!' said Annamaria.

'Did you know the young lady who lives in the flat above you? I imagine you did, Annamaria,' said Beppe with his heart in his mouth, fearing an emotional reaction.

'Not Laura! PLEASE tell me it's not Laura!'

The look of alarm and desperation on her face heralded the onset of grief.

'I'm sorry, Annamaria...'

The blind woman threw herself at Beppe with her head resting on his chest. She was weeping uncontrollably. Beppe instinctively put his arms round her body and held her tightly in a gesture of consolation. She pulled herself free after only a few minutes.

'I'm sorry, Beppe. She was the only real friend I had in the whole *palazzo*. I am so sorry I lost control. It was such a shock. But you know…I'm not altogether surprised,' she added, as she got her tears under control.

'Annamaria, what do you mean by saying you're not surprised? This could be so important…'

The blind girl had been transformed – in an instant – from a grief-filled woman into a valiant warrior.

'Come on, *Commissario* Beppe. Take me up to Laura's flat. I need to get a sense of what has happened. It will only take a few minutes…and then I will be able to tell you what I know.'

'But the forensics team will be there very shortly. I'll get lambasted if I allow anyone to…' began Beppe feebly.

'*Dai*, Beppe! [25] I only need a minute or so in the room. What harm can it do? I can go up there on my own if you're scared of getting into trouble.'

Annamaria was already opening her front door.

'What the hell!' thought Beppe. 'Who knows what light this woman might shed on this already weird case?'

'Wait, Annamaria. We'll go up together. I have one of my officers standing guard outside in the corridor.'

Agente Donato Pavone's mouth fell open at the sight of the dark angel walking towards him in the company of his chief.

'This is the victim's neighbour from downstairs, Officer Pavone. She needs to have a quick…' Beppe had to stop himself using the word 'look'. But no suitable word sprang to mind.

'You had better be quick, *capo*. The forensics team will be here in a matter of minutes.'

Beppe shrugged his shoulders in a gesture of resignation in the direction of his junior officer and held Annamaria's elbow gently as he guided her into the apartment.

'Don't worry, *Agente* Pavone. This won't take long.'

---

[25] Dai = Come on!

They were on the threshold of the living-room where the body was lying.

'That's far enough, Beppe,' whispered Annamaria. 'An awful murder has been committed in this room. I feel the hatred and sadistic pleasure of the murderers...and the absolute terror and pain that Laura suffered in the space of a few minutes...'

'You said 'murderers', Annamaria. In the plural.'

'Oh yes, Beppe. There were two of them. I am sure of that.'

'Something you won't be able to see, Annamaria. But they put quite a big statue of the Virgin Mary near the...Laura's body. It makes the scene even more macabre.'

'A statue!' said the blind girl. 'Really? Now I know that I can help you, Beppe. Come on, we can go downstairs to my apartment now. Before you get into trouble.'

Annamaria even took the time to thank Officer Pavone for his understanding. He was speechless, but watched mesmerised as her shapely rear view swayed along the corridor in the company of his chief before disappearing down the stair-well. Later on, he was astounded to be told that this woman was blind.

Back in Annamaria's apartment, Beppe's surprise turned into a sense of wonder at the direction which their conversation took.

'I need a strong drink, Beppe. *Grappa,* I think. Will you join me? I feel mentally drained. Please say you will.'

She had to feel the shape of the bottles before she selected the right one and poured the colourless liquid accurately into two shot glasses.

'Now please come and sit next to me, Beppe. I don't like talking to someone I can't see who is the other side of the room.'

Beppe sat down next to Annamaria and took his glass, chinking it carefully with hers.

'I'm speechless, Annamaria. How could you possibly know there were two killers?'

'Well, it was partly instinctive but it tied up with something that happened to me as I was stepping out of the lift on the ground floor. Do you know how long ago poor Laura was murdered, Beppe?'

'No. We shall have to wait for the forensics team to...'

'It was three days ago, *Commissario*. I can tell you that for certain.'

'*Sono tutto orecchi*, Annamaria.' [26]

She giggled sweetly at his choice of words.

'It's not just your ears that are appealing, Beppe,' she said flirtatiously.

---

[26] I'm all ears (exactly as in English)

5: *Astonishing insights...*

'As I was telling you, I had just stepped out of the lift on the ground floor and I was aware that there were two men waiting to take the lift to go upstairs. I was just going out to the local delicatessen shop.'

Beppe had so many questions he wanted to ask about how his new acquaintance coped with life, that he interrupted her vital account with a silly question.

'But how do you...? I mean, you don't have a dog, do you?'

'No, *Commissario,* because I prefer cats.'

'I meant...'

'I know what you meant, Beppe. And the answer is I have a sister. Now do you want me to help you solve this murder, or not?' she said sharply.

Beppe uttered a gentle laugh.

'Mi dispiace, Annamaria. No more interruptions.'

'I sensed immediately that the two individuals were strangers to the block. I did not like the aura they gave off and I must have side-stepped to avoid getting too close to them. One of them said *Buonasera, signorina.* But it was said sarcastically, almost lasciviously...'

'Did he have a local accent, Annamaria?' interrupted Beppe despite his promise not to stop the flow.

'No, it was not local. But he didn't say enough to allow me to identify where he came from. But listen to this, Beppe. The other man who didn't speak was carrying something heavy. I heard him dropping a heavy object on the floor of the lift – almost as if he had accidently let go of what he was carrying.'

'The statue!' said Beppe, understanding immediately where Annamaria was going with her narrative.

'*Bravo,* Beppe. But now I'll tell you something else which might interest you. The man who was carrying the statue smelt!'

'You mean…a bad smell?'

'Yes, he gave off an unpleasant odour of sardines – sardines that were no longer fresh. It was on his clothes, on his skin. I even picked up a hint of it in Laura's flat just now.'

Beppe was speechless.

'You *can* say something now, *Commissario!*' said Annamaria playfully.

'I'm astounded, Annamaria, at your memory, at the precision with which you interpret your sensations of life in a world you can only sense but not see.'

'That's not bad, Beppe, for a *first* compliment, I have to say.'

Her words were accompanied by a return to that little trill of teasing laughter.

'You are a remarkable woman, Annamaria. I would say unique.'

'That sounds a bit more promising, Beppe.'

And you are the most beautiful woman I have ever set eyes on, he felt like adding.

But the *Commissario* was not going to fall into that trap.

'Thank you for what you are *not* saying, Beppe.'

Annamaria had surprised him all over again. It was uncanny.

Instead, Beppe asked another pertinent question.

'A few minutes ago, before you told me about the smell of sardines and the men getting into the lift, you hinted you were not entirely surprised that Laura had been…'

Beppe realised by then that he would not have to complete the sentence.

Annamaria emitted a heavy sigh.

'This is no more than an impression I got during our many shopping outings and walks round the *pineta...* ' [27] She called herself Laura Ianni – the most *Abbruzzese* surname there is! But I always got the impression that this was not her real name. She had a southern accent – just like yours, Beppe, now I come to think of it. Where are you from originally? I'm not all that good at identifying regional accents – even if I can tell instantly that they are different.'

Annamaria immediately sensed that her lovely visitor had tensed up – as if the minute shockwave that he had felt had travelled the distance between himself and this extraordinary woman.

'I'm from Calabria,' he said quietly.

'*'ndrangheta* land, Beppe. I see!'

'In the space of half an hour of knowing you, Annamaria, you have given me so much insight into a murder that I have not even begun investigating. You are a truly remarkable person...'

And you are unbelievably alluring...

'Let's talk about something else, Beppe,' she said gaily. 'Please don't leave me just yet. I know you must be busy, but you and I could easily become friends. I sense this so strongly.'

'So do I, Annamaria,' admitted Beppe, despite himself.

And so, Beppe set about finding out all he could about Annamaria. He learnt she had been blind from birth, that she had a married sister with two children who lived in Pescara very near her apartment.

'But you must have a profession, Annamaria?' Beppe asked.

---

[27] There is a famous pine-tree 'forest' in Pescara – a well-known beauty spot.

'Well, I was a fashion model in Milan for several years. I only fell off a podium once and broke an ankle. I made a lot of money but in the end, I got tired of the fashion world – it's just a lucrative form of slavery really. So I came to live near my sister. Nowadays, I have set myself up as a kind of *maga* [28] a white witch, you might say. My 'patients' come here and I help them see themselves as they really are. Ironic, isn't it, *Commissario?*'

'Dare I ask you if you have a *fidanzato,* [29] Annamaria? I don't like to think of you being alone.'

'Or a *fidanzata, Commissario!* I might be a Lesbian. Had you considered that possibility?' asked Annamaria challengingly. 'I'll tell you something amusing, though. It's the one advantage of being blind, I suppose. I can sleep with anyone whom I like and it doesn't matter if they're ugly, because I can't really tell – at least in the early stages. But the funny thing is, which I have discovered over time, that it is very often the nice-looking ones who are the kindest.'

Their conversation went on without a break for what seemed ages. Annamaria had refrained from asking Beppe any questions about his personal life.

'I really do have to leave you for now, Annamaria.'

'I know we shall meet again soon, Beppe. I feel this strongly. But now you should go back to your lovely wife – and two children? Or is it three? Oh yes, I knew you were married.'

'Is it that obvious to you?' asked Beppe.

'Yes, you give off a comfortable aura. You are obviously not alone in life. Besides which, you are famous in Pescara, don't forget. I have followed your career through the news. And your family is often mentioned.'

---

[28] A wise woman : a sorceress
[29] Fidanzato = boy-friend / fiancé. Fidanzata = girl-friend / fiancée

She laughed that gay laugh as she revealed that the source of her information about Beppe had nothing to do with her being a mystic – blind or otherwise.

She came up to Beppe and placed a hand on each of his shoulders. He kissed her on each cheek – not the standard *bacio* which involves minimal physical contact. His lips felt the softness of her cheeks before their bodies separated.

She was smiling radiantly.

'Alla prossima, Commissario!' [30]

* * *

There was no sign of the forensics team, Officer Donato Pavone – nor even Officers Campione and Cardinale. Laura Ianni's apartment was locked up and police tape denoting a crime scene was attached to the door lintel in the shape of an X. Beppe walked back to the *Questura* trying to digest all that he had learnt during the last two hours. Inside, he felt that hint of dread. Why had Annamaria been so certain that 'Laura Ianni' – which would certainly turn out not to be her real name – was from his native Calabria?

'Not again!' he prayed – thinking of his last case which had sent him scuttling back to his native Catanzaro to confront the local *'ndrangheta* clan. [31] He entered the *Questura* with the intention of going upstairs to speak to his *capo,* Mariastella Martellini, He must phone Sonia first to let her know that he was likely to be home late that evening.

'We will wait for you to get back before we have dinner. Veronica and Lori are not in the mood to go to bed early, *amore.'*

---

[30] Until next time
[31] The Vendetta Tree

'I'll be there within an hour,' he promised rashly. Beppe had more than an inkling as to the reason for the upbeat mood that he had detected in Sonia's voice.

Fortunately, his chief, the *Questore,* gave every sign of wanting to leave early too.

'Can we meet up at 8 o'clock tomorrow morning? You look as if you have had a stressful day, Beppe.'

'Not so much stressful as mind-blowing, Mariastella.'

'I understand from Officers Campione and Cardinale that you might have been seduced by a beautiful blind woman, *Commissario!* Can you reject this hypothesis before you go home?'

'No, I can't, Mariastella. Since it is more-or-less the simple truth - but more on a spiritual level than physical.'

'Then I shall look forward to your explanation with great curiosity tomorrow morning, *Commissario.'* concluded the lady *Questore* with quiet irony.

A quick phone call to his friend Bruno Esposito, who had accompanied the forensics team to the murder scene.

'It had all the flavour of a bloody, devilish, medieval tableau, Beppe,' said his friend Bruno.

'We had the same impression,' said Beppe simply.

'I'm glad you are the one investigating this crime, Beppe,' concluded the chief toxicologist.

6: *Life-changing revelations...*

The excitement in the air as soon as he stepped into his parents-in-laws' kitchen and headed for the stairs leading up to their two floors was tangible. Roberto and Irene, Sonia's father and mother, were sitting round their supper table studiously trying to appear neutral. Knowing what pleasure Veronica and Lorenzo would have imparting their 'secret' news, Beppe would feign ignorance until the last moment and then do his best to look surprised at their news.

When he entered their kitchen on the third floor of the house, Sonia was putting the final touches to their dinner and had her back to Beppe. She turned her head round and flashed a brief, conspiratorial smile in Beppe's direction. What a beautiful smile and sparkling eyes she had! Beppe headed for the stove, removed the wooden spoon from her hand and kissed her passionately on her parted lips.

'You haven't heard what the children have to tell you yet, *amore.*' protested Sonia.

Beppe could not reveal to Sonia the hidden motive behind his passionate gesture.

'*Mamma* has bought a pony, *papà*. It's in the garden eating all of *Nonno* Roberto's roses!' said Veronica – always unable to resist the temptation to make up tall stories.

She was gratified to receive an unrestrained laugh from her parents. Her brother merely looked disgusted by his sister's habitual attempt at trying to make some 'clever' joke at the most important moments in their lives.

'*Mamma's* going to have a baby, *papà*. I'm going to have a little brother,' he announced solemnly.

'You don't know that, *scemo!*' [32] stated Veronica scornfully.

---

[32] Silly!

'Well, if it *is* a boy, there'll be more of us than *you!*' retorted Lorenzo tartly.

Nobody had ever heard Veronica's seven-year-old brother answering his sister back in this manner. Veronica looked so shocked by his retort that everybody else began laughing. Veronica's good nature prevailed and family harmony was restored as the special dinner was served.

'*Gallina 'mbriaca,*' [33] Sonia informed them. 'I've never tried making it before. From the lack of response from her family, Sonia supposed that they were happy with their food. It was past nine o'clock and they were all too hungry to bother what the dish was called.

As their hunger was satiated, they began the inevitable discussion as to what the new addition to their family should be called.

'As long as it's not Calògero or Penelope,' stated Beppe, who had been given the middle name of Calògero by his doting Calabrian mother.

'If it's girl, I would like her to be called Annamaria,' stated Veronica out of the blue.

The shock to Beppe's system was to swallow his mouthful of wine down the wrong way as he had a brief choking fit and had to drink mouthfuls of water to aid his recovery.

Everyone looked temporarily shocked, but it was Sonia who said:

'It's a lovely name, Veronica. I was just wondering why the name Annamaria should bring about such a reaction from your *papà.*'

She was looking intently at Beppe.

'*Amore?*' she asked.

---

[33] 'Drunken chicken' – a dish from Le Marche

Beppe was looking solemn – almost guilty – thought Sonia.

Beppe had to come clean.

'I have, as it happens, spent the whole afternoon with an extraordinary blind woman, whose name just happens to be Annamaria.'

'I suppose she was young and beautiful, Beppe?' said Sonia. 'That might explain why you have been looking so guilty since you came home.'

Beppe had the grace to look even more uncomfortable than before.

It was late – especially for Veronica and Lorenzo. In accordance with the family ritual when something important needed airing, the children were dispatched to the bathroom to get ready for bed. A meeting was then convened on the parental king-sized bed and Beppe had the unenviable task of describing everything that had happened to him on that day in great detail.

'A meeting of The Secret Four.' [34] Veronica had declared in a conspiratorial voice.

'The Secret Five,' corrected her brother.

The scene was set. Beppe began to relate the events of the day to his enthralled audience.

Even though he gave a watered-down description of the murder scene, it was Lorenzo who was the most shocked by the description of the dead girl. He was by far and away the more sensitive of their two children.

'Will we be able to meet this Annamaria?' asked Veronica. 'I've never met a blind person before.'

'She is my only witness to this murder. So who knows, Vero? One day you might meet her.'

---

[34] 'Una reunione dei quattro nell'ombra' – A meeting of 'The four in the shadows'. *(translator's note!)*

It was Sonia who, after Lorenzo and Veronica had finally been dispatched to their bedroom, spoke the words which summarised the fear which Beppe had been suppressing from the moment he had left Annamaria Intimo alone that afternoon. 'But, Beppe, if this young woman has been seen by those sadistic assassins, won't *her* life be in danger too? After all, *they* don't know she's blind, do they?'

* * *

'But aren't you jumping to somewhat premature conclusions, Beppe?' asked the *Questore* hopefully, as they were discussing the case in her office the following morning.

Mariastella Martellini had already conjured up images of a horrific mafia killing as her second-in-command had gone into reluctant details. Beppe's hint that their only 'witness' to this murder had been a blind woman, sent shivers of apprehension down her spine.

Beppe's brief conversation with Officers Campione and Cardinale earlier that morning, had confirmed that none of the remaining inhabitants of *I Tulipani* were aware that a murder had been committed in their *palazzo* – or were simply unwilling to become involved.

There was a brief interruption as *Agente* Danilo Simone came into the *Questore's* office and handed her an official brown envelope.

'The forensics team's preliminary report, *Signora Questore,*' said Danilo. 'I've been told to warn you to be prepared for a shock by *il Dottore* Esposito.'

'*Grazie, Agente* Simone,' she replied as she slit open the envelope with a lethal-looking paper knife. She took one look at the photo and decided that Beppe had not exaggerated the weirdness of the murder scene.

'I agree with you, Beppe,' she stated. 'This is no ordinary crime. It looks like a brutal act of revenge. I can only conjecture that one of the mafia clans is involved – or it's the work of a deranged psychopath...'

'That could well amount to the same thing,' Beppe pointed out.

'True, Beppe. But I am wondering if this girl, Laura Ianni, had been given police protection and a new identity – which has somehow been unearthed by one of the clans.'

Beppe nodded.

'My only witness, the blind girl, whose name is Annamaria Intimo, detected a southern Italian accent – she thought it might be Calabrian ...'

'Let's assume for now that this is the work of one of the *'ndrangheta* clans. How do you think we should proceed from here, *Commissario?*' asked Mariastella, reluctant to admit the truth of her own words.

'*Ispettore* Pippo Cafarelli – who is so grateful to you for overseeing his promotion, Mariastella – has taken on the responsibility of going to the scene of the crime to see if the CCTV cameras picked up the arrival of those two mobsters who Annamaria ran into as she was stepping out of the lift. He should be reporting back at any time now.'

'But what do you make of the fact that the killers went to the trouble of leaving a statue of the Virgin Mary at the crime scene, Beppe? It is almost more macabre than the killing of the girl.'

'I find that the most puzzling aspect of this pitiless murder. I've got our new recruit to do some research on the matter. Officer Pavone is a genius at surfing the internet. I hope he will come up with *something*. But we really are groping in the dark, at the moment.'

'So, Beppe, tell me more about this blind woman who you spent such a long time with. So long that Officers Campione and Cardinale gave up waiting for you and returned back to base without you.'

Mariastella Martellini had a playfully wicked glint in her eyes as she spoke.

The *Commissario* let out a sigh.

'You must meet her in person, Mariastella. She is an exceptional human being. Yes, she is physically stunning – she was a fashion model in Milan until a few years ago. But she has a perception of the world which is more astute than that of a sighted person. She is so aware of her surroundings. She has a sense of humour and an ironic perception of her own affliction. She knew the victim well. And she immediately came to the logical conclusion that she had accidently run into the two men – she was sure they were both men – who must have been the killers. She 'sensed' their evil presence and identified one of them – simply because he smelt of sardines…'

The lady *Questore* was looking incredulously at her second-in-command.

'Sardines?' she exclaimed in disbelief. 'How on earth is that going to help? Unless, of course…'

'You need to meet her, Mariastella. She is one of the most positive human beings I have ever come across. It may be a far-fetched reaction. But there is a risk that the two killers might come back and eliminate the one person who, as far as they know, saw them coming into the building. It would make sense to keep her somewhere safe – even for a few days. She is our only witness so far. And I would never forgive myself if something bad happened to her.'

'I would like to accompany you next time you go and visit her. If we can persuade her to leave her apartment, then can you suggest where we might hide her, Beppe?'

Beppe gave her two alternatives.

'Yes, I agree. But there is only *one* place where she would be truly safe, *Commissario* – from ALL interested parties! She can stay with ME!'

Mariastella had that mischievous glint in her eyes once again. Beppe treated her to one of his hard stares – much to her amusement.

'Maybe we should give her the choice, Beppe. But if she opts to stay with you and your family, it will have to remain unofficial, *Commissario.*'

'If I am right, it should only be for a matter of days,' said Beppe.

'Can we both go and see this Annamaria as soon as possible? Tomorrow even?'

'Good idea - I'll phone her straight away, Mariastella.'

* * *

Beppe went downstairs and headed for his office. He made his phone call to Annamaria Intimo, who was delighted that she would see Beppe again the following morning.

'I shall be accompanied by my *capo,* the *Questore,*' Beppe warned her.

'I hope he is as agreeable a man as you are, *Commissario,*' she added playfully.

'Much more so than I am, Annamaria – he's a 'she'!

Once again, Beppe was treated to a delighted peel of laughter.

'*A domani, Commissario!*'

And PLEASE, Annamaria, do not open your door to anyone! If you have an unexpected visitor before we get there, please treat it as an emergency, and do not open the door. Call me directly on the number I gave you.'

There was a lengthy silence as Annamaria digested Beppe's words of warning. Finally, in a subdued voice, she said: 'This murder doesn't end here, does it, my *Commissario?*'

'*A domani, Annamaria,*' he repeated.

'I shall go and pack a suitcase, Beppe. That is what you and your colleague are going to tell me to do, *vero?*'

Yet again, this unique lady had grasped the situation without having to have it spelled out.

Someone was knocking discreetly at his open door. Beppe's friend and colleague, *Ispettore* Pippo Cafarelli raised an eyebrow by way of permission to come in. Beppe beckoned him in with his free hand.

'Any eye-opening revelations to report, Pippo?'

'Anything concrete, you mean, *Commissario?* No, I fear not. The *portinaio* [35] was quite elderly – and, incidentally, deeply affected by the fact that a brutal murder has been carried out under his watch. It was as if he felt that he was personally responsible for what happened. It took me a good ten minutes to persuade him that the police needed his help – not to hear his confession. He himself had not paid particular attention to the CCTV screens. He saw a Fed-Ex mail delivery van pull up and the two occupants bringing in a heavy cardboard box. He watched them getting into the lift.

'That blind lady in flat 24 was getting out of the lift as the delivery men arrived,' he told me. 'She's a stunner!'

---

[35] Caretaker : concierge : janitor

'I got the impression that he was looking at her rather than our suspects, Beppe.'

'A pity you didn't take more notice of the delivery men, *Signor* Marino, I told him, they were probably the ones who murdered Laura Ianni...'

'That set him off again, Beppe. But we did notice from the CCTV footage that the two 'delivery men' did not come back downstairs again until some twenty minutes later.'

'But didn't you think that was odd, *Signor* Marino?' I asked him. He told me he had assumed they had had trouble finding the right flat – or had stayed to help her unpack the parcel... Not a lot of help, I'm afraid, Beppe. But we've got the new boy, *Agente* Donato Pavone, looking at the video footage.

With perfect timing, there was a discreet knock on Beppe's office door. Their newest recruit was standing almost apologetically on the threshold.

Beppe beckoned him in.

'Nothing very startling, *capo,*' Officer Pavone was saying, 'but you might be interested in this bit...' The young man plonked his lap-top on Beppe's desk and swivelled the screen round so it was visible to both of his senior colleagues.

They were astounded to see their local traffic warden standing looking at the offending Fed-Ex delivery van for almost five minutes, waiting in vain for the driver to reappear. Finally, he stuck a parking-ticket on the windscreen – and walked off, looking self-satisfied at a job well done.

'Bravo, *agente!*' exclaimed Beppe. 'Get on to it straight away. You know what to do!'

'*Ci sono, capo!*' [36]

'Smart kid, that!' was all Beppe said to Pippo as he strode out of his office.

---

[36] I'm on it, chief

'I'm off home, Pippo. We'll be having an unexpected house guest tomorrow. I need to forewarn Sonia and the children. *A domani!*'

'My Mariangela [37] had a phone call from Sonia, this morning, Beppe. I understand congratulations are in order.'

'Or commiserations,' replied Beppe as he swept out of his office. *'Grazie,* Pippo!' he called out as he disappeared down the corridor without once turning round.

Pippo smiled bitterly to himself.

'He's secretly thrilled about having a third child,' he concluded. But Pippo was also thinking it was about time that his *capo* delegated more of the responsibilities, which he always shouldered himself, onto his team – and more specifically, on to his recently-promoted second-in-command. 'It will never happen!' he muttered philosophically.

Pippo closed his eyes and let out a sigh of deep frustration. He was astounded, on re-opening his eyes, to find his *capo* standing in front of him. Beppe had returned in silence and was looking intensely at him.

'Thank you for what you have achieved already, *Ispettore*...Pippo. I am really going to need your skills and your support before this murder enquiry has run its course. I feel it in my bones.'

Pippo was lost for words – until he realised that copious amounts of pointless recriminations were the last thing that were needed. He stared back at his chief without blinking.

'Era ora, capo,' [38] he said firmly.

The next thing he knew was that he was being hugged warmly by his friend, the *Commissario.*

---

[37] Pippo's wife
[38] It was high time

'Now, I really must be off!' Beppe said – and vanished once again without a backward glance.

Something had just altered his chief's perception of life. 'WHAT – or more likely WHO - had brought about this transformation?' Pippo was wondering.

He had not yet made the acquaintance of a blind girl, who, the *Commissario* repeatedly claimed, was their *only* witness to this bizarre assassination.

7:   *In a safer place…?*

After a discussion with Mariastella, it was Beppe, on his own, who fetched Annamaria from her apartment at eight o'clock the following morning. Mariastella Martellini had pointed out that two people arriving at the apartment would look too conspicuous. It would be better to get Annamaria out of her flat and talk to her at the *Questura.*

As arranged, Beppe phoned their *protégée* from outside her door rather than calling her on the TV intercom system at the main entrance – an act which could be noticed by any of the residents of *I Tulipani Gialli* going off to work or going to fetch their daily loaves of bread and brioches from the local *pasticceria.* News of the killing had not yet been revealed to the media and Beppe was happy to keep it that way for as long as possible.

He slipped into her hallway even before the door was fully open without saying a single word of greeting to a subdued-looking Annamaria.

'This is serious cloak-and-dagger stuff, isn't it, *Commissario?'* she whispered, trying to cover up her anxiety with a flippant comment. She had already packed a modest-sized turquoise-coloured suitcase, which would be retrieved later on by one of Beppe's team of police officers.

Wishing to reassure her, Beppe held her by placing his hands gently beneath her elbows. She instinctively moved one step closer to him. He could feel her breath on his face.

Did she notice that he had responded by tightening his grip on her arms? He spoke quickly, wishing to sound business-like.

'It's not that bad, Annamaria. I know it all feels a bit furtive – but we are really only taking precautions in the unlikely event that, whichever clan those two men you ran into belong to, they won't be able to do you any harm.'

'But how long do you think I will be away, Beppe? I will need to tell my sister that I've gone away – or else she'll panic like some neurotic schoolgirl who thinks she's going to be abducted by a would-be rapist! I know her too well!'

Beppe laughed softly at the image she had conjured up, as he released his grip on her arms and took a diplomatic step backwards.

'Don't be concerned, Annamaria. We shall take care of all that for you. And I would be surprised if you are away for more than five or six days. If those two individuals are despatched to make sure you can't identify them by whoever their *boss* is, it will happen over the next two or three days – based on previous experience of such events.'

'But where am I going to stay, Beppe?'

'Well, I believe you will be given a choice, you lucky girl!' said Beppe laughing to further lighten the solemnity of the moment. 'You'll either be staying with the lady *Questore* in her country house. Or…if you prefer, you'll be staying with my family in Atri. If you want my advice, you would be better off…'

'I want to stay with *you* and your family, *Commissario*. There's no choice to make.'

Beppe did not bother to tell his *protégée* what his advice would have been. She had already made her preferences clear, despite not yet having met their lady *Questore*.

'I'm much happier when there are lots of people around me,' she added. 'Especially children.'

'Well, it is certainly the case, that you will be surrounded by people of all ages throughout a lot of the day time – and the night time, of course. Plus one middle-aged Labrador.'

'*Perfetto, Commissario,*' stated Annamaria, looking considerably relieved.

'Now, this is how I want us to proceed once we are outside in the road, Annamaria…'

* * *

'But why all the secrecy, Beppe?' Annamaria had begun asking as they made their way downstairs to the ground floor.

'If the clan *have* already sussed out that someone as easy to recognise as you are, Annamaria, has seen those two men coming into the *palazzo,* they won't waste time before sending one of their people to spy on the residents who come in or out of the main door. I expect I'm being over cautious – but one never knows when dealing with the mafia. They are generally far more efficient than the average Italian policeman. And ten times more ruthless.

'*O Dio mio!*' muttered Annamaria. 'I guess I was wishing for something out-of-the-ordinary to break the monotony of my life, but…'

'Here we are, Annamaria. Don't worry. This will all be over in a minute,' promised Beppe as he held open the main door as if he was being formerly polite to a lady who happened to be leaving the apartment block at the same time that he was.

Annamaria, following Beppe's instructions, had her mobile phone pressed to her ear as she began walking along the pavement away from the apartment block – looking like any other pedestrian. With the big difference that Beppe was 'guiding' her down the street whilst he remained vigilant just outside the entrance to *I Tulipani Gialli.*

'OK Annamaria. You've reached the car. It's only a *Cinquecento* [39] so the door handle is quite low down...that's it. *Bravissima!* Now you know what to do. I'll join you in just a minute.'

Annamaria felt the thrill of an adventure as she went through the motions of inserting the ignition key and starting up a car engine for the first time in her life.

Beppe made out as if he was still talking to someone as he stood patiently waiting for an event which he was almost certain would not happen.

It was, therefore, with a degree of self-satisfaction that he noticed a car door opening a few metres down the road from where he was standing – in the opposite direction to Annamaria's exit. A woman in her forties, holding an innocently empty shopping bag was getting out of the driver's seat. She began to walk along the pavement, apparently intent on going shopping. She did not register Beppe's presence. She reached the light blue *Cinquecento.* Her step faltered for barely a second as she glanced inside the car at the young woman who was ferreting inside her handbag, checking to make sure she had her purse or driving licence. The shopper continued walking away from Annamaria's car without a backward glance.

Coincidence – thought Beppe? There was so little to go on. He covered the distance to the *Cinquecento* in a few strides, tapped on the car window which Annamaria had partially opened.

'*Brava* Annamaria! That was perfect. You should have been an actress.'

'I was once, *Commissario!* I had a brief role as a blind woman. It was the easiest piece of drama I have ever

---

[39] Fiat 500

performed,' she said with a brief return to a lighter mood. She had not moved into the passenger seat as planned.

'Are you sure you wouldn't like me to drive, *Commissario?*' she asked pertly. 'You could tell me when to turn left or right.'

'Dai, Annamaria! This is not the moment for...'

She shifted herself into the passenger seat with one graceful movement, accompanied by a brief trill of laughter.

Beppe set the car in motion. Out of the corner of his eye, he noticed the 'shopper' standing outside a chemist's looking at their *Cinquecento* as it drove by. She would notice that the driver was NOT the woman who had first stepped into the car. Beppe felt very smug. He had been right to take precautions.

Less than forty-five minutes later, *Agente* Cristina Cardinale, wearing almost identical clothing to Annamaria's, got out of the same *Cinquecento,* driven by one of the male officers, and walked back along the same stretch of pavement as Annamaria had done earlier on. She paused as if looking for her house keys in her handbag. The *Commissario* had instructed her to wait outside the apartment and look out for the middle-aged lady shopper and her car. Cristina could not stare at their suspect, but she was fairly certain that the woman held up her smartphone for a couple of seconds as she took a photo of her through the open car window. The bait had been taken. Cristina was aware that the occupant of the car had got out and was following her casually into the apartment block, slipping in before the main entrance door closed. Cristina got into the lift quickly and went up to the second floor. The lift indicator would show at what level she had got out.

Cristina Cardinale waited outside the door until the woman got out of the lift and began to walk casually down the corridor towards her. Cristina was under instruction from Beppe to make sure the follower knew which apartment she was entering before she opened the door and disappeared inside.

Cristina retrieved the turquoise suitcase. She threw off the outer garments she was wearing and donned a conspicuous red coat left out by Annamaria before she had departed. *Agente* Cardinale hung around long enough for the 'stalker' to have disappeared downstairs again before she marched down the corridor with a completely different gait and took the stairs down to the ground floor.

As Beppe had predicted, their 'stalker' was talking to the janitor, showing him the photograph which she had taken from inside the car.

The janitor had received an urgent phone call from that scary *Commissario* a few minutes previously, warning him that he should be very wary of any strange woman who asked him to 'identify' a girl looking like Annamaria. 'Tell her she's called – I don't know – Sofia Rossi! But for heaven's sake, say NOTHING about her being blind. Do you understand that?'

The janitor was in awe of this police officer and brought the conversation with the woman to a rapid close – so as not to accidently divulge any other information.

Cristina returned with Annamaria's suitcase to the *Questura* in Via Pesaro and met her chief by the reception desk.

'That woman was definitely trailing Annamaria, *capo.*' She told Beppe about seeing the woman talking to the janitor. 'And this is her car's registration number,' she said, handing him a piece of paper on which she had scribbled down the vital information.

'Grazie Cristina…*sei stata bravissima!'*

Beppe climbed upstairs to Mariastella's office, where she and Annamaria were waiting for him, seemingly chatting inconsequentially about life in general.

'We *were* followed, Annamaria. I think you should know that. Now you can breathe a sigh of relief and leave the rest to us.'

'Am I supposed to feel safer now, Beppe?' she asked with an ironic smile on her face. But there was a look of unease in those oh-so-vivid but sightless eyes.

'Probably not, Annamaria. But at least we know that the bait has been taken. You will be safely out of the way.'

'Thank you, Beppe. But…'

Beppe and the *Questore,* Mariastella Martellini knew exactly what question was coming next.

'We will be putting two of our team in your flat to see who turns up over the next few days. The intruders will be in for a very nasty shock.'

'I'm not sure whether I shall ever feel safe there again,' said Annamaria Intimo in a very subdued voice.

It was Mariastella who was overcome by emotion for this girl, who had become embroiled in this case – almost through her own volition. She came round from behind her desk and gave the blind girl an affectionate hug.

'This will all blow over soon enough, Annamaria. We won't ever abandon you – you may be certain of that! Now, Beppe is going to drive you up to Atri, where you'll be as safe as houses with his lovely family. Leave the rest to us. We've got your sister's address and we shall pay her a visit today to reassure her that you are safe. We will not be able to tell her where you are, I fear. But you will be able to phone each other very briefly every day.'

'Come on, Annamaria,' said Beppe. 'It's time to go home. You're going to be so welcomed by Sonia and the children. They will all want to adopt you as their own.'

Annamaria smiled and looked a little more relaxed.

There was a discreet knock on the *Questore's* door. It was *Ispettore* Pippo Cafarelli who entered, looking as if he had important information to impart.

'You might want to hear this just before you go *Commissario,*' said Pippo.

'But would Annamaria like to hear it?' asked Beppe pointedly.

'Yes, she *would, Ispettore!*'

It was Annamaria Intimo herself who had uttered these words. Pippo was still hesitant to divulge what was on his mind in front of this fragile-seeming beauty in their midst.

'*Dai, Pippo! Spiffera tutto!*' [40] ordered Mariastella Martellini with a sigh. 'Annamaria has as much right as we do to know what is going on in this drama.'

'Well, I have just returned from the *Municipio,*' [41] continued Pippo reluctantly.

'I'm as much a part of this investigation as you are, Pippo. You don't have to mince your words with me.'

It was, once again, Annamaria who had spoken with a degree of asperity which took everyone's breath away.

'You are right, *signorina.* I apologise,' said Pippo humbly. 'We tracked down the traffic warden who had spotted that Fed-Ex van which those killers arrived in. And you'll never guess what...'

'*Ispettore,* we are not here to play guessing games!' stated the lady *Questore* sharply.

'I apologise, *Signora Questore,*' stammered Pippo.

'No, Pippo. It is I who should apologise. I am just impatient to know what you discovered. You are an Inspector

---

[40] Come on...spit it all out!
[41] Town Hall

now. You don't need to keep apologising for what you say!' said Mariastella Martellini in a kindlier voice.

'*Grazie, Signora Questura*...Mariastella,' said Pippo before continuing hurriedly:

'They must have borrowed – or purloined – the Fed-Ex van from their depot in Reggio Calabria and driven it all the way up here to Pescara. The number-plate is definitely from that city...'

'Well,' said Beppe. 'That confirms the *'ndrangheta* connection. But I'm surprised all the same. It might even give us a lead if we can find out who acquired the van in the first place. It would seem that someone in whichever clan is involved has been very careless.'

'Or over-confident, maybe?' suggested Mariastella.

'Or maybe it was done deliberately in such a way as to point the finger of suspicion at a rival clan?'

There was total silence in the room which lasted for as long as it took for Mariastella, Pippo and Beppe himself to hold their breath. It was Annamaria who had offered this explanation.

Her tinkling laughter broke the silence.

'I know you are all still in the room,' she said. 'I can feel your presence. I'm sorry if what I said sounded preposterous...'

It was Beppe who finally spoke.

'You, Annamaria, should apply for a position with the police force. We could do with someone with a brain like yours working with us.'

Mariastella and Pippo simply began to clap their hands together in applause.

'I'll think about it,' said Annamaria, with another little burst of delighted laughter.

'What we must do without delay,' said the lady *Questore,* coming back down to earth, 'is to put a couple of police officers into Annamaria's apartment tonight. From what you have told me today, Beppe, whoever is behind all this is not going to waste time. We need to get a couple of our team in there without delay.'

It was the recently appointed Inspector Cafarelli who spoke next:

'May I suggest that I do the first watch, *Signora Questore*. I can take my wife, Mariangela, with me. That will take care of the problem of sleeping arrangements until we can set up some more flexible rota. My Mariangela has proved to be as good as any cop, as I am sure you remember, Beppe.' [42]

Beppe looked at his *capo* and nodded in approval.'

Annamaria, who could not see the gesture, immediately endorsed the idea.

'Yes, I like that idea. I trust *Ispettore* Pippo absolutely. I can tell by his voice that he knows what he is doing.'

Annamaria could not see that Pippo's face had turned red. He was prone to blushing at the most trivial of compliments. Beppe and Mariastella laughed and shrugged their shoulders. The plan was approved.

'I'm sorry, Pippo,' laughed Annamaria. 'I see I have embarrassed you…'

Once again, Beppe remained open-mouthed at this girl's ability to sense what was happening in the visible world. Pippo and Mariastella merely stared in wonder.

'I had another idea, *Commissario…Signora Questore…*' began Pippo. 'You remember how we fooled those American crooks with a life-size image of Professor Pisano? [43] Maybe a similar image of…Annamaria… would fool whoever turns up at

---

[42] A reference to 'A Close Encounter with Mushrooms'
[43] A reference to 'The Vanishing Physicist'

her apartment? Afterall, they might well arrive at night time…What do you think, *Commissario?*'

What his *Commissario* thought was: 'Is this man getting ready to step into my shoes?' What he said, as casually as he could and looking at Mariastella for approval was: 'I suppose it might just work. Maybe it's worth the try.'

'I like the idea,' stated the lady *Questore*. 'It might well provide us with one additional line of defence. We'll do it!'

The *Commissario* stifled his baser instincts and said a trifle stiffly:

'I'll take Annamaria down to the technicians in the basement for the photograph before we go back to Atri. And, Pippo, I would like to call a general meeting of all our team tomorrow at eight o'clock sharp. See to that, will you?'

'*Con piacere, capo!*' [44] replied Pippo Cafarelli, totally aware of how his friend Beppe Stancato was feeling beneath the surface.

Mariastella Martellini was doing her best to stifle a desire to giggle. She too, had correctly read the signs.

'Poor Beppe,' she thought, affectionately. 'His one and only Achilles Heel!'

---

[44] With pleasure, boss!

8: *On the darker side of Italy...*

Grazie mille, Nunzia. You have proved yourself to be a loyal member of the Talarico family. This woman even has a name, I see, Sofia Rossi - and an apartment number. Most impressive! How did you manage to get her name?

Oh, I got it easily enough from the janitor. He was obviously overawed by the fact I was a woman. I think I made him a bit nervous.'

You did well, Nunzia. I will be showing you my gratitude in person if ever we are fortunate enough to meet up again...

Nunzia grimaced silently at the thought, but said nothing. She knew what was in store for her if ever she let the ageing Mafia *boss* get within a metre's distance of her body. His notion of *'le droit du seigneur'* as an accepted law of nature was deeply embedded in his distorted philosophy of life.

Now I must leave you, carissima. [45] *I have to arrange another little trip up north for those two stronzi[46] who allowed themselves to be spotted in broad daylight. It's true what they say, isn't it Nunzia? If you want a job doing properly...*

Arrivederci, *Zio* [47] Fausto,' she said. *'Buona fortuna* with your mission.'

Oh, it has nothing to do with luck, I can assure you, Nunzia.

---

[45] Dearest one – often used as a conversational 'sweetener'
[46] Arseholes – a strong and vulgar term
[47] Uncle

He hung up without waiting for her to utter any further inanities. He replaced the receiver on its cradle, swore briefly under his breath at the time-wasting task ahead of him of organising yet another assassination trip; so far away from his native Reggio Calabria too - where the fear that he could instil in others had a name and a face to go with it. He picked up the phone again and dialled a local number which he had had encrypted. He tutted impatiently when the man whom he knew must be standing near the phone did not answer immediately.

'Stronzo!' he muttered under his breath. Why had he ever agreed to take this cousin - twice removed – under his wing? Just to keep those useless 'hangers-on' from sinking into obscurity? But that was what the *'ndrangheta'* did, he reminded himself. The strong were there to protect their weaker brethren. At least, he could exploit them for some time to come before their inevitable 'expulsion' became a necessity.

'Pronto, Don [48] Fausto!' said the voice.

May the Blessed Virgin look kindly on our works of charity, caro collega.

'Amen,' retorted Gregorio Giuffrè.

Was that a note of impatience that Don Fausto Talarico detected? He decided to ignore it for now. He needed this underling's complete cooperation if he was to remove this new threat of exposure following his latest costly act of self-vindication.

I have another job for those two colleagues we sent up to Pescara to take care of that female Judas. But it must be done

---

[48] 'Don' is a title used by the mafia clans – the same title which is accorded to priests!

immediately. Seems they were spotted going into the apartment by some young woman as she got out of the lift. I've texted you her details...

But, *Zio Fausto,* Danilo's got a job in that fish canning factory we run. We can't keep taking him out just because he...

Tell the owner he'll be compensated in the usual way, Gregorio. I want this taken care of immediately. And tell them to make sure nobody sees them this time. Do it at night time... I'll see you next week at our Festa dell'Immacolata. [49] We shall be out in full force this year!

'Va bene, capo. Leave it with me,' said Gregorio Giuffrè, with all the signs of subservient acquiescence in his voice.

To the mobster standing near him, he said:

'You heard, Niko. Drive up to Pescara by car this afternoon and finish off the job – no elaborate frills to worry about this time. And take Mimo with you, as soon as he gets out of the canning factory. You'll be back by tomorrow morning if you're quick. *E non fate cazzate questa volta!' [50]*

'There *was* a woman who walked past us, *boss.* She was young and very beautiful but she never even looked at us. It was almost as if she didn't see us. I dunno...'

'Just get the job done and let's keep *Zio Fausto* happy for another week or so.'

The mobster merely nodded. He had barely taken in that woman's presence as they were about to get into the lift with

---

[49] The festival of the Immaculate Conception
[50] Don't cock it up this time

that ridiculous statue. But she did look extremely sexy. Maybe they could have a bit of fun first...

'But above all, remember, Niko, if you run into any trouble, you make sure you say you were sent by the Talarico clan - *chiaro?*' snapped Gregorio Giuffrè.'

The mobster, Niko, sighed. *'Sì capo.* Very clear!'

'And for goodness' sake, don't use that Fed-ex van this time. Somebody might well have spotted it last time.'

Mimo had been too petrified of the inevitable reaction to mention to his *boss* that he had received a parking fine from the Pescara authorities that morning.

'Soon,' thought Gregorio Giuffrè proudly, as soon as his assistants had departed, 'they will be calling ME Don Gregorio!'

It had been a stroke of genius, he considered, to get his minions to plant that statue of the Virgin Mary at the crime scene. Sooner or later, someone would make the connection between the statue and his uncle's obsession with his version of Mary the mother of Jesus. A pity that the Pescara media had not publicised this murder as yet. The police must be keeping the details of the crime firmly under wraps so far. Perhaps he should subtly give the local TV station or their local newspaper *una spinta* [51] in the right direction?

---

[51] A push

9: *Pippo Cafarelli takes over...*

It had never happened before. Pippo received a text message from his *Commissario* only ten minutes before the 8 o'clock meeting in Via Pesaro was due to begin. Inspector Pippo Cafarelli read the message with a twinge of anxiety.

Ciao Pippo. We have a minor incident to contend with at home. Could you please start the meeting without me? I shall be delayed. Not sure how long for. Bring the team up to date with developments. Make sure you and Mariangela are in Flat 24 **well before** *nightfall. A dopo.* [52] *Grazie mille!*
Beppe.

Pippo was unexpectedly in charge of the team of thirteen officers – including the newest recruits. It struck him just how much this team had come to rely on the *Commissario* for their sense of cohesion. He forced himself to stand up in front of the group, trying very hard to muster a sense of authority.

'Have you been promoted again, Pippo?' called out *Agente* Gino Martelli.

'Silence for our *Commissario* in waiting,' someone else called out cheerfully. This produced a brief outburst of uncomfortable laughter from a few of the more experienced team members.

'Beppe has been delayed by some family matter,' stated Pippo in a quietly unassuming tone of voice. 'He has asked me to bring you all up to date on our present – and very complex – murder case. A number of you are certainly only half aware of the horrific and bizarre nature of the death of a young woman whose name is Laura Ianni a few days ago. Our limited research into this girl's identity might indicate that this is not her real

---

[52] See you later.

70

name. We are looking into this possible scenario. For those of you who might not yet be in full possession of the details of her death, I would ask Officers Cardinale and Campione – Cristina and Emma – to say a few words. They were the 'lucky' ones who were first called to the scene of the crime.'

'It was ghastly,' said Cristina. 'She had been strangled, covered with crudely applied make-up and left lodged against her living-room wall.'

'And there was a statue of the Blessed Virgin Mary with her arms held out in supplication plonked down just by the body. It was grotesque!' added Emma.

A horrified silence had settled over the group. Pippo Cafarelli continued to explain the case without any interruption. He was nevertheless relieved when the *Questore,* Mariastella Martellini, stepped unobtrusively into the room and sat down with the body of officers. Her presence added to the solemnity of the gathering and more or less guaranteed that nobody else would attempt to make facetious comments.

Ispettore Cafarelli continued to expound on the extraordinary developments of the last couple of days.

'Matters came to a head just a couple of days ago when we realised that our only 'witness' to this gruesome murder was one of Laura Ianni's neighbours on the floor below. Her name is Annamaria Intimo…'

Pippo was expecting the customary titters whenever this unusual surname cropped up in conversation. [53] But he was relieved when the attentive silence remained prolonged. The severe frown on Mariastella's face might just have quelled any desire to be flippant.

---

[53] Intimi – as well as 'intimate' the plural word also means 'ladies' underwear'

'Annamaria is, as I guess some of you are aware, completely blind. She is in her thirties and watching her dealing with everyday life is a revelation. It is difficult to realise she cannot see. Unfortunately for her, but happily for us, she crossed the path of the two killers just as she stepped out of the lift and headed out through the main door of the apartment block. She sensed they were strangers and that they were carrying something cumbersome – the statue of the Virgin Mary, we assume. She detected that one of the men smelt of sardines. So, we may be looking for someone who works in a fish-canning factory – down in Calabria. We discovered where they came from because, by sheer chance, the Fed-ex van the killers arrived in was spotted by our local *vigile urbano* [54]. It had a number plate from Reggio Calabria and he gave them a parking ticket. The situation for Annamaria Intimo has become threatening simply because the gangsters assumed they had been seen by a witness and reported this to their *boss* in Reggio Calabria. We became aware that Annamaria was being followed by a woman in her late thirties or early forties, pretending she was on a shopping trip. This woman went into the apartment block and asked the janitor for information about Annmaria, showing him a photo she had taken from her car. A photo of our Cristina Cardinale, in point of fact – because we had already substituted Cristina for Annamaria.'

'Do we have this woman's car registration number, Pippo?' asked Giacomo D'Amico – the oldest member of the Pescara team. 'That might help us to identify the *'ndrangheta* clan involved in the killing.'

'*Appunto,* [55] *Giacomo.* And the answer is 'yes'. With his usual foresight, our *Commissario* had warned the janitor to give

---

[54] Local town police who deal with everyday 'offences' such as illegal parking.

our witness a false name should anyone ask for specific details about Annamaria. We will be sending two of you round to pick up this lady for questioning as soon as this meeting is over. Interrogating her might just identify the clan involved. But this is far from certain...'

'I think I might know which clan is involved,' said a nervous voice from somewhere in the middle of the row of police officers.

It was the *novellino,* [56] *Agente* Donato Pavone, who had turned red with embarrassment at his own temerity.

'I was going to tell the *Commissario* about it when he came in this morning...' he stammered.

'We shall all be very happy to know what you have discovered, *Agente* Pavone.'

It was the *Questore* herself whose gentle but firm voice was inviting the young officer to continue. Mariastella Martellini had been reassured by Beppe's repeated claims that this timid-looking newcomer concealed a very active and perceptive brain.

'I was the officer who accompanied our *Commissario* to the crime scene,' explained Officer Pavone as if the involvement of their *capo* would lend credence to his words.

'Just like Cristina and Emma, I found the murder scene nauseating. But it was the statue of Our Lady which struck me as being so uncomfortably incongruous...'

One of the newer recruits muttered something like: 'Keep it simple, Donato' which produced titters from the others.

Mariastella Martellini interjected sharply:

'Go and buy yourself a good Italian dictionary, Flavio!'

---

[55] Precisely
[56] The 'new boy'

The titters ceased abruptly and the new recruit, Flavio, was blushing in embarrassment at being castigated by this awesome goddess.

'Continue please Officer Pavone,' said the lady *Questore.*

'At the *Commissario's* suggestion, I started to research the various *'ndrangheta* clans in Reggio Calabria. Finally, I came across one particular clan – the Talarico clan – who exploit their local version of the Virgin Mary for their own ends. Their *boss* deliberately holds clan meetings inside the Sanctuary dedicated to *Santa Maria di Polsi* – an ancient church nearby – in defiance of the local parish priest. And this *boss,* Don Fausto Talarico, finances processions round their district carrying a huge statue of Mary the mother of Jesus. They stop in front of all the houses where the Talarico clan members live and the statue is made to bow in front of each house – as a sign of respect from the Virgin Mary for the 'holy' work carried out by this clan. The locals just refer to this ceremony as the *inchino.* [57] It simply reinforces the power of the *boss* and the superstitious fear of the locals. *Il Papa Francesco* [58] is up in arms about what is going on. I believe he has even excommunicated this Don Fausto from the Church.

This clan is ruthless and obsessed with their connection to the Blessed Virgin. It seems to me to tie up with our murder...' Officer Donato Pavone's voice died out – as if he suspected his audience must have lost all interest in his far-fetched account. He blushed and sat down again in the midst of the stony silence. It was a full ten seconds later when someone – probably Mariastella Martellini herself – began to applaud him

---

[57] The bow
[58] Pope Francis. This part of the story is factual

loudly. The whole meeting joined in and somebody called out: *Bravo, Donato! Bravo davvero!* [59]

'It should be *you* who tells the *Commissario* what you have discovered, *Agente Donato,* as soon as he gets here. I am certain he will attach great importance to your discovery. Well done!'

'*Grazie, signora Questore!*' said Officer Pavone – who was now blushing with pleasure.

'Excuse me, *Signora Questore,*' said Officer Giacomo D'Amico. 'There have been many surprises so far this morning. But possibly the biggest surprise of all is that our *Commissario* – Beppe – has missed a meeting. I cannot remember such a thing ever happening before during Beppe's time with us. Is it something serious?'

Mariastella Martellini laughed.

'From what I have gathered, since Annamaria Intimo went home with Beppe yesterday evening, Beppe's daughter Veronica has invented a new version of the game Blind Man's Bluff – inspired by Annamaria herself, it seems. Veronica asked her in all innocence what it felt like to be blind. Annamaria – who never refuses a challenge - took Veronica and Lorenzo out into the garden yesterday evening, got the children to stand apart in different areas of the garden and demonstrated how she could sense their presence by their smell or the sound of their breathing – or just their 'aura' as she drew close to them. Veronica, Beppe tells me, was so impressed that she forced her little brother to get up early this morning and made him walk around the garden blindfolded while she stood still as a statue. The poor kid tripped over a rock in the garden and maybe broke his wrist. Beppe had to take him to hospital while Sonia escorted a very guilt-ridden and tearful daughter to school. I'll

---

[59] Truly

leave Beppe to tell you the outcome when he gets in later. But I suspect that our *Commissario* will have other matters on his mind. Pippo - would you like to put everybody in the picture about what is happening tonight? You should all listen to this, *ragazzi*. You will be asked to volunteer for the devious scheme that Beppe – and Pippo - have proposed in the light of our precious blind witness having become inadvertently involved in this investigation. Pippo...?' concluded Mariastella inviting him to explain what plan they had devised.

'It can hardly justify being called a 'plan', *ragazzi* – simply because we have no inkling as to how events will turn out,' Pippo began. 'We are certain that the clan responsible for this apparently motiveless murder will send someone to deal with the one witness to their previous visit – namely Annamaria Intimo. Our plan is to set a trap for them. We are assuming that the killers will be the same couple as before – because they will recognise the woman who stepped out of the lift. They will have a name – albeit the wrong one – and Annamaria's apartment number. I and my very courageous wife – who has proved her ability to protect her husband against attacks by the mafia in the past [60] - will be taking up residence in Annamaria's apartment and hopefully provide a suitable reception committee for the killers of Laura Ianni. We will set up a rota so that there will always be two officers present near the apartment throughout the night. The *Commissario* is convinced that the mobsters will arrive over the next couple of days – even tonight.'

The *Commissario* in question arrived with perfect timing looking slightly out of breath but smiling. He was greeted by a quiet round of ironic applause by the whole gathering.

---

[60] See: 'A Close Encounter with Mushrooms'.

'Thank you Pippo for standing in for me. I gather you have managed to fill everybody in already? Please continue, *Ispettore.* Don't mind me,' said Beppe affably.

'I think everybody would like to know how your son Lorenzo is, Beppe,' said Mariastella Martellini.

'Poor lad! He was a victim of his elder sister's overly vivid imagination. But he has only strained his wrist. No broken bones. He is back in his classroom with his arm in a sling – enjoying all the attention he is getting. Pippo?'

'I was on the point of asking a couple of officers to bring in the lady stalker, *Commissario.* Do you still consider...?

'I've been thinking about that while driving down from Atri. I'm glad you haven't brought her in yet. I think I was too precipitate. It might be safer to let her stay ignorant that we know about her. Let's wait and see who turns up at Annamaria's flat first.'

This reflected precisely what Pippo had worked out in his own mind. So much easier when the words came from the horse's mouth, considered his diplomatic second-in-command.

'Before you go back home again, Beppe,' said the lady *Questore,* 'I think you should have a word with *Agente* Donato Pavone. He has some very significant information that he has unearthed for you.'

10:   *The Commissario's volta face...*

Talking to Officer Pavone was not the first thing that Beppe did. He retired to his office. He needed time to think on his own. He had barely slept the previous night and had only woken up from a fitful sleep because of the sound of Lorenzo crying in agony in the garden below. He had kissed Sonia and hugged Annamaria just as they were both setting off on foot to accompany an anxious and tearful Veronica to school. Beppe had carried a subdued Lorenzo in his arms and placed him gently in the family car and strapped him into the front passenger seat before setting off to the local hospital - driving very slowly.

His ill-defined nocturnal fears about allowing Pippo and his wife to stay on guard overnight in Annamaria's apartment were becoming more insistent.

'I'm missing some important element in all of this,' he said under his breath as he entered his office, uncharacteristically closing the door behind him – usually a sign to his fellow officers that he did not want to be disturbed. It was almost unheard of for this to happen during a major investigation. 'What is it? There is some obvious facet about our plan to seize those mobsters that is escaping me,' he thought. He was feeling mentally frustrated by his own obtuseness. He sat down with his hands pressed tiredly to his forehead. The niggling sensation in his mind would not go away.

Pippo, about to set off and pick up his wife, Mariangela, before they ensconced themselves in Annamaria Intimo's apartment, took one look through the rectangular glass panel set into the closed office door, and saw only Beppe's head resting on his hands apparently fast asleep. He left his *capo* alone. He could phone him later from the apartment which they were about to occupy.

Beppe woke up with a start. He looked at the time on his mobile phone - since he had always refused to wear a wrist watch. He was astounded to see he had slept for over thirty minutes. But he felt invigorated. He had just had a dream – or was it one of his much less frequent 'visions'? His friend Don Emanuele – the Archbishop of Pescara – had appeared in this quasi-prophetic revelation as if he had been God-the-Father in heaven rather than a mere corporeal prelate.

'Beppe, just think!' Don Emanuele's soothing voice had stated. 'What would Annamaria do differently if she was in her house at night time?'

The answer to this ethereal question struck him within a few seconds of waking up. Of course, her whole apartment would be in total darkness! Their idea of having a lit-up image of Annamaria Intimo to fool the mobsters was completely irrelevant! She could use the placard afterwards to promote her business if she wanted. But it would make total sense to turn all the lights off in the apartment from the main control panel – even if that meant temporarily switching off the other appliances too. That way, the attackers would have no way of turning on the lights. It also meant that the armed supporting officers could stay in the apartment alongside Pippo and Mariangela, whose eyes would be accustomed to the darkness when (*If*, he reminded himself) the mobsters arrived. He sighed heavily at the prospect of a highly probable negative outcome to their elaborate plan.

He phoned Pippo as soon as he had digested the implications of this unlooked-for revelation in full. He told Pippo about his 'vision', hoping and praying that his younger colleague would not utter the dreaded words: 'I had already worked that out, *capo.*'

However, there *was* a noticeable pause on the other end of the line as Beppe held his breath. Finally, he heard Pippo saying in a quiet voice:

'*Geniale, capo!*' [61] 'That changes everything, doesn't it! And it will give us a clear advantage over the aggressors - when they arrive.'

Beppe made no comment. Sonia – had she been with him – would have told him that his hunches always turned out to be well-founded. He did not go home that night, but slept in his office on a camp bed which was kept there for emergencies. A cheerful phone call from Sonia reassured him that their house guest had effortlessly charmed the whole family – including Sonia's mother and father. Roberto, in particular, was showing signs of wanting to spend an inordinate amount of time in Annamaria's presence.

'Annamaria can already find her own way around on the top floor of the house – with Veronica's help. But our daughter insisted on wearing a blindfold during suppertime – she is punishing herself, it seems, for causing harm to Leo. He says he has already forgiven his sister and told her she's just being babyish in insisting on wearing a scarf round her eyes.'

'Talking of babies – which we weren't really talking about…?' asked Beppe.

'*Sì, amore. Sono incinta.*[62] I've just carried out the test. Come home soon, won't you!'

Beppe slept through the night. When he woke up, it was daylight. Why hadn't Pippo phoned him? He dialled Pippo's number and waited impatiently for the inspector to answer.

'Nothing happened, Beppe. Sorry.'

---

[61] Brilliant, chief!

[62] Pregnant. Pron: *inCHINta*

With a great effort of will, Beppe made light of this piece of news.

'Well, our precautions were a bit premature, Pippo. I'm sure something will happen tonight – or even earlier.'

'Gino and Danilo are asleep here on Annamaria's armchairs. They both insist on staying here – even though the mobsters are unlikely to arrive before nightfall. They both feel that, in the past, they've messed up a bit every time you've given them a crucial job to carry out. They want to prove to you that they are worthy of your trust, I have the feeling.'

After a suitable pause, Beppe said to his colleague:

'I could come and relieve you later on if you wish.'

'No need, *capo*. As far as my Mariangela is concerned, Annamaria's apartment is like living in a palace compared to our flat on the sixth floor of a seven-story block. She even dared to suggest she would be quite happy if the mobsters didn't turn up tonight either.'

Beppe smiled at his words – invisible to his junior colleague – and closed the call with a brief *'ciao'*.

* * *

Beppe's first port of call, after receiving Pippo's negative report, was to visit his *capo* on the top floor of the *Questura.*

'It appears that our occupation of Annamaria's flat might turn out to be a damp squib, Mariastella,' said Beppe. He had the unpleasant feeling that he had gone too far on this occasion.

Mariastella's reaction was unexpected.

'In the relatively short time I have known you, *Commissario,* you have dreamed up plots far more outlandish than this one. I have, on many occasions, been tempted to ignore your flights of fantasy. But on every single occasion, you have turned out to be right. So, I absolutely intend that this crazy idea of yours should run for at least two more nights. You are, as usual, showing your habitual tendency to become impatient when nothing seems to be happening.'

'I just feel we could move things along more quickly if we arrested that woman who was tailing Annamaria. She must have some idea of whom we are dealing with…'

The lady *Questore* held up her hand to stop Beppe's flow of words.

'I have thought about that too, Beppe. But the trouble is, she could all too easily come up with some innocent explanation, and we would be forced to release her from custody. She would then be free to inform whichever mafia *boss* who is involved in that gruesome murder that they are under suspicion.'

Beppe let out a sigh. He knew that his *capo* had made a valid point. He himself had unconsciously rejected this course of action a short while ago.

'You might not like what I am going to say, Beppe, but I shall say it anyway – for the umpteenth time since I have known you. Go home and be with your family – and your house guest! I myself will stay here tonight – when it is far more likely that something will happen *chez* Annamaria. Since your absolutely brilliant 'dream', there will be three armed police officers present – with pistols and torches – who should be able to deal with any visitors who turn up at Annamaria's flat tonight – or tomorrow night. I faithfully promise to phone you at whatever time of night it is when the mobsters arrive. And, yes, I did say *when* they arrive. Beppe.'

'Are you ordering me to go home, *Signora Questore?*'

'Yes, for once, I *am, Commissario!*' stated Mariastella. 'You need and deserve a day and night off, Beppe,' she added kindly. 'We will try very hard not to mess up in your absence!'

'*Grazie mille,* Mariastella. I would like to spend time at home today. Sonia has just announced that she is expecting our third – and final – child.'

'Are you sure about that, Beppe?'

'Absolutely! If she has a fourth child, I shall be forced to take up the post of *Questore* out of sheer financial necessity!'

Mariastella let out a cheerful laugh.

'Well, Beppe, I shall certainly not be praying for such an outcome. Now, please go and ask *Agente* Donato Pavone what he has unearthed about a certain *'ndrangheta* clan in Reggio Calabria – you will find it fascinating. I hope to be in touch with you tonight with some more concrete news.'

* * *

Beppe had been known to hug members of his team when he had felt particularly moved by their insight or devotion to the cause of justice. He had even been known to kiss the female members of his team on the forehead; 'like an uncle would', he claimed by way of justification for such an 'unprofessional' gesture. But he was aware that hugging Donato Pavone *and* planting a smacking kiss on his forehead was the first time he had bestowed such gestures on a male colleague.

Officer Donato Pavone did not have time to react before his *capo* was complimenting him warmly on his revelations concerning the Talarico clan.

'That is the best news I have heard since this investigation began, *Agente* Pavone. *Bravo...bravissimo,* Donato! Just make sure you never decide to go off and become a chef instead of a policeman!' he added to his already bewildered colleague.

The reference to a certain officer called Remo Mastrodicasa was lost on Donato Pavone. Never mind - he could seek out Officer Giacomo D'Amico and ask for enlightenment from their oldest and most approachable colleague.

'He resigned from being a *sbirro* [63] because he didn't like shooting people. He went off to run a restaurant near L'Aquila. Beppe – our *Commissario* – really valued his intelligence and his ability to solve problems online,' Giacomo explained to his tenderfoot junior colleague. Donato Pavone felt warm inside at the implied compliment.

'But, unlike this Remo guy, *I* won't hesitate to take a pot-shot at those thugs who murdered Laura Ianni,' he informed Giacomo, who smiled and patted Donato's shoulder.

'I think we all feel the same way deep down inside, Donato…'

---

[63] A cop

11: *Annamaria's love of water…*

How to fill up the afternoon and take his mind off what might – or worse, might not – happen that night? He felt anxious that he must have omitted some other vital precaution in anticipation of the mobsters return visit to Annamaria's *palazzo*. It had only been thanks to a last-minute phone call from Pippo Cafarelli, just as Beppe was leaving the *Questura* before driving home to Atri, that a potential hitch in proceedings had occurred to him.

Pippo, Mariangela and Officers Martelli and Simone were already ensconced in Annamaria's flat for their second night time vigil. How – should the gangsters arrive after dark – would they gain access through the main door if it was locked to outside visitors?

'Well, *capo,*' said Pippo. 'I was assuming they would simply buzz through to Annamaria's flat from outside the main door. But I'll have a word with the concierge [64] to make sure the doors can be opened from the outside.'

'*Grazie, Pippo. In bocca al lupo!*' concluded Beppe, entrusting the whole operation to his younger colleague without too many qualms. He had been 'ordered' to go home by his *capo*. He was powerless to change the course of events – maybe for the first time in his role as *commissario*.

It was still well before lunchtime when he arrived home. The kids were not at school since it was a Saturday morning.

Annamaria was looking a little bit lost for the first time since her arrival.

'I'm serenely happy to be here, Beppe,' she assured him. 'You'll get used to my short periods of meditation – they are just a part of my coping with not being able to see.'

---

[64] Italians use the French word for the 'live-in' person who looks after a block of flats.

Veronica looked as if she was about to cry on hearing those words. She went silently up to Annamaria and threw her arms round her neck. By whatever sixth sense that Annamaria possessed, she simply said:

'Grazie, grazie, Veronica. *Ti voglio bene.'* [65]

Piqued that his sister had reacted with this gesture before him, Lorenzo ran up to Annamaria and hugged her clumsily because of his small size. His expression clearly showed a gentle *mélange* of pity and affection.

As if she had been expecting this reaction from Veronica's younger brother, Annamaria gave a little laugh and said without any hesitation: *'Ti voglio bene anche te, Lori!'*

Beppe and Sonia were patently deeply moved by their children's spontaneous reaction towards their 'guest'. It marked an important moment in their children's emotional perception of somebody outside the immediate family circle. Beppe decided to break the spell before anyone had time to feel embarrassed by the unexpected silence that had ensued.

'How would you like to go for a boat-ride on the sea, Annamaria? I assume, as you do not seem to be scared of anything that life has to offer, that you are not afraid of water?'

'No, *Commissario.* I can even swim – you may be surprised to know!'

He was being gently reprimanded, yet again, for assuming that being blind cancelled out all other forms of human activity.

He did not have time to formulate a suitable reply because Sonia was smiling and Lorenzo and Veronica had reverted to childhood and were jumping up and down enthusiastically on the spot. They had never even seen their father's boat – let alone been allowed on board. Sonia had

---

[65] 'I love you' – to a family member or close friend. Cf 'Ti amo.'

always upheld the belief that being on a boat required that their two offspring should be able to swim – life-jackets or not.

Sonia set about organising a picnic with the help of two enthusiastic helpers. Annamaria turned to face the spot where Sonia's voice was coming from.

'I didn't think to bring my bikini with me, Sonia. I don't suppose you could…?'

'I'm sure I have countless unused swimming costumes of various shapes and colours for you to choose from, Annamaria.'

Only then, did she realise what she had said.

'I'm sorry, Annamaria. I don't suppose you mind what colour it is…'

Annamaria laughed her engaging laugh and said:

'Oh yes, I do, Sonia! There will be four other people looking at me, don't forget – not even counting the seagulls. So I would be grateful if you and Veronica could choose me something appropriate. I don't want to look out-of-place, do I?'

Veronica had a happy smile on her face that their guest had considered her to be important enough to help her out of her dilemma. In point of fact, Sonia told Veronica to take their guest into their bedroom to choose a costume while she went on preparing the picnic.

It was much closer to lunch time than breakfast time before the 'family' - as Beppe already thought of his four *protégés* – set off on the short ride to Silvi Marina, where Beppe's boat was moored.

'FIVE *protégés*,' he reminded himself.

* * *

The initial thrill of finding themselves on a boat was temporarily dampened when it was discovered that the battery was flat so nothing more than a reluctant churning sound was made by the engine. Beppe had to call on the marina staff to help him out. By a general vote – excluding the boat owner – it was decided to ignore the pangs of hunger until they were out of the harbour. Lorenzo and the three 'girls' played silly word games while Beppe went off to get help. A cheerful marine mechanic accompanied Beppe back, pulling along a cumbersome-looking piece of apparatus which made the old engine spring to life within minutes.

'Don't turn the motor off, *Signor* Stancato,' said the mechanic. 'We don't want to have to charge you for coming out to sea to rescue you later on! And I would advise you to fill up with fuel before you leave the port. Apart from that, you have chosen a perfect day for being out at sea. It's as calm as a millpond out there! *Divertitevi ragazzi!'* [66]

He lumbered off, trailing the recharger behind him.

And then they were off out to sea. Sonia ordered everyone to don life jackets – which was alright until they discovered that they did not have a fifth jacket. An oversight for which Beppe blamed himself.

'*Commissario* – I will sacrifice my own life rather than run the risk of one your family drowning! Don't worry about me. I'm simply overjoyed to be with you and to feel the movement of the water all around me.'

'But Annamaria…' Beppe began to protest.

'*Non ti preoccupare,* Beppe. [67] I was a mermaid in a former life!'

---

[66] Enjoy yourselves
[67] Don't worry

This revelation caused an outburst of mirth from Veronica and Lorenzo – who could not resist making comments they would never have dreamt of making to anyone other than their new 'big sister'.

'I can just see you with a tail, Annamaria,' said Veronica cheerfully. 'I bet it was a bright blue like the sea'.

'I prefer seeing your legs, Annamaria!'

This appraisal of their guest came from the lips of Lorenzo, to everybody's surprise.

'Lori. You're far too young to be eyeing up girls' legs!' scolded his mother – hoping to restore a bit of parental law and order.

But it was too late. The happy atmosphere was catching as they sat down to devour the cold meats and cheeses which appeared from Sonia's picnic basket.

'No swimming for anyone for at least one hour,' stated Sonia.

That, for Sonia, was one of the few Italian rules of life that had to be obeyed without exception. Beppe dropped the anchor. They were far enough out to sea so that the land no longer looked near enough to be able to swim back. He left the engine running, turning up the throttle from time to time, only risking turning the motor off after the hour's wait had come to an end.

After they had eaten their fill – achieved within a few minutes after the first bites – they were surprised that Annamaria began singing a popular song, as if to herself.

'I know that song, Annamaria,' said Veronica. But I can't remember who sang it.'

In no time at all, it became a game of guessing the titles of popular songs – and the artist who had sung them.

Beppe sighed happily, leaving the three girls to continue the game. Lori shared his father's complete ignorance of popular songs. He was happy sitting with his *papà* tweaking the throttle from time to time to make the engine rev. How quickly, thought the *Commissario,* one could forget the circumstances behind the reason for which the five of them (No, six!) were there without an apparent care in the world.

Well before either Beppe or Sonia had felt like swimming, the children had been asking every five minutes or so, whether the appointed 'hour' after eating had arrived. In the end, they simply received a hard look from Sonia.

'Pazienza, ragazzi!' was all they got by way of an answer from their father. Annamaria had felt her precarious way to the prow of the boat, clinging on to the metal hand rail as she went. Reaching her destination, she had stripped down to her yellow bathing suit. She appeared to be singing a song to herself, standing up and moving in time with whatever music was in her head. She looked serenely happy, thought Sonia.

Veronica had become so fascinated with Annamaria's undulating body that she forgot to ask if their hour was up yet – giving the rest of the world a five-minute period of peace and quiet.

It must have been a gust of wind striking the side of the boat that caused the prow to move suddenly to the port side.

Veronica let out a cry which was followed instantly by a loud splash as Annamaria hit the water.

'NO!' cried Beppe, galvanised into action as he grabbed an inflated buoy from the deck of the boat and launched himself, still dressed in shorts and T-shirt, headlong into the sea from the side of the boat. Lorenzo, the better swimmer of the two children, had to be restrained by his mother before he leapt into the water after his father – struggling in vain to free himself from his mother's grasp.

'*Lasciami, mamma!*' he begged. 'Annamaria needs help – and I'm wearing my life jacket. Sonia, despite her strongly held convictions, relented and let go of her son.

'Where is she, *papà?*' called out Lorenzo in alarm as soon as he had drawn level with his father. Beppe shook his head and took a deep breath as he prepared to dive under the surface of the water.

No sooner had his father disappeared, when a radiant-looking Annamaria broke the surface of the water without even causing a ripple, it seemed.

As soon as Beppe opened his eyes, he saw a moving figure pass in front of his line of vision. For a split second, he could see Annamaria's legs, moving in an undulating rhythm – seemingly with her legs pressed together.

'Maybe Vero was right,' he thought. 'She turns into a mermaid as soon as she dips under water. He followed the legs to confirm his suspicions. But no, she was treading water like ordinary people do - and he could see his son's legs as he swam the few metres which separated him from the blind girl.

'You gave us a fright, Annamaria! Did you hurt yourself?'

'Not much, Beppe. As soon as I knew I was going overboard, I launched myself outwards over the rail. I knocked my right knee but it doesn't really hurt.'

'Let's get you on board and warm up a bit,' said Beppe.

'O no, Beppe. Not yet please. I want to swim round the boat a couple of times before I give up. I haven't been for a swim in the sea for… since I was a teenager. You can shout at me if I start swimming out to sea by mistake.'

'No, Annamaria. I want to swim with you.'

It was Lorenzo who had spoken. Annamaria kissed him on the top of his forehead – she seemed to know where it was without hesitation.

'Grazie, Lori. Sei un angelo!'

There were moments when Annamaria - simply accelerating herself gracefully forward with a powerful overarm stroke while her legs effortlessly displaced the water - left Lorenzo behind.

'Wait for me, Annamaria!' he called out as she appeared to be heading for the horizon.

Veronica was looking furiously at her younger brother. Sonia came to the rescue:

'We'll go for a swim together when they get back on board, *tesoro.'*

After two laps round the boat, Annamaria could tell that her little guardian angel was running out of breath. She was sure her knee was bleeding, so she allowed Lorenzo to guide her to the submerged ladder at the prow of the boat.

It was Beppe who dried her knee and stuck a large plaster on the superficial wound, while Sonia and Veronica did a slow lap round the boat. Veronica had insisted they swam anticlockwise round the boat – just to mark her independence and do the opposite to her 'baby' brother.

'Had you really been a mermaid as we suspected, you would not have had a knee to bruise,' suggested Beppe with a smile.

'But I would not even have been on your boat, *Commissario!'* she pointed out playfully.

To her humiliation, Veronica had felt she had reached her absolute limit after only two circuits round the boat. It had been her intention to do three laps round the boat in order to recover her self-esteem.

'Don't be upset, Vero!' said her mother as they hauled themselves out of the water. 'You are much better than your brother at almost everything else. But *please* don't ever tell him I said that.' Veronica's fragile confidence was restored.

'*Grazie mamma. Ti voglio bene,*' Veronica whispered.

They all sat round in a circle on the seats in the prow of the boat. They talked and talked until the sun was low in the sky. They were feeling hungry again.

'It's nearly sunset,' stated Annamaria. 'Tell me what it looks like, *ragazzi,*' she pleaded.

'How do you know that if you're...' Lorenzo began, but stopped short as he realised what he was saying.

His mother looked at him proudly. He was amazingly sensitive for a child of seven.

Annamaria seemed not to have noticed.

'I can sense light even if I can't see anything else,' she explained.

'We're going to eat out this evening, *ragazzi*. We all deserve a treat after today.'

The boat engine sprang to life as if it had a new lease of life and Lorenzo, standing on an upturned box, held the helm and steered the boat back towards the shoreline under his father's supervision. For once, Veronica was looking affectionately at her brother. Somehow, the events of the day had altered their perspective of family life.

'*Che meraviglia!*' thought Sonia, instinctively placing a hand over her belly.

* * *

Beppe had not given a thought to what was happening in Pescara. He had fallen into a deep slumber and dreamt of wondrous sea creatures swimming around him in the depths of some warm ocean.

It took him several seconds to work out what the intrusive noise was – out of place down there in the blue depths of his dream. Somebody was shaking him. It turned out to be Sonia.

'Answer your mobile please, *amore*. It must be urgent - it's only half past four.'

Beppe took one bleary look at the screen. He was beginning to realise that he was soon going to have to visit an optician to acquire a pair of reading glasses. As soon as he deciphered the caller's name, he was instantly wide awake.

He struck the green icon aggressively with his index finger as if it was the source of a deliberate attempt to thwart him.

All he could hear was a cacophony of voices – of which one was a tirade of words being shouted out in Calabrian dialect.

'Pippo! *Che diavolo sta succedendo?*' [68]

Pippo's voice asserted itself. Beppe heard the sound of a door closing and the hullabaloo becoming a muffled background noise.

'Sorry about that, *capo!* Just to let you know that we've got those two bastards here in the *Questura*. The shouting you could hear is the older one of the two protesting at being arrested 'just because they went to visit a friend after dark.' You wouldn't believe the language issuing from his gob, Beppe. Luckily, it's all in dialect...'

'Put them in separate cells, Pippo. I don't want them to collude even for a second!'

---

[68] What the hell is going on?

'I wasn't born yesterday, *Commissario!*' stated Pippo indignantly. 'See you later on today. No rush – we'll let him cool off in the cells.'

'But the other guy…' began Beppe, concerned that the lock-up cells in the basement were all down the same corridor.

'He just looks bewildered.'

'But you've got to make sure…' Beppe began.

'Set your mind at rest, Beppe. Our *Questore* has got him locked up in her private toilet on the top floor with *Agente* Rapino keeping guard. Mariastella is going to keep him there until you get here – so you can interview him together. Our *Questore* looks as if she is really enjoying herself.'

Beppe was looking in wonderment at a now wide-awake Sonia.

'Can you believe it, Sonia! My inspector has just hung up on me.'

Sonia was laughing gayly at the astonished expression of mild outrage on her husband's face.

'Eh! Le cose cambiano, Signor Commissario!' [69] said Sonia philosophically. But she bestowed a noisy kiss on his forehead before getting up and going to the kitchen to make the first coffee of the day, knowing full well that there would be no more sleep until the following night. The other members of the household remained soundly asleep. It was Sunday, after all!

---

[69] What do you expect! Things are changing, Mr Commissario!

12: *Annamaria Intimo's sense of smell...*

Sunday or not, there was no escaping the fact that he – and Annamaria – would have to spend at least the morning at the Pescara police headquarters.

Annamaria did not look happy about the journey back down south for reasons that Beppe could not decipher.

'There is nothing to be scared of, Annamaria,' Beppe reassured her tentatively.

'Oh, I'm not afraid, Beppe. I just didn't want to leave you all just yet. I love being with real people for a change. My sister's apartment is too small, so I have to go back to my place every night. Besides which, she's so fixed in her ways. Her husband is, frankly, quite boring. But I love being 'Auntie Annamaria' to her two kids. There's still hope for them!'

Beppe and Sonia were smiling at her engaging frankness.

'The way you talk about life is very refreshing, Annamaria,' said Sonia, realising that she could not see them smiling – even if she might sense it.

Beppe looked silently at Sonia. He raised a quizzical eyebrow in her direction.

'We don't want you to go home yet, Annamaria,' said Sonia. 'You can stay with us for as long as you wish.'

Annamaria was moving her arm slowly from side to side at waist level as if searching for something that she expected to be near at hand.

'So, I don't need to say goodbye to Veronica and Lorenzo, right now?' she asked.

Sonia realised why their guest had been sweeping the empty air with her hands.

'They are still fast asleep, Annamaria. You will see them later on today.

Annamaria was smiling contentedly.

'In any case, Annamaria, the forensics team may have to go over your apartment thoroughly – and I'm sure we shall have to clean your flat properly before you return. So, you just stay with us until you feel like going back to Pescara,' added Beppe. 'You are safer here with us for the next few days – or weeks even.'

'*Mille grazie, Beppe, Sonia.* So I didn't need to pack my suitcase after all, did I?'

'Come on Annamaria. Let's get the business part of today out of the way first,' said Beppe kindly, placing a hand under her elbow and leading her out to the car.

* * *

On arrival at the *Questura,* Beppe, with Annamaria Intimo by his side, was met by Pippo, waiting for him at the reception desk. She had hooked her left arm under Beppe's right arm, looking for all the world as if she thought she belonged there. Officers Gino Martelli and Danilo Simone were hovering in the background looking unduly pleased with themselves, considered the *Commissario.* Gino Martelli – always less inhibited than his colleague – even stuck a thumb up in the air for Beppe's benefit. Gino received nothing more than a curt nod from his chief. Danilo had switched his attention to studying Beppe and Annamaria with a degree of amicable curiosity. The *Commissario* gently disengaged Annamaria's arm from his own. She seemed to sense Beppe's unease and turned to him with a sweet smile and said: '*Grazie mille, signor Commissario*' in a voice loud enough to be heard by all present.

'OK, Pippo. Spill the beans!' Beppe ordered.

'Mariastella is upstairs with the younger of the two crooks, *Commissario*. He is handcuffed to the banisters at the moment. Mariastella needed a shower. She had to get the cleaners upstairs to clear up the mess left by him on the floor – and spray the whole bathroom with deodorant before she deigned to use the toilet or the shower. I think it upset her usual composure. She ordered us to take you both upstairs just as soon as you arrived - even earlier, if possible, I had the impression...'

'Tell us anyway, *Ispettore*. I am sure another five minutes' delay won't matter. I need to know what happened before we interrogate the 'prisoners.'

'Probably less than five minutes needed, Beppe...sorry... *Commissario*. It was all over in a trice, thanks to Gino and Danilo - and my wife, Mariangela. She was the *real* star...yet again.'

Officer Gino Martelli was nodding in agreement and looking too smug for Beppe's way of thinking. Beppe simply pretended to ignore Gino, turning impassively to his friend and colleague.

'Dai! Get on with it, Pippo!'

As Pippo's brief account unfurled, he felt Annamaria's arm gently re-engaging with his. She was squeezing his skin tightly. He made no move to disengage contact this time.

'It was all over so quickly, *Commissario*. There was a ring on Annamaria's door bell. My Mariangela, with me by her side, walked up to the door. She had a torch in her hand, because we had doused the lights as soon as we heard the doorbell.

'Chi è?' she asked.

'We have a delivery for Sofia Rossi, signorina. Is she there?'

Because the guy used the name you had supplied to the concierge, *capo,* we knew it must be THEM. Mariangela said *she* was Sofia Rossi and then moved rapidly to a safe place behind the sofa. After a few seconds, I unlatched the door and disappeared rapidly into a dark corner – where Gino and Simone were armed and waiting. Those two idiots were inside the door in an instant…'

'But they must have wondered why they couldn't see anything, surely?' asked Beppe.

'Ah, but that's where Mariangela's stroke of genius came into play, *capo.*'

'We can't see you, *signorina.*'

'Can we put a light on?' the two crooks asked.

'No, just leave the package on the floor near the door,' Mariangela told them.

'But we *want* to see you, *signorina!*'

It was the younger guy talking. He spoke with a heavy *calabrese* accent – but even so, I could tell by the lascivious tone of his voice what he had in mind for her before they killed her. It was sickening, Beppe. But Mariangela did not lose her nerve for a minute.'

'Here I am *ragazzi,*' she said cheerfully. We had decided to use that placard with your photo on after all, Annamaria, rather than let it go to waste. Mariangela briefly flashed a torch on – just for a couple of seconds – to illuminate your figure. We reckoned that it would distract them for long enough to put them completely off their guard. Those two forms of low-life were completely taken in by your image – maybe because it was the one and only thing they could see clearly.

'Why are you living in total darkness?' asked that young scumbag, in what he hoped was a wheedling tone of voice. 'We want to see you close up, Sofia.'

'Oh, I'm so sorry... What's your name? I don't need a light on, you must understand, because I'm totally blind.' I was simply flabbergasted by Mariangela's words, Beppe. We hadn't rehearsed such a scenario at all beforehand. It was her spontaneous reaction to the situation.'

There was a stony silence for all of five seconds before the older man started talking in dialect to the younger bloke.

'Come on let's get out of here now.' He was saying to his side-kick. 'We don't have to kill her. She can't identify us if she's blind, Mimo.'

'Oh come on, Niko! We can't just let it go like that. She might be lying. We didn't come all this way for nothing. Let's have a bit of fun with her first.'

Mariangela piped up again – beautifully simulated panic in her voice.

'Who are you? What do want with me? I'm going to scream the place down!'

She shone the torch in their faces to blind them – so that Gino and Simone could get hold of them from behind. *Dio mio!* You should have heard the language they used – all the way to Via Pesaro, Beppe. The older guy was the worst – as you probably heard when I phoned you at home from the *Questura...*'

'Bravi, ragazzi!' said Beppe. 'You did it! Without a shot being fired too!'

'They didn't stand a chance, *capo!*' said Gino, quite convinced that he had redeemed himself for most – if not all - of his past shortcomings.

Annamaria found her voice.

'I would like to meet your Mariangela, Pippo. She sounds just my kind of woman. Is she here with you now?'

'No, Annamaria,' said Pippo. 'She stayed behind in your flat to tidy it up a bit before she went back home. But don't worry, I shall tell her you want to meet her. I'm sure she'll be delighted. I think she fell in love with your apartment.'

Beppe's heart sank. The forensic team would have a more difficult task lifting finger prints from light switches and door handles as a result of Pippo's wife's unforeseen zeal for cleanliness.

Still looking amazed by Annamaria's reaction to the drama that had taken place in her home, Beppe led her up the stairs to the *Questore's* office on the top floor.

'We had better not keep our good lady waiting any longer,' said Beppe. *'Di nuovo,* [70] *bravissimi ragazzi!'* Of the younger of the two crooks, there was no sign. Presumably, he was being held in one of the smaller rooms upstairs, so that Annamaria Intimo would not have to cross his path before the official interview.

The *Questore,* Mariastella Martellini, stood up as Beppe and Annamaria entered her office. She must have been really angry, Beppe realised, looking at the tension in her normally relaxed facial muscles. She was instantly aware that Beppe was looking at her in a quizzical manner.

'Well, *Commissario,'* she began. 'I shall never allow my bathroom to be used as an additional prison cell again, that's for certain!'

'I apologise, Mariastella. It was my fault for being so insistent that the prisoner should be kept as far away from his older accomplice as possible.'

'Not your fault, *Commissario.* Annamaria, it is so good to meet you again. I hope you are surviving spending the whole weekend in the company of my miscreant second-in-command?'

---

[70] Once again...

'Just about, Mariastella. It was made easier by the presence of Sonia and their two engaging children,' stated Annamaria in similar vein.

The lady *Questore* found the ironic response highly amusing. She began to walk round her desk to where Beppe and Annamaria were standing. The blind girl's arms opened well before Mariastella had reached her – in anticipation of being hugged.

Mariastella stopped in her tracks.

'How did you know…?' she began.

'I got a whiff of your perfume as you moved through the space towards us,' was Annamaria's simple answer. 'And you are wearing high-heeled shoes!'

The lady *Questore* smiled knowingly at Beppe as she hugged their principal witness. 'I see what you mean, Beppe,' her expression inferred.

'Well, Annamaria. We have deliberately not allowed that form of low-life to wash or change his clothes before you meet him. We are hoping with bated breath that you will be able to identify him.'

She was gesturing towards the open door to officers Cardinale and Campione who were dragging their reluctant prisoner through the doorway.

'Right, just leave him standing where he is now and step to one side, ladies. Now, you cheap murderous villain, stand still! This lovely lady – whom you were intending to rape and kill last night - is about to put you behind bars for the foreseeable future. After which time you will be an old man. Got that, *stronzo?*'

Beppe was astounded at the rashness of his chief's assumption that their blind witness would be able to identify this total stranger. It seemed like a very long shot indeed. This youth really must have wound her up to her limits! Beppe was praying fervently that her rash words would not spoil their chances of an easy conviction.

Then, in a sudden flash of enlightenment, he understood the motive behind her seemingly reckless verbal abandon.

'Of course! Mariastella was simply one step ahead of him. Even his friend Pippo had begun to show signs of acting independently of him. Beppe resigned himself to the inevitable feeling that he was no longer 'top dog' in Via Pesaro. How irksome!

The youth in question was cowed by the unfamiliar situation, but not to the extent that he would remain speechless. With any luck, the mobster was being slyly manoeuvred into incriminating himself. Maybe his *capo* had already thought this opening gambit through and was laying it on thick just to wind their prisoner up. Mariastella was looking hard at Beppe as if to warn him off from interrupting prematurely. He nodded imperceptibly in her direction.

They only had to wait for a few tense seconds before the youth opened his mouth in protest.

'You can't pin anything on me, *voi sbirri.* [71] This bitch ain't nothing like the one we visited last night. *She* can't identify me! She's more like the *bambola* [72] what we saw when we first....'

He had realised seconds too late what he was inadvertently admitting to. There was a stony silence for ten seconds. The youthful *mafioso* caught sight of the wicked grin that had appeared on that policeman's face.

'You are right, Domenico Canino. Thank you. You have just saved us a lot of trouble and wasted time interrogating you.

---

[71] You coppers
[72] The dame (vulgar)

This is the lady you ran into when you came to Pescara during your *first* visit.'

'*Cazzo!'* the youth muttered in a vulgar whisper. He had turned very pale. Force was added to this detective's accusation when the prisoner registered that he had an unmistakable Calabrian accent. But he was searching for ways out of his entrapment. He had spent all his young life denying every accusation of wrong-doing that he had committed. He was not about to change his habits now.

'Annamaria,' said the lady *Questore* in a calm voice, 'can you identify this young man as the one you met entering *I Tulipani Gialli* appartements on Wednesday of last week?'

Annamaria Intimo took two steps towards the spot where the crook was standing. She held out her arms from the elbow as she 'felt' her way towards him.

The youth let out a vulgar cackle.

'She's blind! You cops must be out of your minds! You can't frame me for this. I want a lawyer present.'

Annamaria had stopped in her tracks, less than two metres away from the youth.

'Can you identify this man as the one who was lugging that statue of the Virgin Mary into the apartments, Annamaria?' asked Beppe emphasising every word.

The lady *Questore* was looking approvingly at Beppe.

'Yes, I can, *Commissario* - I don't need to get any closer. He reeks of sardines, just like he did last time.'

'*That's* what I thought I could smell as we brought him along the corridor!' muttered *Agente* Cristina Cardinale as if to herself.

Beppe smiled appreciatively in her direction.

'You work in a fish canning factory down in Reggio Calabria, don't you Domenico Canino? Don't bother denying it – we will check that out in the next few hours.'

'*Cazzo, cazzo!*' swore the youth under his breath.

The youth, was sat unceremoniously on a hard chair facing his two inquisitors – plus Annamaria - across the *Questore's* desk. He was handcuffed once again by his wrists which were resting uncomfortably on his lap. He was being stared at fixedly by the senior plain-clothed detective – who seemed to be reading his confusion with great relish.

'Now, Mimo, let's have a serious talk, shall we?'

The voice was soft, the words spoken in a kindly tone of voice. It threw him entirely off track being addressed – in Calabrese dialect - as if by his own granddad on his birthday back in their home in Reggio Calabria.

Beppe was feeling good. He felt as if he was back in charge again – on familiar territory, doing what he always did best.

Domenico Canino, instinctively preparing to defend his weakened position, despite this detective's unthreatening stance, was so taken aback by the first words Beppe had uttered that he felt his jaw dropping. His initial reaction was followed by the sensation that he had been skinned alive like a freshly caught fish. Who *was* this detective? He had never felt so helpless even when being bullied by the police in his native Reggio Calabria. Domenico Canino felt obliged to give in without a struggle and tell this *Commissario* what he wanted to know. With him, arguing back appeared to be pointless. This *sbirro* seemed to be already in possession of all the necessary information to finish him off.

'Who *are* you?' he asked.

'Just call me *'Commissario'*, Mimo. Now, this is what has been puzzling me...' began Beppe in all innocence.

The silence in the *Questore's* office was total as everybody held their breath, wondering where their *Commissario* was going.

Beppe continued speaking with hypnotic calm. 'Mimo' was mesmerised, looking at Beppe with unblinking eyes, his mouth slightly open.

'We know your clan *boss,* Don Fausto Talarico is devoted to the Virgin Mary, Mimo. It's public knowledge. So what really puzzles me is why you were ordered to leave a statue of the Virgin Mary next to that young woman you strangled. It was tantamount to a confession of guilt on Don Fausto's part...'

Beppe had paused to let his words sink in. 'Mimo' Canino's face had turned ashen.

'Unless, of course,' continued Beppe Stancato relentlessly, 'you are under orders from another clan *boss* who wants to usurp Don Fausto's position. Maybe you could help me out here, Mimo?'

'I can't help you, *Commissario,'* stuttered the youth. 'I'm dead meat if I tell you *his* name.'

Beppe simply nodded at Mariastella. He had obtained a virtual confession from this minor mafioso. There was nothing to be gained from continuing the interrogation for now.

'Take him down to the cells,' officers,' Mariastella ordered *Agenti* Campione and Cardinale, who had been sitting in spell-bound silence during this one-sided interrogation.

'Make sure he gets his breakfast. It might be the last decent one he gets for a long, long time' ordered Mariastella Martellini. 'And bring that other murdering bastard up while you're there. Keep them well away from each other. Hold on to

Signor Veraldi downstairs and bring him up in about twenty minutes – when we've had a breather.'

Apparently, Mariastella Martellini's outrage, provoked by these two gangsters from the South of Italy, had not yet been totally assuaged. Beppe could not think of a time when his chief had been so roused by the evil doings of Italy's criminal underworld.

She must have been more deeply affected by the photo depicting the gruesome demise of a young woman called Laura Ianni than Beppe had realised.

Beppe was even more convinced that they would need to take steps to discover the murder victim's real name, preferably before the crime was reported to the media. He let out a long sigh as the complexities of this case fully dawned upon him.

Agenti Campione and Cardinale were looking at their 'hero' with undisguised admiration as they led their prisoner out of the room. They had been present on many occasions when Beppe had been interviewing suspects. But they had never witnessed anything quite like their *capo's* latest performance.

'I hope they remembered to record that interrogation in its entirety,' said Claudia Cardinale to her friend.

'It should go down in the history books of police interviewing techniques,' added Emma Campione. 'I'm going to suggest that we have a replay next time we have a general meeting. Everybody who works in this *Questura* should get the chance to hear it.'

Bianca Bomba and Marco Pollutri, the technicians in the basement who were recording the interrogation, were of the same opinion.

'*È geniale, quest'uomo!*' [73] declared Officer Cardinale in conclusion.

---

[73] He's brilliant, that man!

13: *How to interrogate a suspect...*

Annamaria Intimo was frowning. Who knows what she is thinking,' thought Beppe as he stared at the deeply serious expression on her face. Her sightless eyes looked like polished jet.

Beppe noticed that Mariastella was looking at *him* intensely. She too, seemed to be frowning - in disapproval? Yet, her eyes were alight with mischief.

'That must rate as the most god-almighty shot in the dark of your whole career to date!' she declared. 'What a good job it paid off!'

'You didn't do so badly yourself, *Signora Questore,*' retaliated the *Commissario.* 'It has to be noted that it was only possible to take the risk I did, thanks entirely to our new recruit, Donato Pavone. Without his research, we would not have got anywhere with that crook. I am expecting some additional information from *Agente* Pavone about the other villain – if we could possibly hold off interrogating him for a little while longer, Mariastella?'

The lady *Questore* nodded.

'Let's keep him on the back burner for as long as possible. It'll wind him up nicely.'

'You handled that smelly little bastard brilliantly, Beppe!'

Mariastella and her second-in-command looked in astonishment at the woman who had uttered those words out of the blue, fuelled by what appeared to be pure contempt.

'You deserve more than half the credit, Annamaria. We could not have achieved any of this without your help. You were brilliant too!'

This, from the lady *Questore.*

'Maybe I could come and work for the police force?' suggested Annamaria, returning to her usual happy-go-lucky self.

'That is not such a bad idea, Annamaria,' said the lady *Questore* in all seriousness. 'I am quite sure there must be a precedent somewhere in our peninsula for such an arrangement.' [74]

'And now, I must ask you if I could visit a toilet before we resume interrogating that other bastard,' said the blind 'policewoman' politely.

'Of course, Annamaria. You must use my private toilet. I'll take you there myself,' said Mariastella, smiling to herself. 'It has just been thoroughly cleaned,' she added at the irony of her personal space being invaded for the second time that day by such a totally contrasting human being.

Whilst the ladies were otherwise engaged, Officer Donata Pavone knocked timidly on the open door. He handed a sheet of paper to Beppe.

'Not much, I'm afraid, *capo* – but I think you'll find it interesting. It's an old article from the archives of *La Gazzetta di Napoli.*'

'*Grazie infinite, Donato,*' said Beppe. '*Sei un genio!*'

'I fear I still have a long way to go, *Commissario,* before I deserve such an epithet,' replied Donato modestly.

* * *

Just over an hour later, Mariastella phoned the reception desk to request that the second mobster should be escorted upstairs. Beppe could hear the older crook mouthing off somewhere in the background, swearing in *Calabrese* dialect – as was his wont. Beppe had had ample time to digest the

---

[74] *See note at the end of the story.*

contents of the newspaper report which Officer Pavone had given him. He had already decided what his opening gambit would be.

To Beppe and Mariastella's astonishment, the elder of the two 'arrestees', Nicola Veraldi, was led into the *Questore's* office by *Agente* Luigi Rocco, who was holding his prisoner up by the collar of his jacket, so that his feet appeared to be barely touching the ground. Even this swarthy individual was dwarfed by the *Orso Bruno's* [75] massive frame. The prisoner's official escorts followed them into Mariastella's office, trying hard to suppress their mirth.

'We apologise for our unconventional arrival, *Signora Questore... Commissario.* This gentleman was proving to be reluctant to come up and meet you all,' explained Officer Emma Campione gleefully to their two chiefs.

The crook, Niko, was dumped unceremoniously on the wooden chair by Officer Rocco, who raised his eyebrows quizzically in Beppe's direction whilst holding up the handcuffs.

Beppe shook his head.

'Please stay, *Agente* Rocco. You may be needed to subdue our prisoner if he gets out-of-hand during his interrogation.'

'Grazie, capo. Con piacere! [76]

Luigi Rocco sat down on the row of chairs alongside officers Campione and Cardinale.

The *Commissario* was already staring fixedly at their suspect. Beppe succeeded in keeping it up for a record twenty-five seconds without blinking. The recipient of the stare merely continued to look aggressively at his opponent. But he broke eye contact before Beppe did.

---

[75] The Brown Bear – Luigi Rocco's original nickname in Via Pesaro.
[76] Thank you, boss. With pleasure

'Hands flat out on the table!' Beppe ordered sharply. Before being escorted upstairs, Nicola Veraldi had had his finger prints taken down in the basement where the technicians were housed. The tips of his fingers still bore the smudge marks. He had refused to be subjected to a mouth swab test.

'Don't worry, Bianca,' he had told the lady technician over the phone. 'We'll find a way of getting his DNA during the interview.'

'Hands flat on the desk, please, Niko,' repeated the *Commissario.*

The man was sullenly refusing to do as he had been ordered.

'Luigi?' said Beppe quietly to *Agente* Rocco, as he beckoned his colleague over. That was enough to bring about a complete change of mind on the part of the *mafioso,* who obligingly spread his hands on the desk, palms downwards.

'A fisherman's hands, *Signor* Veraldi!' stated the *Commissario.* 'Tough work hauling in those nets every day of your life, I would imagine.'

'So, what of it?' he snarled.

'Powerful hands, I would say, Niko!'

The *Commissario's* tone of voice had subtly altered when he uttered the mafioso's nickname. The atmosphere in the room was electrified. Officer Emma Campione nudged her friend's elbow.

'Look at the blind girl's face,' she muttered in a fierce stage whisper. Emma Campione was shocked to notice that the malicious grin on Annamaria's face vanished in a trice. Emma was being 'observed' by those coal-black eyes. Officer Campione had underestimated the blind girl's hearing ability. Annamaria was simply 'looking' in Emma Campione's direction. The police officer instinctively waved her hand weakly in Annamaria's direction by way of an apology – forgetting that the gesture was invisible to her.

'So, it was *you* who strangled the girl in Apartment 34 last week. Not your spineless, little mate, Mimo Canino. He was probably more interested in sexually assaulting the young woman – before you strangled her.'

Beppe had spat out the words viciously in the silent office. Everybody in the room was staring fixedly at the mafioso – even Annamaria Intimo, it seemed.

Only the *Questore,* Mariastella Martellini, seemed to be anxious at the risk-laden path her second-in-command appeared to be taking.

'You are talking nonsense, *Commissario.* This is my first visit to Pescara. And I hope it will be the last,' stated Nicola Veraldi boldly.

His attempt at denial was followed by a stony silence. The *Commissario* simply shook his head from side to side in disbelief.

Beppe broke the silence gently. He remained sublimely unruffled.

'Do you recognise the lady who is sitting over there at the end of the table, *Signor* Veraldi?' said Beppe indicating Annamaria.

'Yeah, of course I do. It was the girl who we tried to deliver a parcel to last night. Only, we couldn't see her properly 'cos all the lights were off.'

'There *was* no parcel, *signore.* You came to eliminate her – just as you had done with the other girl last week.'

'You are fantasising!' shouted the mafioso. 'I want a lawyer present.'

'Don't you recognise this lady from your first visit? She was coming out of that apartment block just as you came in with the statue. That's why they sent you two goons back again – just to get rid of the only witness to your visit to those apartments. In point of fact, she cannot see you, because she is blind.'

'I've never been to Pescara before!' raved the man, Niko.

'Don't waste any more of our time, *Signor* Veraldi. This lady has already identified Mimo Canino as he came in carrying that statue of the Virgin Mary….'

'You're lying! She's as blind as a bat,' raged their captive.

'That's as maybe… Niko! But your little mate stank of sardines. That is how he was identified. And save your breath, *Signor* Veraldi - your accomplice, Mimo, has already admitted that you visited the apartment block last week. And if that is not enough, we identified *you*, thanks to your stupidity in arriving in that Fed-Ex van. Are you even aware that you were issued with a parking fine by our urban police? You left your van parked there for over twenty minutes. Your name showed up as the owner of the vehicle.'

Their prisoner lost his self-control and began mouthing insults in Calabrian dialect. He had half stood up and was leaning over the desk, muttering menacingly at Beppe. *Agente* Rocco was up on his feet in a second. The mafioso found his left arm being pinioned painfully behind his back as Luigi Rocco forced him to sit down.

Beppe began speaking even more quietly.

'Let's simply turn to the death of the young woman you strangled. We know her as Laura Ianni. But we suspect that this is not her real name. It is far more likely that *you* are more aware of her real identity than we are – and that you know the motive behind her killing much better than we do. Some kind of vendetta, I suspect.'

'You are groping in the dark, *Commissario,*'

'Not so, *Signor* Veraldi. It would appear that you were told to carry out that ghastly assassination under the orders of the boss of the Talarico clan. But I suspect that the background story is a little more complicated than that.'

The gangster was sneering at Beppe across the desk, his hands tensed, with fingers splayed out rigidly, as if he wished they were gripping this detective's neck.

Beppe's reaction made everybody in the room jump with shock. He had slammed an enlarged photo of the murder of Laura Ianni down on the desk.

'THAT is what is going to send you to jail for the rest of your life, you cheap-jack mafia killer!' pronounced the *Commissario* in stentorian tones - as if the day of the Last Judgement had arrived.

'I've never murdered anybody!' cried out the enraged man, with panic in his voice for the first time.

Once again, Beppe's voice changed to a casual, almost apologetic tone.

'Well now, *Signor* Veraldi. That is not quite accurate, is it?' said the soothing voice with a tone of underlying menace.

'Wot you getting at?' hissed the mafioso suspiciously.

'I was thinking of the time you pushed a rival lover overboard off your fishing boat – after you tried to strangle him,' replied the *Commissario*. 'You thought your woman had had an affair with him while you were out on a long fishing trip. True?'

'That was never proved in court!' snarled the man called Niko. 'I was let off the hook.'

'Guilty as charged was the general opinion of the good people of Reggio Calabria, I gather,' said Beppe waving the copy of the newspaper article. 'Your lawyer – or rather Don

Fausto Tallarico's lawyer – got you off on a technicality, I believe. Besides which, one of the other fishermen on your boat, was a witness to your crime. Naturally, he never survived long enough to denounce you to the *Carabinieri.'*

The man, Niko, raged and swore in dialect at this policeman who was tying him into knots. He was further disturbed to find that this *sbirro* was offering him a cigarette with an innocent smile on his face. Beppe even had an unlit cigarette in his own mouth.

'Come on, Niko. You need to relax a bit. We know you didn't murder the girl, Laura Ianni. We just had to go through the motions.'

The two lady officers, Cristina Cardinale and Emma Campione were looking at the scene with mouths open in shock. Neither they, nor the relatively new lady *Questore.* had ever witnessed this favourite trick of Beppe's.

The *Commissario* held the lighter in his left hand as he lit his own cigarette. He held out the lighter to the man who leaned forward towards the flame. Dazzled by the closeness of the flame, the mobster was too late to catch on to what was happening as Beppe's right had whipped the cigarette out of his mouth and popped it into a plastic evidence bag.

'There, *Signor* Veraldi! I am sure the traces of DNA on this cigarette will confirm your *innocence* – don't you think?' stated Beppe with cold sarcasm.

The man, who had been so neatly tricked, was trying to leap over the desk. The fingers of his bare hands were curled rigidly in front of him. Officer Luigi Rocco was out of his seat in a trice. Officers Campione and Cardinale were applauding enthusiastically.

Signora Questore?' said Beppe. 'Will you do the honours?'

Maristella smiled – the look of admiration on her face was replaced by her official, solemn face.

'Nicola Veraldi, you are under arrest for the murder of Laura Ianni – and the attempted murder of *Signorina* Annamaria Intimo. Have you anything to say?'

The prisoner was struggling to free himself from the Mountain Bear's grip.

'Take him away, Officers. The penitentiary police are outside in the street. You are going to take a long ride into the countryside, *Signor* Veraldi – well away from any danger you will be facing from your own bosses in Reggio Calabria.'

'Niko' understood the implications of the *Questore's* words all too well.

* * *

'So, what is our next step, my dear *Commissario?*' asked Mariastella Martellini. 'I somehow feel that this case has only been partly solved.'

Beppe was pondering deeply how he should reply to his *capo's* crucial question – especially since he was harbouring the same ill-defined doubts.

'We could quite safely wash our hands of the whole scenario, Mariastella. We could pass the buck – and nobody would criticise us for doing so. But…'

'Ah, Beppe. So, *you* feel there is a 'but' too!'

'I personally would dearly love to know the true identity of the victim of that ghastly massacre. It feels as if we will not have done justice to Laura Ianni if we do not take steps to find out who she really was – and why she had to suffer such a gruesome form of torture before she died strangled.'

'*Appunto,* Beppe.[77] And do you consider that it is safe to let Annamaria Intimo return to her apartment?'

'She, herself, would love to stay with me and my family for a while longer, Mariastella. We are happy to have her company until we are sure it is absolutely safe for her to return.'

'That reassures me greatly, Beppe. I didn't want her to go back to her apartment until we know precisely who the driving force behind these crimes really is. And then, there is the question of identity of the woman who tailed Annamaria. We should really follow up on that aspect of the case too – at present she is a bit of a loose cannon.'

'I agree. I suspect she must have some connection with the mob,' added Beppe.

At this point, their discussion was interrupted by the *Questore's* phone ringing. Mariastella picked up the receiver as if she found the interruption to their analysis of the situation unwelcome.

The first words she heard transformed her annoyance to a look of total disbelief.

'Just a minute *Signora* D'Arcangelo. I have my *Commissario* with me. I would like him to hear what you have to say to us. Would you mind repeating what you have already told me for his benefit too? It sounds incredible.'

'It's the chief editor of our local Pescara newspaper *'Il Centro',* Beppe. I'm putting her on loud-speaker mode. You need to hear this from the horse's mouth.'

---

[77] Precisely, Beppe.

14:   Cat out of the bag...

'As I was saying, *Signora Questore,* I have just received an email from someone who is evidently giving a false name, depicting the most macabre murder scene I have ever seen throughout my career as a journalist. It is simply horrifying. So much so that I thought at first it had been 'staged'. Do I need to go into details...?' Diletta D'Arcangelo asked.

'Not if, as I suspect, it depicts a statue of the Virgin Mary staring down at the molested body of a young woman, *Signora* D'Arcangelo,' stated the lady *Questore.*

'Please call me Diletta – it's far less cumbersome. And yes, *Signora Questore...*'

'Mariastella, will do just fine.'

'*Grazie...Mariastella.* We have been sent that photo - just as you describe it. I believe it just about comes under the category of an item of public need-to-know. But I wanted to check with you first.

'Did the email come with any explanation as to why it was sent specifically to *Il Centro Pescarese,* Diletta?'

'The message simply said: *The people of Pescara have a right to know what goes on in their city. It seems the police are hiding the truth from you all. You must print the photo for all to see – so they know the consequences of betrayal.* There were a few spelling mistakes and a couple of words written in dialect – Calabrian, I think. I wanted to ask your advice before committing myself to any course of action.'

'Thank you, Diletta. You have acted very responsibly – as one would expect from the chief of a newspaper of such renown as *Il Centro.* What I *can* say to you is that this crime was committed about a week ago. We have arrested the two assassins – mafiosi from Calabria – about fifteen minutes ago. But we are very unclear as to why the girl concerned was singled out for such a horrendous death. We are not even sure that the name we have for the victim is her *true* name.'

'So, you would wish me to hold off the publication of this photo, I would guess?'

'I shall discuss the matter with my *Commissario*. I will let you know what we decide after our discussion. In fact, I will send an officer round to *Il Centro* before the end of the afternoon. I see my *Commissario* making urgent signals to me, Diletta. He obviously already has a clear idea as to how we should proceed.'

'*D'accordo, Signora Questore.* I look forward to meeting whoever comes to our offices later today.

* * *

'So, my *Commissario.* What do you think of this dramatic twist to the story? I confess this latest development leaves me totally perplexed...'

'No, Mariastella. I am thinking that we *both* understand perfectly well what is going on. However, I am less certain as to how we should react.'

'I have the distinct impression that you are, as usual, one step ahead of everybody else, Beppe.'

'Maybe only half a step, Mariastella. It was obvious that both the perpetrators of this crime are more afraid of some other shadowy mafia *boss* than they are of Don Fausto Talarico – who is 'officially' behind the whole grisly set-up. But you will recall how the younger thug hinted he would be 'dead meat' if he told us the name of the other individual behind this gruesome drama.'

'So, what should we do about the editor of *Il Centro* in your opinion, Beppe?'

Beppe let out a deep sigh and fell into one of his long silences. Mariastella Martellini knew better than to interrupt her colleague's train of thought.

The two minutes' silence which ensued seemed like an eternity to her. But the silence was broken by Beppe, whose brain had sifted through every aspect of the case in a matter of only one hundred and twenty seconds. A record on his part reckoned the lady *Questore*.

'I feel certain that we are up against a very complex game that is being played out down there in Reggio Calabria,' began Beppe. 'Think about it, Mariastella. If this assassination had been perpetrated solely by the Talarico clan, there would be no point in bringing it to the attention of the media. So...there is some other shady individual who wants to stir up trouble for Fausto Talarico – for reasons which are not yet clear to us. I suspect that our two assassins are in thrall to the unknown *boss* - probably carrying out a revenge killing on behalf of Fausto Talarico. That is what I am guessing.'

'So, what shall we say to the editor of *Il Centro,* Beppe?'

'The details of this murder are certain to come to light in the near future, Mariastella – even if we block its publication today. It might serve our purpose better if the story is released now - in diluted form. Somebody will filter the news down south to Reggio Calabria. That way, it will look as if we have been fooled by their ploy. I can go and meet this Diletta D'Arcangelo and suggest a suitable wording to accompany the photo if you wish, Mariastella. She is relatively new to the post – so it would be good diplomacy if I took this opportunity to get to know her.'

The lady *Questore* looked gratefully at her second-in-command.

'Thank you, Beppe. Meanwhile, I think I should make a very discreet preliminary phone call to a certain organisation in Reggio Calabria. We need to find out exactly who Laura Ianni really is. I suspect she might have been sent to Pescara as part of some witness protection scheme – which, subsequently, went wrong.'

'I take it you are referring to the DIA, Mariastella?' [78]

She simply nodded.

'I imagine that the DIA will clam up if there is any hint that they are being accused of a security breach within their system,' said Beppe gently. 'I don't envy you the task ahead of you, Mariastella. But they are likely to be the only ones who can shed light on Laura Ianni's identity – if our assumptions are correct.'

'Well, I may have to throw my weight around to break their code of secrecy. I am certain they will find it in their hearts to help us, if they are in a position to do so,' said the lady *Questore* with a strained smile on her face.

'*In bocca al lupo,* Mariastella,' said the *Commissario,* before he set off to make the acquaintance of the lady editor of Pescara's local paper – who, he recollected, had only taken up the position of editor-in-chief two months ago, following the retirement of a gentleman who had run the newspaper for a commendable fifteen years.

* * *

At the end of the day, Beppe had rescued Annamaria from the clutches of her sister before briefly calling in at her apartment in *I Tulipani Gialli* to collect some fresh clothing.

---

[78] DIA – the Anti-Mafia Police *(Direzione Investigativa Antimafia)*

'I can still smell those sardines, Beppe,' Annamaria stated, turning up her elegant nose as they triple locked her apartment door.

'We'll fumigate your living space and make it smell like roses before you return, Annamaria,' said Beppe only half-jokingly. Annamaria giggled at the suggestion.

On the journey up to Atri, Annamaria related how she had valiantly refused to tell her sister Angela where she was staying, and even less so, who she was staying with.

'She would have become hysterical had she known I was hiding in a policeman's home, Beppe,' Annamaria explained to Beppe on the road up to Atri. 'And it would have been common knowledge in the whole of Pescara by tomorrow,' added Annamaria with a wicked edge to her voice. 'I love my sister, Beppe. But she's so terribly conventional – and quite unreliable.'

'Certainly not like her younger sister, then!'

'I'M the elder sister, *Commissario.* Although you would not think so,' Annamaria pointed out just as they arrived outside the house in Atri. Veronica and Lorenzo were hovering outside waiting to greet them.

'I've got a new game for us to play, Annamaria. You are going to love it!'

'Let me get changed into fresh clothes, first,' said Annamaria.

'And have dinner,' added Beppe eying his daughter severely. 'After which it will be bedtime, young lady.'

As usual, Veronica smiled disarmingly at her *papà,* feeling confident that she could sway events to her way of thinking. Unless her mother took sides with her father, of course – which she did on this occasion.

'Save your game up for tomorrow, *tesoro*. *Nonno* and *Nonna* have something they want to talk to Annamaria about after dinner. I have no idea what it's about.'

It had been a very long day, thought Beppe – quite unaware as to how the next stage of their investigation was to be played out. Had he known what was in store for him, The *Commissario* might well have agreed to accepting the post of *Questore* in Terramonti on the spot.

15:   *How it's done in Italy...*

Driving back down to Pescara on his own the following morning, the sense of change was palpable. Beppe Stancato had the impression that cars were being driven more erratically than usual. And weren't the pedestrians walking more hurriedly - as if to reach the security of their destinations as rapidly as possible? It was not until he was obliged to drive more slowly through the town centre that he passed a newspaper kiosk and was able to read what was written on the bill-boards.

HORRENDOUS MAFIA-STYLE ASSASSINATION IN THE CENTRE OF PESCARA.

Pedestrians were hurrying along the pavements trying to read the front page as they walked. Beppe even noticed a car travelling in the opposite direction to him in which the driver had folded an open newspaper across the steering wheel, and was trying to read the article as he was driving. Beppe honked loudly – almost causing the idiot to crash into him. If Beppe had been able to stop his car safely, he would have got out and given the man a severe dressing down. No point in getting frustrated - Beppe simply continued to be appalled at the way some of his fellow-countrymen behaved when sitting behind a steering wheel.

'He probably comes from Sicily,' he thought unkindly. He had once witnessed a man driving along on a main road in Sicily holding open the driver's door as he blew cigarette smoke out – so his passengers did not have to breathe in his noxious fumes.

Inside the *Questura*, the atmosphere was electric – even though most of his colleagues had either witnessed the murder scene with their own eyes – or at least seen the photos of the victim. The publication appeared to have had the same effect as the earthquake that had shocked the population of Pescara when he had first arrived in Abruzzo way back in 2009.

As soon as he reached the *Questura,* Beppe was summoned upstairs to Mariastella Martellini's office. A woman in her late thirties was sitting facing the lady *Questore,* talking volubly. She stood up as Beppe walked across the intervening space between the door and the desk. Her face was pallid – despite her darker, southern Italian skin.

'May I introduce you to *Signora* Nunzia Rubino-Talarico, Beppe?' began the lady *Questore.*

The unexpected final part of her surname briefly made Beppe's hair stand on end.

Beppe looked hard at the woman without attempting to shake her proffered hand. Only then did he identify the woman from the photo which *Agente* Cristina Cardinale had taken in front of Annamaria's apartment block - *I Tulipani Gialli.* It was the woman who had been 'stalking' Annamaria Intimo.

Beppe was looking hard at his *capo* – almost angrily.

'And NO, *Commissario,'* said Mariastella with a bright smile on her face. '*I* did not summon *Signora* Rubino-Talarico to the *Questura.* She came of her own accord as soon as she saw the photo in *Il Centro* this morning.'

Nunzia Rubino-Talarico began unburdening her pent-up anger and disgust with her Calabrian relative in one unstoppable verbal tirade.

I would never...never have agreed to follow that second girl - what was her name? - if I had known about how that Laura Ianni was butchered by those thugs. Fausto – my 'uncle' I have to call him – is a lecherous bastard at the best of times. But that murder... I am appalled to the very heart of my being. I just came into the police station here to warn you that the same thing might happen to the girl I was told to tail. I simply could not have that on my conscience for the rest of my life... Not that the murdered woman was called Laura Ianni, you know officers? You must have changed her name before allowing that photo to be printed. I remember some girl refusing point blank to marry one of Fausto's cousins. But she belonged to a different family. I can't remember which one...'

Nunzia Rubino-Talarico had to pause for breath for an instant – during which, Mariastella raised a hand to stem the tide of words.

'Thank you for taking the risk of coming to tell us about your small departure from being a good citizen, *signora.* You have been a great help. I am very confident that we shall track down the killers of Laura Ianni – I am sure *they* must know the victim's real name. We are doing our best to identify those crooks but they did not exactly leave a calling card! Go home to your husband – and children. I imagine you have a fairly young family to look after? I am guessing that Rubino is your husband's name and that he comes from Abruzzo?'

'*Sì, Signora Questore.* But I feel like phoning up that bastard and giving him a piece of my mind,' began the lady all over again.

'You must do as you see fit, *signora.* But I advise against saying anything to Fausto Talarico. You would most likely end up being his next victim!'

It had been the *Commissario* who had intervened with those chilling words.

'And do not worry about the lady you were stalking. She is under our protection all the time,' Beppe added, in a kindlier tone of voice.

Mariastella had stood up and walked round to the other side of her desk. She gently escorted the garrulous lady towards the door of her office. Officer Giacomo D'Amico was there already, waiting to escort the lady downstairs and out of the building.

'Would you be so kind as to leave your address and phone number at the reception desk?' asked Mariastella. 'Just so we can contact you if we need your help again. We shall overlook your brief transgression on this occasion.'

The lady gave every indication that she had not fully understood the *Questore's* final words – the gentle dig at her former stalking activities.

'*Grazie, Signora Questore,*' said Nunzia as she went downstairs with Officer D'Amico who was talking courteously to her and thanking her for taking the trouble to come to the police headquarters.

'Well, that resolves the dilemma as to whether to pull her in – or not,' said Mariastella Martellini, relieved that this was one less decision she had to make.

'Yes, indeed it does. And if she does call Fausto Talarico – which I doubt – she will not be able to tell him how far we have got in this investigation,' added Beppe.

'Now I am going to tackle the DIA in Reggio Calabria. It could take me a long time, Beppe. So, I'll let you know when I've got something useful to tell you.'

Beppe took his leave and went downstairs to 'mingle' with his team, agog to know where the investigation was likely to be heading in light of the revelations leaked by the local newspaper that morning.

'Good question!' thought Beppe to himself. There was a long way to go before the real criminals behind this ghastly assassination were behind bars for good, mused Beppe. For the first time in his career, he was feeling overwhelmed by the sheer weight of evil, which felt ever more present just beneath the surface of everyday life. No wonder people clung to their family life these days, he thought. There, at least, survived a feeling of sanity and loving human bonding, which helped to make sense out of everyday life on the planet at large. He experienced a surge of pity for Annamaria. He felt as if her presence amidst his family should be prolonged for as long as she wanted to be there. How vital physical contact must be for someone who could never 'see' what they were missing! He shook his head to clear such negative thoughts from his mind. He decided to drive home immediately. He would find out the next morning if Mariastella had had any joy with the anti-mafia police in Reggio Calabria. He left a message at the reception desk to be communicated to his *capo* as soon as he had taken his leave. If there *was* something really urgent to deal with, she could text-message him before he drove 'out of range'.

Spirits were running high in their home in Atri. Sonia's parents had obviously fallen in love with Annamaria. They had insisted that she move into a ground-floor annexe in their house, where she could enjoy her independence when she needed it but would still be free to go upstairs or into the garden whenever she wanted.

Beppe discovered Annamaria, Lorenzo, Veronica and Roberto – Sonia's father – sitting round the grandparents' kitchen table, about to play an elaborate game which Veronica claimed she had invented. As usual, Beppe's daughter hoped - often optimistically – that she would never be challenged as to the truth or falsehood of her assertion that her schemes were original.

'Pretend you are a vegetarian,' she began, addressing the question to Lorenzo. 'That's someone who never eats meat, Lori,' she explained to her brother, who merely looked despairingly at the ceiling and then grinned at his *papà* with a resigned shrug of his shoulders.

'You go and have lunch at a friend's house where your friend's mother has cooked a roast chicken. Do you refuse to eat it?'

The person questioned then had to answer simply: *Sì, No,* or *Dipende.* The question-master had to predict what their answer would be – and hold up the chosen prediction card as soon as the person had given the answer.

'Do I have to tell the truth, Vero?' Lorenzo asked with a crafty look on his face.

'Of course, you do!' replied Veronica, looking mildly put out that her brother had asked the question.

'In that case, I say *Sì,*' said Lorenzo.

Veronica had predicted he would say *NO* and simply told her little brother he was a liar.

'That round didn't count,' declared Veronica. 'It was just to make sure you all knew how to play it. Now it's your turn, Annamaria.'

Veronica had thoughtfully given the *Yes, No, Depends* cards with one little ball of plasticine on the 'Yes' card, two balls on the 'No' card and three on the 'Depends' card.

'*Bene, Vero,*' [79] began Annamaria. 'Here's a question for you. *You see a blind person waiting to cross a busy road. Do you go up to the blind person and offer to help her across the road?*'

Beppe complimented Veronica on her adaption of a game which he seemed to remember was called *I Scrupoli.*

'I'll play this game with you another time' promised Beppe. 'It sounds like a brilliant invention, Vero!'

With a smile in the direction of Roberto and Irene, Beppe headed upstairs, where a happy Sonia hugged her

---

[79] Vero – a contraction of Veronica. *cf 'vero' meaning 'true'*

husband warmly. Sonia told Beppe about the new arrangements for Annamaria.

'My mum and dad have really taken a liking to Annamaria. She told me that their offer was a bit risky in her opinion – because she simply wouldn't want to leave at all.'

'That will be fine for us, won't it Sonia – we aren't in a hurry for her to leave,' stated Beppe.

'You just have no idea how wonderful it feels to be home with you!' he added with a deep sense of inner joy. *'Viva la famiglia! – dico io!* [80]

'A difficult day at the *Questura, amore?'*

'You could say that, Sonia.'

* * *

The following morning, Beppe was called urgently upstairs to the *Questore's* office on the top floor. Mariastella Martellini was looking edgy – as if she was about to impart some uncomfortable news to her second-in-command.

Beppe was looking as encouragingly as he could at his *capo*. He had had a premonition the previous evening, which he had not dared to share with Sonia.

'We are going to have to make a journey down to Reggio Calabria, *vero,* [81] Mariastella? Into the lion's den!'

The lady *Questore* looked gratefully at Beppe.

'That is one way of putting it, *Commissario.'* she said, smiling grimly.

'So, you managed to get in touch with the DIA, I take it?'

---

[80] Long live the family – say I
[81] True? : aren't we? (The girl's name, Veronica, means 'one who tells the truth')

'With great difficulty. I had no idea just how secretive they are. In the end, I had to phone the *Ministero dell'Interno* in Rome and badger my few precious contacts in that organisation before I could even begin to think of calling anybody in the DIA. One of my senior contacts – a friend whom I knew from my days in Bologna – had to use *his* clout to ask permission from the DIA in Rome, who then had to contact the DIA in Reggio Calabria, before I could extract a contact number which we could phone directly. It took three hours before I spoke to someone – who refused to give me his full name.

'Just call me Amedeo,' he told me. Honestly, Beppe, it must be easier for a mafia *boss* to get in touch with the DIA than it is for a run-of-the-mill *questore* such as me!'

'They do have a reputation for being obsessively secretive, Mariastella. But their 'secrecy' did not seem to work for Laura Ianni – if it was the DIA responsible for her new identity. So, did you get anywhere with this Amedeo character?'

'I practically had to plead with him. I even suggested it would be safer for him to travel incognito to Pescara. But he wouldn't have any of that. He implied very plainly that HE would be doing us a favour. When I offered to go down alone, he told me that was not the way the DIA worked. *La prassi,* [82] I was informed, demands that I be accompanied by a male officer – and nothing lower down the ranks than a *Commissario,* Amedeo felt it necessary to stress! I shall ask my secretary down the corridor to book us return flight tickets from Pescara to Reggio Calabria. This 'Amedeo' character will pick us up in person from the airport and take us to a secret place where we shall be 'interviewed' – I am sure *he* said 'interrogated'. I am sorry to take you away from your family, Beppe. But please be sure to stress to Sonia that there is no danger involved for you.'

---

[82] A very Latin word for 'standard procedure'. Praxis in English!

'I am sure that Sonia knows you well enough now not to be anxious about my safety when in your company, Mariastella,' said Beppe in what he hoped sounded like a leg-pull. 'I shall break the news to her this evening.'

'I know I keep telling you to go home and be with your family, Beppe. But you have done all you can for the moment. So, please, I beg you, return to Atri. I'll let you know when we are leaving for Reggio Calabria. I am glad you are coming with me. I can never understand the *Calabrese* accent – let alone their dialect.'

'Well, Mariastella, I guess I have the advantage over you – at least in that one respect,' added the *Commissario*.

16: A glimpse behind the scenes...

A cynical leer had appeared on the face of Gregorio Giuffrè as soon as he looked at the screen on his mobile phone. He was surprised that his uncle, Don Fausto Talarico, had taken so long to react to the realisation that the photo of 'his' crime had gone viral across the whole of central and southern Italy. Needless to say, the 'official' Italian media – almost entirely based in the north – had fought shy of publicising the more gruesome aspects of life in Italy. The 'northerners' preferred not to face up to the truth as to who really ruled the roost in Italy. So mused the minor boss of a minor clan somewhere in Reggio Calabria. He, Gregorio Giuffrè, would soon rectify the public evaluation of himself and his family. He was feeling smug as he assumed a tone of subservient pleasure at the sound of his uncle's rasping voice.

Zio Fausto... How can I be of help to you today?

You've messed up, young man. Who told you to plant a statue of the Virgin Mary next to that girl? I just ordered you to 'farla fuori' [83]

You told me to make it as dramatic as possible, *zio*. I thought the idea of the statue was good. It emphasised the sense of your power. Isn't that what you wanted?

What it has done is to point the finger of suspicion at ME and MY family, you idiot! How long do you think it will take some smart cop to make the connection between the statue of the Virgin Mary and my clan?

---

[83] Bump her off. To make her disappear.

I am truly sorry, *zio*. I swear I was just trying to make the scene a bit more sinister. You told me you wanted the whole world to know that the girl who refused to marry – one of our nephews, wasn't it? - would never get away with it. A signal to everyone that the Talarico clan was not to be trifled with.

What you've done is... Sei uno stronzo, Gregorio! Have those two goons returned to Reggio Calabria yet?

(Gregorio Giuffrè allowed the pause to protract itself for as long as he dared before he put on a guilty-sounding voice.)

They haven't been to see me, *zio*. I assumed they would come and report back to you first. After all, you're the boss...

Had it occurred to you that the police might have arrested them? They might be pouring out their little hearts to the cops. Had you considered that?

They won't be doing that, *zio*. I put the fear of God into them before I let them loose up there in Pescara for a second time. Don't worry, *zio*. There won't be any repercussions.

For your sake, you'd better be right, giovanotto! [84] If all this backfires on ME, you'll be the one looking over his shoulder for the rest of his days. Your usefulness to my clan is in the balance. Hai capito, stronzo? [85]

Sì, *zio*. Scusami, *zio!*

---

[84] Youngster – a word loaded with scorn in this context.
[85] Have you got that? Have you understood, you bloody fool?

'It's only a matter of days now,' thought Gregorio Giuffrè, with a feeling of terrifying conviction that the time for action was drawing nigh.

* * *

If this would-be mafioso *boss* had known that an astute *Commissario* in distant Pescara – heading down to Reggio Calabria just as he was patting himself on the back - had worked out the scenario so accurately, he might not have been feeling quite so self-assured. But he, Gregorio Giuffrè, had one trump card up his sleeve that even Fausto Talarico was unaware of.

17: *Into the lion's den...*

Commissario Beppe Stancato and the lady *Questore* were feeling relatively relaxed as the Alitalia [86] flight from Pescara landed at Tito Minniti Airport in the deep south of Italy.

Sonia had appeared to be reassured by the presence of Mariastella on this official journey down to Reggio Calabria.

'We should be back in a couple of days,' Beppe had promised.

If anything, it was Veronica, Lorenzo and their 'house-guest', Annamaria Intimo, who had shown signs of emotion at Beppe's departure – accompanied by a trolley suitcase. Beppe had secretly hoped that Sonia was simply putting on a brave face at his departure. He had been granted only the usual hug and the quick kiss on the lips. Her eyes were dry. One never knew exactly what women were thinking or feeling mused the *Commissario* – even after several years of being together. Sonia had – quite subconsciously, it seemed – placed her left hand over the slight swelling of her belly as Beppe put his car into gear and drove off. Just maybe, Sonia was chiding him silently for his untimely act of desertion?

Mariastella's suitcase was only the third piece of luggage to appear on the conveyer belt. Beppe's suitcase seemed to have gone on a journey of its own. His *capo* suggested she would meet him outside in the main hall – so as not to keep whoever was meeting them waiting in suspense.

She might just as well have stayed with her travelling companion in the luggage area. She looked around in vain for anyone amongst the crowd of people waiting for friends or family to emerge through the exit doors who might be the individual who was supposed to be meeting them. But nobody seemed to show any signs of detaching themselves from the

---

[86] This story takes place before Alitalia was 'renamed' ITA.

crowd. She and Beppe had been obliged to send a head-and-shoulders photo of themselves via their cell phones the day before to a number that had been reluctantly divulged to the lady *Questore* by some nameless individual. The DIA were fulfilling their mission in life of remaining as anonymous as possible, she assumed.

When Beppe finally appeared, trailing his recalcitrant suitcase behind him, the one-and-only person whom Mariastella had subconsciously dismissed walked towards them as soon as Beppe had arrived and stood next to his *capo*. She looked exactly like a maiden auntie who had been dispatched to pick up her nephew and niece in the absence of any other family member.

'*Io sono* Gloria,' announced the maiden aunt, unsmilingly. 'Gloria Rossi. I'm sorry I didn't come over straight away, *signora Questore.* I had to be sure there were two of you before I identified myself. Necessary precautions, you understand...'

Beppe looked at Mariastella. It was obvious that they were both suppressing the desire to giggle at the excessively secretive nature of their 'welcome' to Calabria.

'I was led to believe that we would be met by someone called Amadeo,' said Mariastella.

'Ah, they often do that,' stated Gloria. 'Thank you for telling me. It's a kind of secret code - but I forgot to ask you. It just seemed a silly precaution in your two cases, *signori.'*

Gloria drove fast and very competently through the backstreets of Reggio Calabria. All their driver said during the journey was limited to a few terse words.

'I'm taking you to your hotel first and giving you time to settle in. I shall pick you up at nineteen hundred hours – outside the hotel - for your meeting with *Il Colonnello.'*

Great Aunt Gloria did not add the words 'on the dot' but her tone of voice implied it. 'I trust you brought your uniform with you, *Commissario? Il Colonnello* Procopio will be expecting to meet you officially,' added Gloria.

'I had my uniform especially cleaned and pressed for the occasion, *Signora* Gloria,' stated Beppe with heavy sarcasm. Mariastella smirked but the lady from the DIA merely grunted – whether in approval or not was unclear.

The hotel was comfortable enough but was far from being luxurious. Not that either Beppe nor Mariastella had been expecting anything else. But Beppe had the impression that the hotel owner looked 'uncomfortable' at the arrival of the two officers of the Law.

Beppe and Mariastella had gone out in search of a local restaurant or trattoria still willing to serve them a cooked lunch at this hour.

Beppe had commented on the cool reception they had received from the hotel owner as he had checked his guests in.

'I thought he looked guilty rather than off-hand, Beppe,' Mariastella had ventured.

Beppe had frowned at her words, rather than making light of the situation. Was it because he had in point of fact had the same impression?

They shrugged it off and talked about other matters. The food and the wine were both more than acceptable – and half the price they would have paid for a similar meal in the centre of Pescara.

They both retired to their rooms after lunch and tried to rest in preparation for their encounter with the DIA later on. They both arrived simultaneously one minute before the nineteen-hundred hours which their redoubtable escort had specified.

They laughed at their own punctiliousness.

'I set out early,' joked Mariastella. 'I've been put in a room with a view on the fifth floor.'

'Whereas, I have been given a room on the first floor.'

'Strange!' thought Mariastella.

'Strange!' said Beppe.

'Something is not quite right...'

But Beppe kept the thought to himself. In any event, the maiden aunt had arrived 'on the dot.'

'It's only just round the corner from here, *Commissario...Signora Questore.* It won't take long to get there.'

Odd that the Great Aunt had listed him before his senior colleague, thought Beppe. Socially insensitive? Or was it a subconscious choice?

'Stop being so suspicious, *Commissario!'* he told himself as the car came to a halt.

There was nothing ostentatious about the DIA 'head-quarters'. It was down a side alley and there was no plaque outside with the distinctive *DIA* insignia on it.

'We don't want to appear too obvious in this town,' said Gloria. 'I'll be waiting for you right here.'

Mariastella looked at Beppe. He nodded.

'No need to wait for us, Gloria,' he said amicably. 'We can walk to our hotel.'

'Ah no, *Commissario.* I have my orders, you see.'

* * *

Colonnello Pasquale Precopio had already been ensconced in his office - wearing his full *Carabiniere* regalia – since six o'clock that evening. [87]

---

[87] The DIA does not exist as a separate body of the law. It regularly draws

He was in the company of a young female officer with whom he was in earnest conversation. She was wearing the official dark blue jacket with the distinct, angular motif comprising the letters DIA on the back of the garment.

She was dark-skinned. Her hair was jet black and fell tightly to just above shoulder level. But it was her vivid brown eyes that seemed to illuminate the room – giving out a light of pure intelligence in the spartan office. Her body was perfectly formed, thought the *Colonnello* quite dispassionately. Her face reminded him of a famous young actress – whose name eluded him. The actress in question had been one of the lead characters in a series on RAI Uno. What was the actress's name? Bah! He gave up searching for it. She was already challenging his authority, it seemed, with a direct and fearless gleam in those incredible eyes beneath the perfect curve of her arched eyebrows.

'Are you telling me, *Colonnello,* that you have deliberately sent this *Commissario* – what's his name? Stancato? – to stay in a hotel which you know to be owned by one of the local mafia clans? I cannot quite get my head around this. You have always struck me as being one of the few honest *sbirri* left on the face of this earth…'

This high-ranking policeman had winced at the word *sbirro* [88] shamelessly applied to him by this woman who could barely be more than twenty-one years old. But he had worked with her on a number of occasions before. He had developed a respect for her fierce integrity and blunt honesty, which was never dulled by the presence of higher-ranking officers.

Colonnello Precopio let out a deep sigh.

---

upon personnel from other police forces on a long-term or short-term basis.
[88] The slang word for 'cops' – never used by policemen about themselves!

'Let me explain to you exactly why I am doing this, *Agente* Sposato... Asia. [89] And give you an assurance that I am not abandoning this *Commissario* from Pescara to his fate. Incidentally, as his surname implies, he is a Calabrian born and bred – from Catanzaro. And an outstandingly brilliant *sbirro*, I am told.'

He spat out the word with what he hoped was heavy sarcasm.

'He had to escape to Pescara because he got far too close on the heels of the Spanò clan some six or seven years ago. He was quickly promoted to a full-scale *Commissario,* simply because he showed himself to be such an outstanding detective.'

'I don't suppose he happens to be good-looking as well, by any lucky chance?' interrupted Officer Asia Sposato with an irreverent smile on her face.

'That, you may have the chance to judge for yourself, Asia. Because, if anything goes wrong, I am assigning you to the task of rescuing him.'

Officer Sposato fell silent with shock.

'Maybe you should explain to me what is behind this subterfuge, *colonnello,*' she said simply, secretly thrilled by what she was being asked to do. She was rashly hoping that some mishap *would* occur – just so the monotony of everyday policing might be interrupted by some 'real' mission. But she was listening very intently to the sinister explanation that her superior office was now imparting. He must trust her absolutely to be telling her all this, she considered with a sense of pride. She would certainly not be repeating any of this conversation outside the four walls of this office.

'So, you told this officer, whom you suspect of being our mole, that our guest, *Commissario* Stancato, will be staying in

---

[89] Confusingly – a girl's name in Italy, albeit an unusual one. Pron: AA-zia

that hotel just round the corner, along with the lady *Questore* from Pescara. Have I understood the situation correctly, *mio caro colonnello?'*

'Yes, and he is the ONLY person I have told – apart from you. If anything should happen to the *Commissario,* it can only be HIM who is the informant. And that will settle the matter of the numerous missions over the last couple of years that have inexplicably misfired. Now do you see why I am pushing the limits of decency to breaking point?'

'But you must have tempted him with a bit of extra information – to whet his appetite, surely? Otherwise, why would he bother to…?'

'You are too intelligent to remain a simple foot-soldier, *cara* Asia. Yes, I spoke to the lady *Questore* over the phone before they travelled down to Reggia Calabria. She informed me that her smart *Commissario* already has a shrewd idea which clan *boss* is behind the murder of the girl whom the Pescara police know as Laura Ianni. I might have dropped a hint whilst I was talking to…my 'suspect' earlier on today.'

'And might I know who the officer is who you suspect of being our *talpa?* [90]

'I am absolutely convinced you have a shrewd idea of his identity already, *Agente* Sposato. So, I will resist the temptation of making a premature revelation - even to you!'

'And I have a fairly shrewd idea as to the identity of the woman assassinated in Pescara, *mio colonnello,'* said Asia Sposato teasingly. 'Maybe we should have an exchange of information when you have interviewed this Stancato character – and the lady *Questore?'*

Colonnello Procopio gave her a hard look. Officer Asia Sposato merely smiled in his direction as she stood up to leave.

---

[90] Mole

'*In bocca al lupo,* with your interview, *mio colonnello!*'
'*Crepi!*' [91] he replied, with very little conviction.

* * *

Beppe and Mariastella Martellini shook hands with this imposing *Carabiniere* officer. His hair was rapidly turning grey, Beppe noticed. He had a care-worn expression on his slightly wrinkled face. But he did not try to hide his surprise on seeing this youthful and little-short-of-gorgeous example of womanhood who had confidently stepped over the threshold of his office.

To make matters worse, one look at this *Commissario* with the smiling face and honest brown eyes made his heart sink. The stinging words uttered by Officer Asia Sposato a mere fifteen minutes previously came forcibly back to haunt him. He was going to end up liking this extraordinary couple of police officials. How was he ever going to hold his nerve?

'My name is *Colonnello* Precopio. But please call me Pasquale – if you prefer,' he added despite himself. 'I thank you for taking the trouble of travelling all the way down to Reggio Calabria to meet us 'in the lion's den' so to speak. Please sit down, *signori.*'

There was an awkward silence. It became instantly apparent that neither of the three officers knew how to broach the subject that had brought them together. Mariastella broke the ice with a nervous but merry laugh.'

'This conversation could prove to be very short indeed, *mio caro colonnello,*' said Mariastella, still trying not to laugh. 'Or else it could take us one whole hour, at least. The main

---

[91] See footnote at the end of the novel concerning this very 'Italian' way of wishing one 'Good luck'.

reason for our journey down south is simply because we felt that the gruesome murder of a young woman in Pescara has been partly solved, in as much as we have arrested the perpetrators of the crime. It is out of respect for the murdered girl – and her family – that we would like to know her true identity. It became very obvious that this girl, whom we knew as Laura Ianni, was not a native of Pescara. So, *Colonnello* – sorry, Pasquale – would you like Beppe here to give you a potted version of the events that took place in Pescara? I am sure you will be fascinated by the whole story.'

Pasquale Precopio did not hesitate.

'Naturally I would be interested to know the history behind your investigation. It may seem fanciful to you two – but I have the impression that it is fate that has brought you to my attention – so delightfully,' he added before he could stop himself. 'I have to tell you without prevarication that I have so far not been able to discover the identity of your murder victim. I would have to go through so many hoops with the various ministerial departments in Rome that we would all have reached retirement age – possibly still in ignorance. And yes…'

The lady *Questore* understood the reason for the *Colonnello's* hesitation.

'Beppe and Mariastella is fine, Pasquale. No need to stand on ceremony in private, wouldn't you agree?'

'*Grazie…Mariastella.* I was going to say that I have seen that photo of the murdered girl – which has gone viral all over the south of our beloved peninsula. And I totally understand your desire to get to the bottom of this crime. I repeat, I have so far been unable to discover this girl's true identity, but…'

Pasquale Procopio had paused for dramatic effect. Afterall, he might as well give this engaging couple some hope.

'I have just been talking to one of our younger and smarter officers who claims that she might well know the true identity of your murder victim, Laura Ianni. She was a little reluctant to divulge her name – I imagine that is because she may be related to this girl. If we wait until tomorrow, you could meet her in person. Maybe if she hears the full account of your investigation, she will be far more willing to divulge the name you are looking for. We too, as part of the DIA, would be interested in taking your investigation one stage further. What do you say, Beppe, Mariastella?'

'Tomorrow would be good, *Colo*... Pasquale,' stated Mariastella decisively.

Beppe nodded in agreement. The day had been very long – and he wanted more than anything else to phone Sonia.

'*A domani mattina, allora.* Shall we say at nine o'clock? I bid you both a good night's sleep. Don't forget to lock your bedroom doors! This is not Pescara, you understand,' he said as if it was a joke.

'*Sei un maledetto vigliacco,* Pasquale Procopio!' [92] he accused himself out loud as soon as Beppe and Mariastella had been whisked off into the melee of evening rush hour traffic by Great Aunt Gloria.

---

[92] You are one almighty coward!

18:   *Not such a good night…*

In his first-floor hotel bedroom, Beppe lay flat out on his bed, fully dressed, talking to Sonia, who had insisted that they should switch on the video camera so that Veronica and Lorenzo could see him.

'Our children are missing you, Beppe.'

This observation was followed by a protracted silence on Beppe's part.

'But not as much as *I* am,' added Sonia, almost inaudibly – as if she did not wish to admit it publicly.

Beppe felt a wave of warmth travelling through his body.

'Ah – the power of words!' he thought.

'Anchio, amore.' he said – his reticence unlocked.

Veronica looked as if she was about to protest that a daughter could miss her father in equal measure. But one look at her mother's face made her think better of it.

In her top-floor bedroom, Mariastella Martellini was looking out over the roof-tops of Reggio Calabria at the glowing horizon, still illuminated by the setting sun which transformed the sky into a glorious pinkish-orange backdrop. How hard it was to imagine that the beauty of this vibrant city was tarnished by the presence of the most dangerously efficient criminal minds in the world. *'La 'ndrangheta'* – the lady *Questore* said aloud, as if saying the words audibly would banish their hold over her imagination. Would it be a sign of weakness if she phoned Beppe four floors beneath her? Yes – after all, she was nominally in charge of this mission. She must remain strong. Instead, she triple-locked her door before getting undressed - the parting words of *Colonnello* Pasquale Procopio still echoing in her ears.

'I think he was trying to make a joke of it,' she told herself, fighting off her irrational fears. 'This is still Italy, for heaven's sake – albeit the 'untamed' part of it.'

Nevertheless, after a disturbed night's sleep, her first act after getting dressed the following morning was to go downstairs and knock on her *Commissario's* bedroom door. Her night time fears were rekindled when there was no response from inside his room. She banged on the door with her fist, which only brought a middle-aged male guest out into the corridor. He took one look at the imposing young woman responsible for all the noise and decided to retire back inside his room, stifling the recriminatory words that had sprung to mind.

Mariastella headed downstairs to the reception desk. If the hotel owner had appeared guilty the previous day, he was now looking petrified at the menacing expression on this forceful woman's face as she strode purposefully in his direction. He had heard the sound of someone banging on a bedroom door one floor above him and a female voice calling out the name 'Beppe' with increasing alarm in her voice.

There was no escape.

'The guest in room 13, *signore.* He seems to have gone missing. Have you anything to say about his disappearance?'

'He went out for a walk earlier on, *signora.* He said he was going for a coffee,' the owner stammered. His face had turned ashen.

'You are lying, *signore.* I am from the police department in Pescara. I always *know* when someone is lying. Find your pass key and open up my *Commissario's* door immediately.'

'I…I…cannot, *signora.* I was told not to…'

Never in her professional life had she ever physically attacked anyone – however angry she had felt inside. She found herself striding round to the back of the counter and seizing the

147

man by the neck with both hands. She was alarmed to find her fingers tightening round his throat.

'Open that door!' she snarled with so much venom in her voice that the owner broke into choking sobs.

'Alright, *signora*. I will open the door for you.' he gargled.

His hands were shaking as he walked upstairs, with a red-faced *Questore* hard on his heels.

One look inside the room told Mariastella everything. Her *Commissario's* uniform was still hanging over a chair. She found his mobile phone untouched inside the top drawer of the bedside table, hidden under his underpants. He had been abducted wearing only his pyjamas. She put Beppe's phone into her pocket and headed for the door.

One look at the cowed face of the hotel owner and she knew she would have to adapt her approach to this new and unique situation.

'This room is a crime scene now, *signore*. The police will be along later this morning and seal it off. You will have a lot of explaining to do. What's your name, *signore?*' she asked in a softer tone.

'Marino…Luigi.'

Well, Luigi Marino, were you present when my *Commissario* was abducted?'

He nodded his head up and down continually for several seconds – as if the repeated gesture would mitigate his guilt.

'How many men took him away?'

'Just two, *signora.* '

'I assume it was YOU who let his abductors into the bedroom?'

The hotel owner merely nodded in acquiescence.

'And would you like to give me the name of the individual who is behind the illegal abduction of my *Commissario*...Luigi?'

The hotel owner shook his head violently from side to side.

'Please don't ask me to do that, *signora*. I cannot... I dare not...'

'Is his name – I assume it's a man – Fausto Talarico, by any chance?'

The hotel owner suddenly and inexplicably displayed a look of pure relief on his face.

'*Sissignora.*' He was nodding again with great enthusiasm.

Mariastella Martellini left the man without another word and headed for the hotel entrance door.

'Interesting,' she thought to herself.

The man was lying, of course - almost happy to find a way out of his dilemma.

'*Bravo, Commissario* Stancato – wherever you are. You were right again. There *is* another clan *boss* involved in all this.'

To Mariastella's relief, their faithful chauffeur was waiting outside the hotel.

'The *Commissario* won't be long, will he?' asked Gloria – making the question sound like a complaint.

'Oh, no need to wait for him, Gloria,' said the lady *Questore* airily. 'He's been abducted by the mafia during the night.'

No apparent change in Gloria Rossi's facial expression worth mentioning!

'So, the *colonnello* was right,' were the only enigmatic words that she uttered. But she did manage to drive to the DIA headquarters with even greater urgency than on the previous evening.

* * *

'No *Commissario* this morning?' asked the *Colonnello* as Mariastella Martellini stepped in a determined manner into his office. The expression on his face clearly indicated a degree of surprise, noticed the lady *Questore*. In contradiction to his face, his eyes looked 'shifty' she considered.

'I have to tell you, *Colonnello* Precopio, that my colleague and friend has been abducted by two mafioso hoodlums during the night.

'Ah! So I *was* right!'

The *sotto voce* words had emerged spontaneously - unpremeditated.

'So, you are not altogether surprised, *mio caro Colonnello?*

The words emanating from this simply stunning-looking woman's lips carried more than a hint of menace. Why was it his fate, in recent months, to find himself dealing with forceful women? How times have changed, he thought, nostalgic about a past that had never really existed except in his own utopian world.

He let out a heavy sigh as he gestured to his guest to sit down.

'I shall be entirely honest with you, Mariastella – because you deserve to be told the whole truth. Even if I have known you for less than twenty-four hours,' he added - more than half of him being afraid he was about to get his head bitten off by those oh-so-pearly-white teeth!

Mariastella stopped herself from giving vent to her anger. Twice in one morning would be tantamount to a complete lack of professionalism, she told herself.

'*Mi dica tutto, Colonnello!* [93] It might have been wiser of you to have left unsaid the bit about *only knowing me for less than a day.*'

Pasquale Procopio felt himself blushing.

'You are right, *signora Questore.* I apologise for any unintended inuendo regarding my choice of words.

'Apology accepted, *mio Colonnello.* Please continue – and excuse me for my reaction. I am deeply shocked by my colleague's disappearance. I am already dreading the phone call I shall have to make to his wife and children.'

'*O mio Dio!* I am so sorry. Might I say at this juncture that I do not believe your colleague – Beppe, isn't it? – has been harmed. At least, not yet. Had the clan involved wished him dead, they would have carried out the deed last night in the bedroom. The mafia in these parts doesn't usually have any qualms about assassination. And we will immediately set about the task of liberating him – do not fear. In a short while, my colleague will be arriving. She will be responsible for tracking down your *Commissario...*'

'More importantly, the *Commissario* is a good friend and an outstandingly good policeman. So please tell me why you put us at risk by sending us to that particular hotel – when almost any other hotel in Reggio Calabria would have been safer.'

Colonnello Procopio told her in plain, unadulterated terms why he had embarked on this course of action.

'The irony is, of course, that your *Commissario's* abduction has given me enough proof to arrest this young man – who has been surreptitiously hampering our investigations for

---

[93] Tell me all...

months. He's probably a 'plant' from the clan responsible for Beppe's abduction.'

Mariastella's desire to remonstrate with this man should have got the better of her – but would have done nothing to help the spirit of cooperation prompted by his confession. Mariastella was spared from going down that path by a timely knock on the door.'

'Avanti, Agente Sposato,*'* he called out, with more than a hint of relief in his voice.

'Salvato dalla campana, Colonnello?' [94]

Pasquale Procopio laughed at the comment. Peace and good will had magically been restored.

Mariastella found herself staring open-mouthed at the young uniformed woman who had stepped over the threshold. At first, she thought of Officer Oriana Salvati, back in Abruzzo. But then, it was the image of an actress who had played the role of the teenage Lila from the film of Elena Ferrante's book *L'Amica Geniale.* [95] which sprang to mind.

'I know what you are thinking, *Signora Questore,'* said *Agente* Asia Sposato, without even waiting to be formally introduced.

'Yes, you remind me very vividly of an actress whose name I cannot remember, *Agente* Sposato...'

'Asia, please, *Signora Questore.* And it would be safer for you to remember me as I am in reality – especially as I have frequently been told that I am even less predictable than Lila Cerullo in that TV series.'

Mariastella Martellini smiled warmly at the newcomer. She reminded her of herself at that age – self-assured, wild and determined to be herself every second of every waking moment

---

[94] Saved by the bell?

[95] My Brilliant Friend – see note at the end of the novel.

in her life. Mariastella felt reassured that this person was quite capable of saving her *Commissario* from whatever fate awaited him.

Colonnello Precopio coughed politely from behind his desk.

'As it is plain to see that you two ladies are going to get on like a house on fire, may I suggest you get better acquainted somewhere more inspiring than my office? I need to go through the legal necessities of sealing off the *Commissario's* hotel room and get a forensics team to check for any traces of those two mafia underlings who deprived Beppe Stancato of his night's sleep – and interrogate the hotel owner,' said the *Colonnello.*

'May we join you, *Colonnello?'* suggested Mariastella. 'It would seem a good place to start.'

'Yes, give me half an hour to get things organised and then we'll go to the hotel together. You two, go and have a coffee somewhere. I'll call you when I am ready to leave.'

'*Grazie, Colonnello,'* said the lady *Questore,* as she and Officer Asia Sposato stood up to leave the office.

* * *

Without being asked, Asia led Mariastella past two noisy bars in the immediate vicinity of the DIA headquarters. She took her companion to a tiny tree-lined park with benches scattered around at strategic points. Beneath a lofty palm tree, she stopped and smiled knowingly at Mariastella.

'I thought you might like to make your phone call here, Mariastella, It's almost peaceful here.'

'How did you know…?' began Mariastella.

'The *colonnello* gave me a kind of hand-signal as we left. I guess you have to tell Beppe's partner what has happened?'

Mariastella just looked at Asia almost lovingly.

'I'll make myself scarce,' offered Asia.

'No, please stay with me. I need moral support for this call.'

Moral support, in Asia's book, meant putting an arm round Mariastella's waist – she was too short in stature to put her arm round the lady *Questore's* shoulder.

'*Dai,* Mariastella!' said Asia, noticing her companion's hesitation. Best get this moment out of the way. I am sure that…'

'She's called Sonia,' interjected Mariastella, correctly interpreting Asia's quizzical rising of an eyebrow.

'I'm sure that Sonia is not going to blame you.'

This slip of a girl, with her arm round her waist, had already intuited why she, Mariastella, was hesitating to make the call.

Mariastella just looked at her new companion and quietly mouthed the words: '*Grazie mille,*' before tapping out Sonia's number on the screen.

'*Pronto? Beppe? Sei tu?* [96]

Sonia's voice sounded stretched, agitated. She had been expecting a morning call from her husband for over two hours. She looked at the screen and saw that the caller was Mariastella Martellini. That could only mean one thing, she realised.

Asia could hear Sonia's voice and then a prolonged cry of fear and grief. Her heart went out to this woman whose existence she had been unaware of until a few minutes previously.

---

[96] Is that you, Beppe?

'I'm so sorry to have to break this news to you – and your two children,' Mariastella added, as she heard their alarmed voices in the background.

'I knew that he would go too far one day, Mariastella. I just hoped it wouldn't be this time – because *you* were there with him…'

'This time, Sonia, it wasn't Beppe's impetuosity to blame. We had no fore-warning that this would happen. He was, as far as we know, abducted from his hotel room in the middle of the night.'

'O Dio mio!

'We are not sure why he was abducted – or by whom. But I have been assured that he is still alive. If they had wanted him dead, they would have…'

Sonia could be heard speaking softly to Lorenzo and Veronica. She had managed to get her own emotions under control.

'I don't blame you, Mariastella. Just keep me posted during the day. I'll keep the children at home today – and there's Annamaria here to keep me company too…'

Asia Sposato was making frantic signals to Mariastella that she wanted to speak to Sonia. It was a completely different voice that Sonia heard. In a trice - and without asking for the permission of the lady *Questore* beforehand – a voice full of vitality was requesting that Sonia should switch to a video call.

The face which appeared on Sonia's screen took her breath away. She had no time to reflect on the appearance of the uniformed girl – whose appearance and the clarity of her voice reminded her of Oriana Salvati. Except *this* version of the much-loved policewoman from Pescara was speaking with a pronounced Calabrian accent.

'*Ciao,* Sonia,' said the girl. I'm Asia Sposato – a police officer with the DIA. I'm so sorry we have to get acquainted in such distressing circumstances as this, but...'

Sonia was only aware that the vitality of the young officer was so strong that it was just as if she was *physically* present.

'... I want to reassure you that I will personally find out where your husband is – and I shall rescue him within four or five days. That's a promise that I know I can keep. Trust me!'

Sonia found herself thanking this woman whose supreme confidence was inspiring.

'I do trust you, Asia,' Sonia said simply. 'And now, I must comfort my children.'

Asia could hear another woman's voice in the background as she brought the call to an end.

'That would be Annamaria Intimo,' explained Mariastella to her companion. 'She's blind – but without her, we would never have arrested the two thugs who murdered Laura Ianni.'

'That sounds like a story you can tell me later on, Mariastella.'

'Yes, I will. Right now, we had better return to the hotel, Asia. I see that your *colonnello* has summoned us to the scene of the crime.'

'Sorry, Mariastella. I should have asked if I could switch your phone to video mode, shouldn't I?

'No, you shouldn't, Asia. It seems as if *I* shall have to trust you too!'

All Mariastella got by way of reply was a complicit grin and a look which said: 'That suits me fine.'

* * *

In the hotel, the *Colonnello* was personally demolishing the hotel owner, in public, in the hotel foyer – even if the only audience consisted of Mariastella and Asia stepping through the front entrance door.

'So, *Signor* Marino,' said his inquisitor with petrifying intensity, 'was last night the first time in your life that you had set eyes on the two men who abducted our colleague, *Commissario* Stancato? Come on now, Luigi,' continued the *Colonnello,* altering his tone of voice to cajoling mode, 'You don't have to say a single word. Just nod or shake your head. After all, I now have two eye-witnesses to your answers.'

Luigi Marino finally shook his head once.

'Ah!' said the *Colonnello.* 'Did you meet them before here in the hotel?'

Once again, the question elicited a shake of the head.

'So…Luigi, where have you seen them before?'

The open form of the question appeared to defeat the hotel owner utterly. Pasquale Procopio changed tack immediately.

'Do you know the name of the owner of this hotel, Luigi?'

A far less convincing nod of the head this time, accompanied by a look of pure dread.

'And what might this name be, dare I ask?'

The man's lips were pressed together as if to prevent any accidental, tell-tale words issuing from his mouth.

'Never mind, *Signor* Marino. We can simply go and look up the name in the public records office,' said Pasquale Procopio in such a reasonable voice.

'But, of course, your silence will mean I am bound to arrest you now for obstructing a police investigation – a murder investigation, by the way.'

Luigi Marino looked petrified at these words.

He looked wildly at the three people who were staring intensely at him. The group suddenly seemed to be closing in on him – including that woman who had wanted to strangle him.

Mariastella Martellini was looking admiringly at the *Colonnello*. Only her own *Commissario* could have engineered such a verbal trap any better. But her Beppe would not have had to resort to what Mariastella hoped was a 'white lie!'

A strangulated voice was heard to utter the words:

'Gregorio Giuffrè.'

To her surprise, a yelp of something resembling pure joy broke the tension of the atmosphere. Officer Asia Sposato was nodding her head up and down with a broad smile on her face. It meant quite simply, that her promise to locate their missing *Commissario* was one step closer. Something positive she could relay later to Sonia and family back in Abruzzo.

The lady *Questore* had, out of a habit of correctness of procedure, requested that she and Asia should go and take a look at the bedroom which Beppe had occupied the previous night.

Mariastella was not expecting any further revelations from an examination of the 'crime scene' and she was, therefore, astonished at the manner in which the next half hour unfurled. Her surprise was shared in equal measure by Officer Asia Sposato – who considered afterwards that she had, so far in her short life, given insufficient thought as to what it meant to be blind.

'The intruders hardly left a single clue as to their identity,' the white coated, unmasked, chief crime scene investigator told the *Colonnello* and his two female companions. 'Some prints on the door-handle and the light switches which we've taken might help – but of course, we will need this

Commissario's prints too in order to have a minimum chance of identifying the others,

'That's it, Michele?' asked the *Colonnello,* looking at the scientist.

'Ci dispiace, Pasquale. There's nothing else, I'm sorry to tell you, apart from the smell, that is...'

'Quale odore, dottore?'

It was Mariastella, who had shot the question at the startled chief of the forensic team. She had already learnt about the vital importance of smells during this investigation.

'There's a smell of onions hanging around in the air.'

'That's what I can smell!' stated Asia Sposato, breaking her silence.

'I was about to open the window to let some fresh air in,' said one of the forensics team, with his hand on the window handle.

'STOP!' ordered the lady *Questore.*

'Do as she says, *signore,'* said the *colonnello.* 'She's a *Questore!* he explained. 'She must have a good reason to shout at you,' he added with a smile.

'I could detect the smell as soon as we came into the room. it is still quite strong – I should have questioned it immediately. Just give me time to make a single phone call – please, *signori!'* requested Mariastella.

All the other five people in the room were eaten up by curiosity. Mariastella could see it on their faces. She put her phone on to loud speaker mode, for their benefit.

All the same, Mariastella Martellini was feeling slightly ridiculous as she began to speak.

'Ciao, Mariastella. What a pleasant surprise! Have you got some good news about Beppe? No surely not – it's much too

soon, isn't it?' said the young woman on the other end of the line.

'Annamaria – can you help me please? We are in the hotel bedroom where Beppe was before he was abducted. There's a strong smell of onions in the room – which could not have been given off by our *Commissario.*' she said in all seriousness.

'What a pity nobody has been able to invent something which can teleport smells!' said the voice.

The people in the hotel room smiled automatically, totally intrigued by the oddness of this exchange of words.

It was Annamaria Intimo who took up the dialogue after a thoughtful pause.

'Would you say that this smell of onions reminds you of the town or of the countryside?'

'I..,' began Mariastella. 'Is there a difference, Annamaria?'

'Oh yes! Absolutely,' replied Annamaria in far-away Atri.

In desperation, the lady *Questore* looked at the group of five – all of whom were obviously thinking hard - captivated by the uniqueness of the question.

It was Asia who answered after only a brief pause.

'I would say, the town!'

The others nodded in what they hoped was a convincing manner.

Annamaria Intimo responded to the single voice which had supplied an answer.

'Could it be that he – or is it 'they' – work in a vegetable market?'

'*Grazie infinite,* Annamaria. 'You are a genius!'

Mariastella looked at the puzzled faces before her.

'She's blind, you know,' was all she deigned to say by way of explanation.

'I'll get the hotel owner to describe the men when I've got him back in headquarters,' promised the *Colonnello*.

'Maybe, that won't be necessary, *signori,'* stated Asia Sposato. 'But it would certainly help. That clan *boss,* Gregorio Giuffrè is responsible for supplying at least 70% of the vegetables that find their way to the main market. I am sure you don't need me to explain any further.'

One of the forensics team added:

'There is a surveillance camera just down the road. It won't help to identify the abductors, but you might be able to identify the car they used. There wouldn't have been a lot of traffic on the road at that time of night, The camera should give a good image of any car that was parked near the hotel.

'Thank you, Andrea,' said the *Colonnello,* rubbing his hands in glee. 'Finally, we stand a chance of catching some of those bastards who think they are the Lords and Masters of our wonderful city.'

19:   Small talk...?

'How long will you be staying in our sadly deranged city? Which, incidentally, I love!'

'I have a flight booked to take me back to Pescara tomorrow late-morning, Asia.'

'*Geniale!* That means we've got a whole day – and night – that we can spend in each other's company!' declared Asia with a note of joy in her voice. 'You can keep me company while I find out where they are hiding your *Commissario.*'

Mariastella did not dare ask what this voyage of discovery into unknown territory would involve. It was unlikely to be conventional.

'So, what will be our first port of call?

'We'll walk back and collect your things from the hotel. I'm quite certain you don't want to spend your last night in Reggio Calabria in *that* place.'

'Not particularly, no,'

'Then we'll pick up my car and pay a quick visit to my apartment, Mariastella. I need to change into something which does not advertise my status to all the world. I live a double life in this city. Then we will go and find a place to have lunch. I take it you have not lost your appetite? Personally, I can't miss out on my food in the middle of the day.'

Mariastella assured her new companion that she loved food – especially regional food which was new to her.

'You can stay with me in my apartment tonight, Mariastella. Then I can run you to the airport. You're not a lesbian, are you?'

'Only on Sundays!' stated Mariastella, in mock seriousness.

Asia Sposato burst out into peals of laughter.

'*Ti voglio bene,* [97] Mariastella. I am so happy to know you.'

'And you, Asia? With a surname like 'Sposato...?' [98]

'Well, I'm very much single. To be honest with you, I'm not quite sure what I am, at the moment. But I would certainly not want to marry any of the men I have met so far in Reggio!'

Mariastella felt like hugging Asia – but was not sure what her reaction would be in the light of her earlier question. Instead, she asked:

'And where are you taking me to have lunch? Will that be a place owned by the mafia, as well?'

'No – it's a lovely little *trattoria* near the seaside – which does only local food. Mind you, they probably have to pay their *pizzo* to some clan or other. It's still too close to Reggio,' concluded Asia.

'And after that...?' asked Mariastella with a slight feeling of trepidation.

'When was the last time you went to a night club, Mariastella?' Asia asked with a challenging grin on her face.

'You want to take me to a *nightclub?*'

'It's business – not entirely pleasure,' laughed Asia Sposato, looking at the expression on the face of the lady *Questore* from Pescara. 'The one I have in mind is owned by a mafia crook by the name of Gregorio Giuffrè.

'Ah! *Ho capito,* Asia!'

It's so expensive that only a select few can afford to go there. It doubles up as a high-class brothel and gambling den. I actually work there as a barmaid two or three times a week. Sometimes, I earn more money than I do as a police officer.'

---

[97] 'I love you – as you would say to a friend or family member. Cf 'Ti amo'
[98] 'Sposato / sposata' is an adjective meaning 'married' - which has also become a surname.

'Out of curiosity, Asia – how come you think this visit will help us find my *Commissario?* I do love dancing, by the way. It makes me feel like a teenager again!'

For the first time in their short acquaintance, a guarded expression had crossed the face of the young DIA police officer. She was reluctant to give a straight answer, it seemed.

'Because Gregorio Giuffrè is my uncle, Mariastella.'

Mariastella was taken aback by this admission on her new friend's part.

'But you want to be instrumental in putting him behind bars, don't you?' the *Questore* asked, thinking it was something of a stab in the dark.

'It's where he deserves to be, Mariastella. No…he actually deserves to be in Hell! I was raped by him when I was only fourteen years' old.'

There were no suitable words to convey what Mariastella was feeling – but her face expressed the shocked revulsion caused by Asia's revelation.

* * *

'Do you ever watch Montalbano – that Sicilian detective on Rai 1?' [99] asked Asia as they sat down round a table set for two diners, which was big enough to seat six people.

'Always,' replied Mariastella. 'My Spanish boyfriend loves it. I'm not so sure – sometimes it is almost too close to real life for comfort. Beppe watches the series avidly – even though he criticises Montalbano for being totally sexist.'

'I agree with Beppe,' stated Asia. 'And before I forget to ask you, do you have a photo of Beppe on your iPhone? It would help if I knew what he looks like.'

---

[99] Also shown, 'subtitled' on BBC 4 – and BBC I-player

Mariastella rescued her phone from her handbag and selected a photo of Beppe which she had taken some months previously on the occasion of Beppe and family's visit to her country house. She showed it to Asia, whose eyebrows shot up briefly - accompanied by a secret smile. She quickly reset her features to 'normal'.

'Not bad-looking for his age, is he?' she stated casually. 'Could you send that photo to my mobile please, Mariastella? This is my number,' she said, holding up her phone.

Mariastella remembered she had put Beppe's mobile into her handbag earlier on.

'You might as well have this as well, Asia. You are, I believe, going to meet him before I see him again.'

'Brilliant! Thank you, Mariastella.'

'*A proposito,* [100] why did you ask me whether I watched Montalbano, Asia?'

'Ah yes! Because he always claims that he refuses to talk when he is having a meal in a restaurant – so he can appreciate the food. I agree with him. But I have so many questions to ask you that I know I shan't be able to wait until the meal is finished. That is the reason why I asked the owner – who I know well – to reserve this huge table. I didn't want the other diners listening in,' explained Asia.

'Why don't we order a first course now and then have a long pause before ordering the main course?' suggested Mariastella.

The owner of the *trattoria, La Locanda di Alia,* in a seaside village to the north of Reggio, arrived in person to take their orders. He was very laid back about life in general, it seemed, and very easy about waiting before taking orders for the main course.

---

[100] By the way

Mariastella left Asia to choose the starters.

'There's nothing I remotely recognise on the menu, Asia. I rely on you entirely.'

'The food here is unfailingly good, Mariastella – and do you notice that the name of the place is only one letter different to my first name? It's as if this place exists almost exclusively for me.'

Asia ordered *Cozze ripiene al sugo* and *Crispeddi a lici* [101] – which wasn't even in Italian, noted Mariastella.

'I guess we had better not drink any wine, today,' said Asia. It could be a long day ahead of us. And out of respect for Beppe...' she added. 'It's not yet quite the moment to celebrate, is it?'

Mariastella admired her companion's restraint – so they drank sparkling water instead.

'Why don't we share the starters, Mariastella? That way you get to taste two local dishes!'

The food was delicious and Mariastella hardly spoke until the immediate pangs of hunger had been satisfied.

Asia Sposato was wiping her sauce up with some fresh bread, but decided she could wait no longer to satisfy her curiosity.

'Now, please tell me *everything* which happened in Pescara to make you and Beppe travel all the way down to Reggio.'

And that is precisely what the lady *Questore* did – with hardly a single interruption from her new friend. It was obvious that *Agente* Asia Sposato was absorbing every single syllable.

In the end, it was too late to have a second course, because the cooks had gone to rest before the evening session.

---

[101] Mussels – stuffed with tomato sauce and anchovy fritters. *(See Valentina Harris's Italian Regional Cookbook)*

The owner of the *trattoria* looked mortified. Mariastella gave him a €100 note – ignoring his genuine protestations.

'Please keep it, *signore*. The starters were the best food I've eaten for years. And I would like to treat my friend Asia to a meal next time she comes here. Unfortunately, I have to return to Pescara tomorrow. She is going to deserve the treat a hundred times over before the next couple of days are through. Matter settled!'

'*La ringrazio, signora.* Especially for your compliment about our food. I shall make certain that Asia will eat like a princess next time she comes here. My only regret is that you may not be able to accompany her.'

'*Grazie signore.* But I fear that Pescara is a bit too far away to come just for one lunchtime.'

Mariastella could hear herself talking – and felt self-conscious that her 'posh' Bolognese accent seemed so out of place in the deep south of her motherland.

The two women left the restaurant with arms linked – despite the disparity in their heights. Asia was looking content with life. She tried hard not to think of the ordeal she would have to go through as soon as this tall and confident woman left her standing in the airport departure lounge.

* * *

Asia was driving her Fiat 500 back towards Reggio Calabria at about 100 kilometres per hour. Mariastella could hardly complain. She had a reputation for driving fast herself – her only excuse being that her father had been a professional racing car driver. But she usually drove in silence after the speedometer needle had exceeded 80.

Not so Asia Sposato - who spoke non-stop during the brief ride back to the city.

'I was enthralled by your account of Beppe's investigation of the murder of the girl you know as Laura Ianni. The blind girl – Annamaria… It was simply miraculous how she identified those mobsters – just because one of them smelt of sardines. Everybody who lives near the sea in Reggio knows about that fish canning factory. It stinks to high heaven – especially in summer time. It's owned by the Talarico clan.

But how your Beppe worked out that those bastards belonged to another clan was pure genius. He guessed that they had planted that statue on purpose – just to make it look as if the crime was committed by Fausto Talarico. He has an obsession with the Blessed Virgin Mary. In fact, he's a bit past it as a clan leader. We are expecting a take-over bid by my uncle's clan any time now. That must be why he made them place the statue of the Virgin Mary at the crime scene. I suppose he hoped that Fausto Talarico would be arrested by the police. Simply heart-wrenching that poor girl's face looked, didn't it?'

'But you said you might know what the murdered girl's real name was,' interjected Mariastella.

'It's a bit of a guess at the moment. But there was this girl – a beautiful girl – called Flora Nisticò who absolutely refused to marry some cousin of my uncle, Gregorio. Flora was also related to someone in the Talarico clan too, I seem to remember. Flora shouted at my uncle – in front of several family members – that the cousin was a mobster and that, in any case, she had no intention of going to be bed with some ugly moron like him. She went missing and dear *Zio* Gregorio threatened the parents with death if they complained to the police. The DIA must have decided to give her a new identity – in exchange for information about my uncle.'

'What about the officer who was your *talpa?*' asked Mariastella.

'His name is Officer Davide Russo. It could well be through *him* that my uncle got to know about your and Beppe's visit to Reggio Calabria. The *Colonnello* - Pasquale Procopio - has suspected Officer Russo for months, but he's one of those men who manage to look innocuous – whatever the weather, *si fa per dire...* [102] That's why the *Colonnello* thought the risk of putting you and Beppe in that hotel was worth it. It was a golden opportunity not to be missed.'

'And now, where are we going, Asia?' asked Mariastella during a short break in the conversation.

'To my apartment – down the backstreets of Reggio. I need to have a sleep - and a change of clothes - before we go to the night club. You can relax or watch TV, *cara* Mariastella. My home is yours too!'

'*Grazie,* Asia. I think I shall do the same. I did not sleep all that well last night!'

Mariastella's siesta was interrupted by a call from the *Colonnello.* She listened to what he had to say – and sighed.

'Not finding the *Commissario's* abductors on day one is only a minor setback, Pasquale. I'm sure we will be in a better position to act after tonight. Do you know where Asia is taking me later on in the evening?'

'No idea, at all, Mariastella. Anything is possible where Asia is concerned. But there is usually a very sound reason behind her actions.'

'We are going to a night club called *Il Diamante Nero.*'

'Ah! I see...' was virtually all Pasquale Procopio deigned to say before bringing the call to an end.

---

[102] So to speak

'*In bocca al lupo,* Mariastella!' he added, in a tone of voice which implied that simple 'luck' might not be enough to survive the night club venture.

20: The quick-step...?

'Mariastella Martellini' might enjoy the status of *Questore* when in Pescara, she mused, as she and Asia set out for *Il Diamante Nero* just after 9 o'clock that evening. But it was blatantly obvious that Asia was firmly in charge of operations down here in Calabria.

'Make sure you leave behind in my apartment every document you possess and every credit card that might reveal your true identity, Mariastella,' she had been ordered by this forthright young woman.

'And what if I need to pay for my entrance pass – or buy myself a drink during the evening?' she asked Asia.

Business-like and self-assured in every fibre of her body, Asia smiled her most engaging smile and stated firmly:

'I shall keep you supplied with your favourite cocktails during the course of the evening. And we will be passing a *Bancomat* on the way. You should take out as much cash as you can - up to €700 – even if this means making two transactions. And then give me your credit card to look after – if you trust me enough!'

Mariastella was on the point of asking whether she had a choice in the matter – but thought better of it.

'Don't worry, all you need to do is look confident all the time and flash a wad of cash around if you have to. There must be no sign at all that we know each other, Mariastella. *My* life depends on it as well as yours. You look great in that outfit by the way!'

The compliment was the last kind word that Maristella heard from Asia, who was scantily dressed in a tight skirt which finished less than halfway down her shapely thighs. She was already acting in a brazen manner even before they stepped out of the taxi which dropped them off outside the night club.

'You must go in first, Mariastella. I shall wait out here for five minutes before I follow you in. It will look far less suspicious if you appear before I do. The other way round just might make somebody think there is a connection between us.'

'*Agli ordini, commissario!*' stated the lady *Questore*, saluting the woman whose head only came up to her shoulders.

Asia gave a brief, tense smile before she practically pushed her friend away from her towards the entrance door, from where they were concealed down a shadowy alley some fifty metres from the night club.

'Just go and sit down at one of the tables at the edge of the main atrium. I shall come over and take your order in about ten minutes time. Say you're waiting for a friend if anybody starts to get inquisitive. *In bocca al lupo!*'

And that was it. Maristella waltzed with a confidence she was not feeling, her hips and buttocks swaying convincingly from side to side, as she approached the doorman, who bowed gracefully and held the swing door open. Mariastella, glancing back briefly as she walked towards the main atrium, noticed that the doorman was now on his mobile phone; no doubt informing someone on the inside that a client had just entered whose identity was unknown.

There were perhaps twenty to thirty people already in the night club, Mariastella noted with relief. Mainly couples, but there were some predatory lone males standing at the bar, looking out for any ladies who might walk in. Mariastella sat down, trying to look nonchalant. One or two of the male clients looked more than once in her direction. Despite her nerves, the lady *Questore* was experiencing that dark thrill in the pit of her stomach – a forgotten feeling from her teenage years. She had to remind herself why she was there.

Despite the stimulating sensation that she was being 'naughty', Maristella was quite relieved when – absolutely on cue, Asia approached and placed her 'free' cocktail on the table with a flourish.

'I've been told to ask you what you do in life, Mariastella. I can hardly say you are with the police.'

'Oh, I just happen to be a film director for Mediaset TV – researching the town for a new film production,' said Maristella inventing herself to order.

The 'waitress' smiled mechanically and shimmied back to the bar. Not a single false move, thought Mariastella admiring her new friend's perfectly executed performance. Asia had managed a furtive, few words before she turned her back on her 'customer'.

'I'll walk past your table just before midnight. Give me some excuse to stop and talk to you, Mariastella.'

The lady *Questore* spent the evening telling the various men who approached her that she would not be having sex with them tonight, but, next time who knows! She declared that she was very happy to dance 'close up' with them. 'As long as you really know how to dance well,' she warned each man flirtatiously.

She was surprised how many of them were good dancers, with a good sense of rhythm. She had only had to remove groping hands from her *culetto* [103] on a couple of occasions. Some of them were even good conversationalists during and after the various dances she performed – including a vigorous samba at one point.

She was enjoying the sensation more than she had anticipated.

---

[103] Bottom – usually implying a 'nice' one

Her only dark moment was when a man in his forties made his way towards her table. He was handsome but he walked with an arrogance and self-assuredness which he assumed in the manner of one who never expected to be ignored or disobeyed.

Mariastella found herself being led to the dance floor. What was it that was different? Then she realised the man exuded a sense of malevolent power. It came as no surprise that the man announced at the end of the dance that he was the owner of the nightclub.

She had just danced with the person responsible for her *Commissario's* abduction – and the rape of a fourteen-year-old girl. He had left her with a broad smile, with a wish that her trip to Reggio to research her film was successful. But he had managed to imply by his tone of voice that he was unconvinced by her story.

Seated at her table, she noticed with a deep sense of unease that the man who had pressed his right hand firmly into the small of her back, letting it slide down as far as her right buttock, was climbing upstairs – with *her* new friend and guide, Asia, who was following him a few steps behind. She just stopped herself making the sign of the cross. Instead, she muttered a short prayer under her breath. *Look after her, please!* she said to the God whom she tried very hard not to believe in. Inexplicably, she wanted to phone Don Emanuele for comfort and reassurance – until she remembered that Asia had even forbidden her to take her mobile phone to the night club. She looked at her watch. Still fifty minutes to go before midnight! She went and bought only the second drink that she had had to pay for. Most of her dancing companions had given up on expecting any sexual favours from her – as they drifted off to pastures new.

It was well past midnight before her companion approached her. As Asia had suggested, she waved imperiously at this mini-skirted 'tart' – as if she was the last resort.

'Can you call me a taxi, young lady?' she asked in a loud voice.

'It's alright now, Maristella. No more pretence necessary. I shan't ever need to come back here again.'

Mariastella realised that Asia was smiling with grim satisfaction.

'Let's go home, Mariastella,' she said.

The same taxi-driver who had taken them to the nightclub was waiting outside for her. Mariastella was shocked when Asia climbed into the back seat of the taxi and closed the rear door, leaving her on the pavement. Asia wound down the window and said pertly:

'Would you like to share my taxi, *signora?* I believe we are going in the same direction?'

She had a cheeky grin on her face as Mariastella pulled open the door and shooed her friend over to the other side of the seat.

'This is Marcello, Mariastella. He's a member of the DIA team. They look after me very well...most of the time!'

'Did you manage to...?' began Mariastella.

'Wait until we get home, please,' said Asia. 'I need a good shower first of all. 'I feel contaminated by my contact with that man. He is VILE!'

Mariastella took one look at this beautiful girl and hugged her as she burst into tears of relief. Asia pulled herself away from the contact. But it was obvious that it was not a gesture of revulsion. Asia smiled wearily at her companion.

'It's alright, Mariastella. I know where Beppe is.'

* * *

What could never be reported to a Lady Questore...
- *Give me one good reason why I should tell you where he is, Asia.*

- Dai, zio! I only want a bit of fun with him. I haven't had any free sex like that for months. I could set him a kind of honey-trap – telling him I can make him a free man again, if he does what I tell him. Just think how it will make him feel when he discovers what you intend to do with him. He'll be putty in your hands. Dai, zio! I've been a good girl over the last few years. Let me have this bit of sexy fun with him. He's just some stupid *sbirro,* after all! You know how I hate the cops!

- *You are a wicked young lady, Asia. I like it.*

- You are the one who taught me to be wicked, zio Gregorio. Don't forget that! And I *was* only fourteen!

Gregorio Giuffrè was aware that his niece had this moral hold over him. It was a long time ago. But so far, he had to admit, she seemed to have treated his transgression as a thing of the past. Better to indulge her on this occasion.

- *OK. Go and have your bit of fun. Why not? Just don't let him leave that bedroom whatever you do to him. And now, you can give me my massage...Aaasia!*

* * *

'When you say 'contaminated...' began Mariastella when a bath-robed Asia finally appeared out of the shower room some thirty minutes later.

'I meant, contaminated, corrupted, sullied... I had to give him his 'massage' – not for the first time – and you need to be clear that it was not just my hands involved...'

The lady *Questore* was deeply shocked and wanted to console the girl. Asia correctly interpreted the deep look of pity mixed with contempt for the perpetrator of this bit of wanton abuse.

'Don't worry, Mariastella – I didn't just do it for your *commissario*. I did it for *me* as well. This time he is going to pay the price for his disgusting habits – for the rest of his life. And now, we should get some sleep. I have to get you to the airport tomorrow morning.'

When Mariastella - reunited with all her documents, credit cards and mobile phone - woke up, she was astonished to find the sleeping form of Asia lying next to her in the double bed. Mariastella got up silently, had her shower and packed her suitcase. She went into the kitchen and made herself a cup of coffee. 'Who knows what dark dreams had led this beautiful young woman not to want to sleep alone?' thought Mariastella.

Asia appeared in the kitchen fully dressed some twenty minutes later, looking at peace with herself and the world. She smiled at Mariastella – but never uttered a single word about her sleeping arrangements.

All she said was:

'I know I said it might be five days before Beppe would be free. Make that three!'

It was only when Asia was about to leave her just before she went through the customs control barrier that she hugged

Mariastella tightly, standing on tiptoes to give her a *bacio* on each cheek.'

'*Ti voglio bene,* Mariastella. I'll phone you just as soon as I have taken Beppe to a safe place.'

'If ever you need a place to hide, Asia...' began Mariastella. But her friend was already waving goodbye and walking away from her with a purposefully alluring stride – towards whatever fate awaited her.

'*Ti voglio bene, anch'io,*' muttered Mariastella as she manoeuvred her trolley suitcase towards the conveyor belt which would lead them both to the familiar world of Pescara and her comfortable office on the top floor of the *Questura.*

'Am I naïve enough to believe that this beautiful young woman will be able to save the life of my *commissario* single-handed?' she thought. 'Nobody – least of all Sonia – is going to believe me. They will simply think I have abandoned him!'

21: *The grieving 'widow'…*

There was only one place to go…one human being who could alleviate her fears about her husband, thought Sonia as she woke up on the second day after Beppe's abduction. She had been down this path once before when Beppe had been 'imprisoned' by the mushroom poisoner. [104]

'Come on kids – and you Annamaria,' she said decisively, after the four of them had each picked at the food on the breakfast table and abandoned their drinks after a few desultory sips. 'We're going to church – in Pescara! Annamaria – I want you and the kids to meet the most remarkable man I have ever met – apart from my husband, of course!'

'You wouldn't be talking about the Archbishop, Don Emanuele, by any chance, Sonia?'

'Ah, you guessed! So, have you met him, before, Annamaria?'

'No, I haven't – but my sister is always harping on about him. She drags her husband and her kids off to mass every other Sunday – when he preaches his fortnightly sermons. I'm not really into priests, you know!'

'Well, he won't do you any harm, Annamaria. He's certainly nothing like the average clergyman! You may even be agreeably surprised.'

'Anything is possible, I suppose,' conceded Annamaria, with a smile on her face.

'Do we have to dress up?' asked Veronica, who usually welcomed any opportunity to show off her limited but well-chosen wardrobe. The abduction of her *papà* had come as a cruel blow to her sense of security. She was showing a reluctance to get dressed at all.

---

[104] See 'A Close Encounter with Mushrooms' (Book 2 in the series)

The landline telephone interrupted the despondency that had settled over the little group. It was Lorenzo who got to the phone first and wrenched the phone from its cradle.

PAPÀ? he cried out hopefully.

I'm so sorry. You must be Lorenzo Stancato?

Who are you, *signore?*

My name is Don Emanuele.

Are you a mafia boss? [105]

No, Lorenzo. I'm a bishop – an archbishop.

Are you the one my mum wants to come and talk to?

Yes, that's me. Can you give your mum a message please, Lorenzo?

Yes, Don Manuele. Are you sure you're not the mafia boss that's got my *papà?*

Quite sure, Lorenzo.

The man called 'Don Manuele' had a lovely voice and he laughed softly at what Lorenzo had called him. Lorenzo decided he must be a good man.

What do you want me to say to *mamma?*

Just tell her it's alright to come down to Pescara this morning, Lorenzo. I shall be waiting for you all in the cathedral.

Ciao, Don Manuele. I'll tell her now. We were just going to get into the car when you phoned.

A presto, Lorenzo!

Call me Lori – all my family call me Lori.

A presto, Lori! said the gentle voice.

---

[105] 'Don' is a title that is applied to priests and mafia bosses alike.

Having failed to win the race to answer the telephone first, Veronica had lost interest and retreated back into the living room, where Sonia and Annamaria were getting ready to leave.

'Who was that, Lori?' asked Sonia.

'A man called Don Manuele...he said he was an archer bishop or something.'

His mother's face had turned as pale as a winter's morning.

'What exactly did he say to you, this man, Lori?'

Annamaria was instantly aware of the change in atmosphere. She could hear the shock in Sonia's voice.

'He just said he would wait for us all in the cathedral, *mamma*. Did I do wrong?'

'*No, tesoro,*' she said, the disbelief in her voice still echoing through her words.

'You must have made an appointment to see him,' said Annamaria.

'No, Annamaria. That's just the point. I *didn't* make an appointment. I only thought about the idea of going to see him as I woke up this morning.'

'So how could he have possibly known?' asked a puzzled Annamaria.

'That IS the point, Annamaria! He always knows things in advance.'

Annamaria thought that maybe, after all, she *should* meet this man – so doted upon by her stupid sister!

* * *

Don Emanuele was kneeling on the altar steps, seemingly in deep thought, as the Stancato family plus Annamaria Intimo came into the cathedral – not all that quietly.

'It's much bigger than our church in Atri,' exclaimed the voice of Veronica – and it's got PIPES too.'

'That's an organ, Vero. It's like a piano only bigger!' exclaimed a younger boy's voice, scornful of his sister's ignorance.

'Shhh!' whispered Sonia. 'Don Emanuele is praying – probably for your father!'

Neither Lorenzo nor Veronica had ever met the Archbishop in person. Thus, they were stunned when the white-robed figure, kneeling down on the altar steps rose upwards in one graceful motion to roughly the height of a block of apartments.

They gasped at the smiling figure that strode over to where they were standing in the main aisle – reduced to staring in awe.

'So, this is what an archbishop looks like!' Veronica was thinking.

The two children somehow sensed that they were in the presence of someone 'different'.

'He feels good,' whispered Annamaria to Sonia. 'He smells of something sweet and nice – which I have never smelt before. And he gives off an aura of…yes, goodness.'

Don Emanuele's hearing was as exceptional as his height, it seemed.

'It maybe my housekeeper's cooking,' said Don Emanuele, laughing quietly. 'But more likely, it's the smell of incense. It lingers everywhere in here, from one Sunday to the next. Aren't you going to introduce me to this young lady, Sonia? She reminds me of one of my regular parishioners. She only comes to church on the Sundays when I am giving my sermons. So, she is undoubtedly attending mass for all the wrong reasons!'

Annamaria Intimo couldn't help it. She burst into a peel of laughter which echoed pleasantly round the cathedral.

'That sounds like my younger sister, Don Emanuele. You must be very observant for a member of the clergy!' she said deliberately in a tone of mild sarcasm.

Instead of being offended by her jibe, as she had intended, Don Emanuele laughed in delight.

'This is our dear friend Annamaria, *padre*. She is living with us for now.'

'She's my big sister,' added Veronica.

'And she's blind,' said Lorenzo proudly – as if being sightless was a great achievement on Annamaria's part.

Annamaria could sense that Don Emanuele had taken two steps towards her. She stood still. What she had not been expecting was to feel this man's hands placed on the crown of her head. She froze – but still did not move away.

There was an absence of any words. Afterwards, driving back home, Annamaria explained that she had felt 'strange'.

Back in the cathedral, the Archbishop had spoken softly to Annamaria:

'I do not think you are blind, Annamaria. You see things as clearly as I do – if not even more clearly! You are blessed by beauty and intelligence.'

Annamaria wanted to protest – but the words got stuck in her throat.

Don Emanuele moved away from Annamaria. He hugged Sonia.

'Child number three doing well, I gather?' he asked in a whisper.

'Ah! Beppe has told you I'm expecting another child, has he?'

'No, Sonia,' he replied with dignity.

Don Emanuele then put his hand gently under Veronica and Lorenzo's chin for a brief second.

'*Dio vi benedica!* [106] Your parents are very fortunate to have you, Veronica...Lori!'

'And I'm known as Vero, in family circles!' said Veronica, setting the records straight.

'Why is your first name Don – and not Giuseppe, for example,' Lorenzo felt emboldened to ask.

Veronica decided not to put on her habitually scornful voice when she wanted to chide her younger brother.

''Don' is not a name, Lori. It's a title – like *signore*... or *dottore.*'

'Come on, everybody! Let's go somewhere more comfortable,' said Don Emanuele leading the party through a little door that led to the presbytery. I believe Eugenia has made some pastries for us all. And I'm dying for a cup of coffee.'

Annamaria whispered to Sonia – very quietly - from the rear of the little procession:

'Does Don Emanuele know about Beppe being in the hands of the mafia?'

'Just be patient, Annamaria. You haven't seen anything yet!'

Annamaria was disinclined to comment. Surely, her soppy sister could not have worked out that the Archbishop of Pescara belonged to a different species of mankind altogether?

* * *

The whole group – including Eugenia, her daughter, Alice and Leo, her two-year-old son – were seated at a large round table.

---

[106] God bless you both

'You had a rectangular table last time we came here, I seem to remember, Don Emanuele,' observed Sonia. 'Why the change, dare I ask?'

'Because everybody is equal sitting at a circular table. There can be no 'head-of-table' when it's this shape.'

'I like it,' said Annamaria Intimo,' with a laugh. 'It's a democratic table.'

Democratic or not, it was Don Emanuele who assumed the leadership of the group and the direction that the discussion took.

'Before we do anything else – like eating or drinking – we must remember why we are all here together. Our beloved *Commissario* seems to have landed himself in trouble again. This time, it is slightly more serious. He has disappeared – abducted by the mafia, we understand…'

'But how did *you* find out, Don Emanuele?' asked Sonia.

'It was the very first time that Mariastella Martellini has ever phoned *me,'* laughed the Archbishop. 'She claims not to believe in God, but it seems that her distress at losing Beppe – your wonderful *papà,* Leo, Vero - got the better of her.'

The melodious voice of Don Emanuele seemed to have mesmerised the children. They were staring at Don Emanuele with their mouths slightly open. Annamaria's jet black eyes were fixed on the Archbishop's face – as if she was hearing his words via her eyes.

'But how did you know in advance that we would come and see you, Don Emanuele?'

To Sonia's astonishment, it had been Annamaria Intimo who had posed the question.

'That I cannot explain in words, Annamaria. I often find that these so-called moments of inner vision – something that you undoubtedly experience too – arrive unbidden in my mind.'

Don Emanuele had paused for several seconds. It was Eugenia who broke the silence.

'Go on, Costanzo, tell them what you told me the other day.'

Don Emanuele sighed.

'Alright. I have found a true friend in the physicist which your Beppe rescued from that American gang of so-called secret agents who came to abduct him. [107] Donato Pisano has become my human guiding light. He told me in confidence about his latest crazy idea about physics...'

'It's not all that crazy, *papà!* It has the ring of truth about it, in my opinion.'

It was Alice, Eugenia's daughter – studying physics at Pescara's *Liceo Scientifico* - who had spoken out of the blue.

'Donato suspects that he has found a clue as to the so-far hidden purpose of neutrinos. He believes it should be neutrinos which are called the real 'god-particles'. He doesn't yet dare to talk about this in public. Millions of these nearly massless particles pass through our body every second of our lives...'

The Archbishop had laughed kindly in Lorenzo's direction. Lori had been feeling his chest to see if he could catch these particles before they escaped from his body.

'I don't think you can stop them, Lori,' Don Emanuele said. Sonia put her arm round her son's shoulder and gave him a quick hug. He continued to stare, as if hypnotised, in Don Emanuele's direction.

'NOBODY in the world understands why these particles exist – nor what purpose they might have. Donato Pisano – who *does* believe in a God – has given birth to the notion that neutrinos might be the means by which the spiritual world can contact the physical world.

---

[107] See The Vanishing Physicist

'Whatever the truth may be, I found myself praying before you four arrived from Atri. In my mind I was shown images of an aeroplane that was flying over mount Everest, down south to India and Singapore – and then on across all of the continents beneath the plane – which finally, you'll laugh at this, landed at Pescara airport.'

Strangely enough, nobody felt like laughing at the powerful image which Don Emanuele's words had created.

'I decided,' he continued, 'that I had misinterpreted what I had seen in my vision. That does happen sometimes, I'm afraid.'

Eugenia broke the spell.

'Time we all had drinks and my almond pastries,' she declared. 'Come and help me, Alice!'

Slowly, the powers of speech were returning to the gathering, as they dunked biscuits into drinks – or merely helped themselves to the perfectly baked little almond cakes which Eugenia had prepared.

Only Veronica remained in thoughtful silence. She appeared to be mulling over some idea which was running round inside her head; some girl in her class at school who had an unusual name – which everybody pulled her leg about.

The general chatter was brought to a close when Sonia's mobile phone rang out above the talk.

'It's the *Questore,* Mariastella. Maybe she has some news about Beppe. I'll put her call on loudspeaker.'

'I'm sorry to have taken so long to call you, Sonia – and children? I can hear other voices in the background. I am back in Pescara. I feel so guilty about leaving Beppe to his fate down in Reggio Calabria. But I want to assure you that he has not been abandoned. The most remarkable young female officer I have ever had the privilege of meeting has assured me that she

will personally rescue Beppe within the space of three days. She knows the exact location where he is being held prisoner. She's only twenty-two years old but she is so full of vitality. She has made it her personal mission in life to save your husband, Sonia. Her name is...'

'ASIA', called out Veronica in a loud voice.[108]

Yes, that's right! Asia Sposato. Is that you Veronica? How on earth did you guess that correctly. It's miraculous!'

'Thank you for phoning me, Mariastella,' said Sonia. 'I'll tell you how she knew when I next see you. Before we go back home, to Atri – if you're at the *Questura* at the moment?'

* * *

'It was easy, really,' explained Veronica to her admiring audience. Lorenzo, in particular, was staring in amazement at the accuracy of his sister's usually wild deductions. 'We had studied Asia in geography – and all those places you talked about, Don Emanuele, came back to me. We've got a girl in the class called Asia. We all pulled her leg about her name being the same as the continent. 'Is *that* where you were born?' we tease her every time a new country name comes up!'

For an archbishop, Don Emanuele, was looking mildly pleased with himself. But of all the visitors from Atri, he spent more time saying goodbye to Annamaria than to anyone else.

'I believe your physicist friend's theory, Don Emanuele. It fits in perfectly with a number of strange happenings in my life. Even if I did not think they were anything to do with God!'

'Bless you, Annamaria,' said the Archbishop, briefly making the sign of the cross on her forehead. 'I believe that the

---

[108] Yes, ASIA is the Italian name for that continent – as well as the girl's name. Not a coincidence, I assume. Pron: AAA-zia.

'strange happenings' in your life will continue to manifest themselves.'

* * *

Sonia, Annamaria, Lorenzo and Veronica entered the lady *Questore's* office.

Sonia, with an innate sense of rank, waited for Maristella to utter the first words.

'I told you over the phone a brief account of the situation with Beppe. I am far more intrigued how you, Veronica, knew that my policewoman friend's first name was Asia.'

Sonia and Veronica gave a detailed account of the 'vision' that Don Emanuele had recounted to them – and how Veronica stole the limelight by calling out the name 'Asia' just before Don Emanuele was about to reveal it.

'The more I hear about that man,' stated Mariastella,' the less I want to be an atheist. I'm beginning to have severe doubts about atheism – especially after my visit to Reggio Calabria.'

'What's an atheist?' asked Lorenzo.

Veronica supplied an explanation – reverting to her usual condescending tone of voice when 'teaching' her little brother about the facts of life'

'I now believe with a fair degree of confidence that we shall have good news about Beppe in a couple of days' time, Sonia – and you two kids, of course. Officer Asia Sposato just needs to make sure with her superior officer – a *Carabiniere colonnello* – that the mafia boss who ordered Beppe's abduction won't be able to interfere. I understand he is going to be arrested on some charge or other. Asia might even be able to give me an update this evening. But knowing her for only a day and a bit, she might equally not tell me anything until she has made sure that Beppe is safe. She will more likely want to be the bearer of good tidings. She's very dramatic about everything she does.'

'I have a photo of her on my phone, Sonia. Would you like to see it?'

'No, said Sonia. 'I have already spoken very briefly to this girl on your phone, Mariastella – if you remember. I saw her face for no more than five seconds.'

'Of course, how silly of me to forget, Sonia. Here is a photo of all of her…'

'No thank you, Mariastella! If the rest of her is as beautiful as her face, I would rather not see the photo at all!'

Veronica and Lorenzo took one look at the photo.

'She's not as beautiful as you, *mamma,*' said Lorenzo.

Veronica had immediately sensed the danger of being too honest.

'She's alright, I suppose…' she said with a very casual shrug of her nine-year-old shoulders.

The kids had unintentionally given their mother an impression of this young officer that she would rather not contemplate.

'Shouldn't we tell Mariastella about those Godparticle-things, *mamma?*' asked Lorenzo. 'They sounded rather important.'

'Let's save it up for when your father returns, Lori. I'm sure Mariastella has too many things to do right now – and I want to think about them a bit more.'

The lady *Questore* gave the impression of wanting her curiosity to be satisfied immediately. But Sonia was right – her work schedule had fallen behind during her absence.

They said their fond good-byes to Mariastella and headed back home to Atri. The feeling of despair over Beppe's fate had receded.

They sat out in the sun and chatted, alternating with the kids' favourite board games. Sonia noticed Annamaria rubbing her eyes every so often.

'You don't have any eye-drops, do you Sonia? My eyes seem a bit dry – after being back in the city.'

It was Veronica who ran upstairs to the main bathroom to fetch the tiny bottle of eye-drops, which she insisted on administering – very deftly, according to Annamaria. She had tried to tell Veronica that she *did* know where her eyes were kept, but gave way in the face of Veronica's desire to help.

The children retired to sleep at about ten o'clock – managing not to worry too much about their father. A beautiful young police woman called Asia was going to save his life.

'Do your eyes still hurt, Annamaria?' asked Sonia with kind concern as Annamaria still seemed to be suffering some mild discomfort,

'There's something happening, Sonia,' said Annamaria, puzzled. 'But I'm sure I shall be alright by tomorrow morning. It doesn't hurt at all.'

The following morning, Irene, Sonia's mother, made one of her rare visits upstairs to the Stancato family's part of the house.

'You had better come downstairs and talk to Annamaria, Sonia. She tells me she can see light and shadowy shapes.

Sonia came running down the stairs to find Annamaria in the company of her father, Roberto, who was talking quietly to her.

Annamaria heard Sonia's voice and turned round at her approach.

'I'm not imagining things, Sonia. I can see you – just as a shadowy silhouette. What's happening to me? I'm scared but also…excited. It's unbearable, Sonia. Hold me tight, please.'

'Well, Annamaria – whatever it is that is going on, it beats being blind. Can you wait until Beppe is back here safe and sound? Then we'll take you to see a friend of ours who works at the hospital in Pescara.'

Alerted by some drastic change in the air added to the unexpected lack of parents upstairs, Veronica and Lorenzo came running downstairs in alarm.

'Is it *papà?*' cried out Lorenzo in fear.

'No, Lori. Don't worry!' said Sonia with a smile on her face. 'It's Annamaria – she's seeing things!'

Annamaria appeared to be 'looking' in their direction.

'I can see your two blurry silhouettes, Lori, Vero,' said a terrified Annamaria, taking two steps towards them. She tripped over the dog which had been lying placidly on the floor, half of its body under the table. Roberto, standing near her, managed to catch her before she hit the floor hard.

Annamaria seemed to be crying hot tears as Roberto sat her down at the kitchen table. She was crying and laughing at the same time in a highly agitated state.

Later on in the morning, Annamaria made them *all* laugh by begging them to find her a pair of dark sunglasses.

'That way, I can pretend that everything is back to normal again,' she explained.

22: The end of the road...?

Beppe had had a very rude awakening that night. He had woken up abruptly on hearing the sound of the lock on the door being forced open. He knew instinctively that he was in trouble. He had only just had the time and the nous to shove his mobile phone under his pants in the top drawer of the bedside table before he had found himself being yanked to his feet by two louts whose breath stank of garlic and onions, mingling with the acidic smell of cheap red wine on their breath. They dragged him roughly out into the corridor and down the short flight of steps to the reception area. A knife blade was being held to his throat.

'One word and you're dead, *sbirro!*' growled an uncouth voice in heavy Calabrian dialect.

Even in his state of shock, he knew that the threat was just for show. They wanted him alive. He saw the petrified figure of the hotel owner, Luigi Marino, powerless to react to what was happening.

'Buona notte, signore!' Beppe called out to the hotel owner. 'That was *three* words! What are you going to do about *that?'* Beppe shouted sarcastically to the chief thug - in dialect - before he was yanked through the main door of the hotel, even more roughly than before, and bundled into the boot of a large black Audi, whose driver shot off along the deserted streets of the city as soon as the two abductors had slammed the car doors shut.

'That cop's a Calabrian like us,' said the shorter of the two hoodlums, as if attempting to excuse himself for what he had just helped achieve.

'Not for long, he won't be!' growled thug number one.

'We were told to confiscate his mobile,' said the smaller thug. 'We forgot to look for it.'

'*Porca puttana!*' swore thug number one. 'Stop the car, Mimi. You – get out and search him, Pinuccio. Take my knife, Mimi and go with him and make sure he hasn't got his mobile on him. That's all that matters.'

They opened the boot of the Audi. Beppe, making a supreme effort to conceal his discomfort, appeared to be at ease with his hands clasped together behind his head.

'Looking for my mobile phone, are you? Should be easy to find, *ragazzi*. I'm only wearing pyjamas.'

Beppe took his feeble revenge by not helping the two gangsters as they were forced to frisk him all over with their bare hands.

Gangster number two held the knife to his throat. Beppe gripped the man by the wrist and forced his hand away.

'You're not going to use that on me, *stronzo!* You were in such a hurry to get me out of the bedroom, you forgot to carry out your orders, didn't you? Well, you are too late. I chucked my phone out of the bedroom window.'

The gangsters gave up, swearing at Beppe – who returned the compliments in dialect – just to wind them up.

They slammed the boot shut again and drove off, leaving Beppe to fight his lonely battle against fear and despair. He retained enough resistance to work out that the car was heading northwards out of the city and, judging by the angle of the car, towards the hills. Not that this discovery was of any help to him! But one simply had to resist, he told himself.

* * *

Beppe woke up on day one of his captivity. He had been dumped on a bed whose mattress was of the rustic variety. He had had a nightmare in which he was running naked round a city which called itself Reggio Calabria, but which felt more like the popular quarter of some anonymous far-eastern city. It was still dark outside – or perhaps, they had put blackouts over the windows? He forced himself to get off the bed. He should get dressed if he was going to fight back against his aggressors. But then he remembered he only possessed the pyjamas he was standing up in.

He found the windows and drew back the curtains. It was dawn - somewhere out in the countryside. He could see hills silhouetted against a dark blue sky which was illuminated by the light of the sun as it began to rise above some unknown horizon. The windows would not open. He took his first act of revenge by picking up the bolster on the bed and smashed at a window pane through the coarse material of the pillow. He smelt the cool morning air wafting into the stuffy bedroom. He moved the pillow to the next pane of glass, ready to vent his anger on whoever was responsible for his captivity.

He entertained the thought he could run across the countryside bare foot with only his pyjamas on to seek help in the nearest village. Just as he was about to deal the second blow on the bolster, his heart sank. Looking out of the window, he saw that his 'cell' was at least twenty metres above ground level. Looking at the sloping ceiling above him, he realised he must be on the top floor of a large farmhouse – the sort of rustic dwelling where his parents used to take him and his sister on holiday – 'to escape from the smells of the city' as his mother would repeatedly tell him, even though she knew her offspring would have rather remained in Catanzaro.

Images of his father came to mind, which in turn made him think about Sonia and his three children – one of whom was still unborn. The full force of his perilous situation struck him forcibly. Sonia and the children would be desperate in a few

195

hours' time, when they were told that he had 'disappeared' without trace.

He felt a deep depression settle over his spirit as he lay hopeless and helpless on the crude bed. He remained there, fighting off encroaching despair, until he heard someone turning a key in the lock. He leapt up with fists clenched, ready to take on the thugs who had brought him to this place. But it was a portly farmer's wife who entered the room carrying a tray with a mug of black coffee and a slice of plain country bread by its side – no plate. A burly farmer – her son perhaps – was standing in the corridor.

'Drink, eat!' ordered the man. 'I take you to the bathroom.'

Beppe was struck by the thickness of his local accent – a different one to his home town of Catanzaro – which, ironically would be only a matter of fifty-or-so kilometres further north.

'Closer to my mother than to my wife!' was the ironic thought that sprang to mind.

All too soon, he was back in his state of solitude again.

'Forza, Beppe!' he told himself aggressively. 'You've been in worse situations than this.'

But, he reminded himself, this was simply untrue! He would be obliged to draw on mental resources which he had never needed to conjure up at any point of his previous life. He was surprised to find an image of a beautiful blind woman, called Annamaria Intimo, who was exhorting him to survive and be strong as she had had to be throughout her sightless life. And what wise words would Don Emanuele have whispered fiercely in his ear to make him have faith in his omnipotent deity?

No, he would not allow despair to engulf him!

* * *

It was well into the evening – after a basic fish stew for lunch and a long siesta to catch up on his sleep – that Beppe was faced with the first challenge to his newly-found resourcefulness.

The door was being unlocked by someone who was not fumbling with the key. Someone younger, Beppe correctly predicted.

The man – in his early forties – walked in with an arrogance which instantly put Beppe on his guard. The man had a leer on his face. A clear indication of the sadistic pleasure which he was sure he could extract from this encounter.

A pyjama-clad Beppe was in no doubt as to the kind of man who had just walked through the door.

Beppe Stancato had the audacity to sit down on the one-and-only semblance of a single-seater armchair in the room. He crossed his legs and waved an airy hand in the direction of the mafioso – as if inviting him to say what he had to say and clear off.

The man looked mildly surprised by his reception but recovered his composure within seconds.

'I trust you are satisfied with your accommodation, *commissaaaario?'*

'Not really, no!' replied Beppe indifferently. *Take the initiative, Beppe Stancato,* an inner voice urged him.

'I take it you are the mob leader who initiated the killing of one Laura Ianni in Pescara, *signore…?'*

'The mafioso was astounded at the verbal directness of his victim.

'Followed up a few days later by a failed attempt to murder a woman in the same block of flats. You assumed this woman – Sofia Rossi – had seen your two goons enter that apartment block. But your 'witness' was blind! I bet you didn't know that, *signore...?'*

'Talarico!' said the mafioso without even thinking about the lie he had just uttered.

His captive laughed mockingly in his face.

'That is what you wanted everyone to think.'

Beppe shot the words at his visitor at point blank range.

The mafioso felt deflated. It was as if this policeman was holding *him* captive and subjecting *him* to an interrogation.

'Why don't you just turn round and leave me in peace, *signore.* I don't want to listen to any more of your inanities.'

'Wouldn't you like to know what fate awaits you, *commissaaario?'* asked the mafioso with cruel irony – hoping to regain the power to reduce this wretched policeman to pulp.

'Not really, no, *signore.* I won't be staying here for more than a day or so.'

'No, *Commissario.* You are right about that. I have put you up for auction. You will be sold off to the highest bidder. As things stand, you will be shipped off to Catanzaro where the Spanò clan will be welcoming you with open arms.'

If the mafioso had intended to sow the seeds of fear in his captive, he had succeeded well beyond his wildest hopes.

But Beppe managed to applaud sarcastically as the mafia boss turned on his heels and departed, slamming the door shut and locking it behind him – leaving his victim with a feeling of utter despondency. Beppe was fated to spend another forty-eight hours in a state of dread. This time, he knew that he might really never see his family again. How vital human love became when the risk of losing it forever loomed over one.

'Oh, Beppe! This time, you really have gone too far!'

He found himself digging ever deeper into his reserves of mental strength. He could not turn his back on the last remnants of courage, faith and hope of survival. Was it at that point in his thinking that he made a kind of decision about his future career – as a kind of bribe offered to his elusive God, who yet might come to his rescue?

Commissario Beppe Stancato could have saved himself hours of agony had he known to what extent *Colonnello* Pasquale Procopio – and company – were labouring on his behalf.

* * *

Beppe had even resorted to removing the remains of broken glass from the ancient window frame and singing anything that came to mind in the loudest voice he could muster out across the valley. He gained some comfort from the way that his voice echoed feebly off a nearby hillock. But he could see the nearest village was at least five kilometres away.

The large lady who brought his lunch the following day even left him a bottle of rustic red wine with his lamb stew.

She shot a brief, weary smile in the prisoner's direction.

'The wine is to help you keep on singing, *Commissario*. Though I'm sorry to say that there's nobody out there to hear you – except us. *Buon appetito!'* she added kindly.

His spirits were lifted for a good fifteen minutes. Human kindness had managed to trickle out – even in this remote *'ndrangeta* stronghold.

The longer his solitary wait became, the harder it had become to bolster his failing morale. On waking up, following a broken sleep two days after the visit from the mafioso, he had a vision of his family sitting round the breakfast table in Atri. Nobody was eating, nobody was talking, Veronica was sobbing and Sonia could not even find the strength to comfort their daughter in her hour of need. Beppe found involuntary tears were pouring down his cheeks – any semblance of courage having ebbed away.

He hastily dried his eyes on the sleeve of his pyjamas when he heard the key turning in the lock. This was it. The moment for the journey which would seal his fate had finally arrived. It was almost a relief. So convinced was he that this was the end of the line for him that he could only stare in disbelief at the figure who had just entered the room. The shock was so great that he remained lying on the bed – whereas, normally, good manners would have dictated that he stand up.

'Buongiorno Commissario Beppe Stancato. I'm not sure whether your troubles are over – or whether they are just about to begin,' said the vision of loveliness that had just entered his prison cell.

'My name is Asia - and I'm here to get you out of this mess – God willing!'

23:   A 'date' with destiny...?

Asia simply walked over to the bed and sat down next to Beppe's feet. She had dumped a ruck-sack on the floor and began rummaging through its contents.

'Item number one,' declared Asia to a bewildered policeman, handing him his mobile phone. 'With the compliments of Mariastella – who sends you her love, by the way.

'Your lap-top is in here too. And here is a complete change of clothes for you, Beppe. Including a track-suit and a nice warm outdoor jacket too – it's going to be cold outside when we escape this evening. Best not to use the mobile phone though – at least not until you are well on your way up north.'

Beppe finally recovered from his shock and realised he ought to say something appropriate. Half of his mind was busy working out whether this was some subtle form of honey-trap – to make him believe that salvation was at hand, only to find that the hope was to be dashed before despair finally triumphed.

This girl – young woman, he corrected himself – seemed to understand what he was thinking.

'Don't look so concerned, Beppe. Gregorio Giuffrè – that mafioso crook who came to visit you two days ago - has been arrested. He won't see the outside world for quite some time...'

'Arrested? What is be being held for? Surely, you didn't manage to...?'

'He's been arrested for rape, Beppe. And also, for a failed attempt to kill off a rival mafia boss. For now, we only want him out of the way for long enough to get you safely out of Reggio Calabria.'

'But you...?' began Beppe, feebly, trying to grasp the reality of his rescue at the hands of this girl, who could only be twenty-five at the most.

'Ah, sorry, my dear *Commissario*. May I introduce myself? I am *Agente* Asia Spostato – of the DIA. But I'm certainly not married – despite what my surname implies.'

With these words, Asia was looking at him intensely. She gave him a radiant smile – her eyes alight with humour and... something akin to passion, thought Beppe. The expression on her face was so intense – radiating some kind of inner joy at simply being alive - that Beppe felt he had to accept her at face value. His next words might seal his own fate if he had misjudged this compact yet voluptuous angel, sitting a mere metre away from his upper half.

'I would like to get rid of these pyjamas, please Asia. I've been wearing nothing else for nearly four days.'

'Good idea, Beppe. *I* want you to take them off too! Because I have a favour to ask you.'

Now, that expressive face, those sparkling brown eyes, were full of dark passion.

'Please, Beppe. Don't judge me too hastily till you understand why I am asking you this favour. I want you to make love to me!'

There! The words were out! She was now looking deadly serious – and so desperately anxious not to be misunderstood or rejected that Beppe stifled any words of protest.

'In fact, *I* want to make love to *you!*' she added, in a little voice.

The inner conflict was impossible to resolve. If he did what this girl was asking him to do, would he feel guilty afterwards? Would he tell Sonia what had happened or would he go through life endlessly debating the rights and wrongs of what he knew was about to happen?

The dilemma, such as it was, resolved itself in an eerie moment of clarity. He felt some force travelling up through his body and into his brain. He found himself asking Asia a question – no, the question turned itself into a statement:

'It was *you* who was raped by that man, Asia. *Vero?*'

The tears welled up and trickled down her cheeks. She nodded wordlessly – only bursting into speech after she had brought her sobbing under control.

'You are a lovely man, Beppe. You have so much compassion. I fell in love with you as soon as Mariastella showed me the photo of you. I told myself *you* were the man I wanted to make love to for the first time in my life. I've been dreaming of meeting a man who could make me forget what that bastard did to me. Thank God he wore a condom – otherwise I would have felt too sullied to go on living. I have been waiting eight years to meet a man like you, Beppe. And now…'

Beppe did not hesitate – any guilt he might have felt was subconsciously drowned out simply because Sonia's long pregnancy had left him yearning for physical contact. There was no time to indulge in any inner debate. This girl was going to save his life.

'I would love to make love to you, Asia. You are a beautiful woman and I owe my life to you. But I insist on having a shower first.'

Asia smiled and waved a hand to indicate he should get on with it without further excuses.

When Beppe returned from the bathroom, wearing a borrowed dressing gown, Asia was already lying naked under the bed cover.

* * *

He stroked every curve of her body and kissed her neck and breasts. He could smell her naturally scented skin at every breath he took. She had begun to respond, very slowly and silently at first. Only after she finally began to emit low gasps of pleasure from her now parted lips did Beppe take it to the next stage – by which time any fleeting thoughts of 'protection' had been overwhelmed by the passion he too was feeling towards this young woman who had thrown herself at him in desperation. He should let Mother Nature take her course.

After what seemed like hours, they were lying together on the narrow bed – Asia on top of Beppe, due to the narrowness of the bed. She was staring lovingly into his eyes. Beppe was thinking how the act of love-making felt so 'different' with someone unfamiliar; one of life's ineffable mysteries.

It was Asia who finally broke the spell.

'That was beautiful, Beppe! Next time, I shall have no fears. You have saved *my* life too.'

She kissed him passionately on the mouth. Beppe briefly felt her tongue delving into the inside of his mouth. But she withdrew quickly, realising via some hidden instinct that he was becoming sexually aroused again.

And then it was over. She got resolutely out of the bed and slipped into her clothes.

'Be ready as soon as it gets dark, Beppe. And get warmly dressed with those clothes I brought you.'

'Why, Asia? Where are we going?' asked the *Commissario.*

'It's not *where* we are going, *amore.* It's how!' whispered Asia, wishing to sound mysterious.

She was nearly out of the room by then. But she turned round at the last minute and, with a mischievous grin on her face once more, said:

'If I manage to come back a bit earlier this evening, maybe we could do it again!'

But she had disappeared down the stairs before Beppe could reply. He got dressed in his new clothes.

Left on his own again, he was haunted by the fear that she would never return. But he smothered such unworthy speculations. Her love-making had been passionately sincere. Of course, she would return! She had given him his mobile phone back – and, he noticed, she had even recharged the battery for him.

Any remaining doubts were dispelled by the lady of the house, who brought him his lunch just as the ancient church clock was striking twelve times – quite out of tune with the church bells ringing out the midday angelus. Strange that, only now, was he consciously aware of the bells echoing triumphantly across the valley.

'I'm Elsa,' the lady announced, placing a tray with his lunch and a glass of wine on the little table. 'This is the last meal I shall be serving you...*Commissario*. I shall be sorry to see you go this evening.'

'What about the other man who was here when I first arrived?' asked Beppe.

'My son?' said Elsa. 'Don't worry about him, *Commissario*. He's gone back to his wife and kids in the village.'

'But what can you tell me about Asia...Elsa?' asked Beppe out of curiosity. 'Did you know her before today?'

'Oh yes, *Commissario*. She is my favourite great niece. She's the most beautiful and courageous girl in the world in my humble opinion. Do you know how she found out where you had been taken to – so she could come and rescue you?'

Beppe shook his head – although he had a vague inkling as to how Elsa would reply. Better coming from the horse's mouth.

'She made her uncle – Gregorio Giuffrè – tell her where he was hiding you…by persuading him to let her come and 'take advantage' of you. Nobody but Asia could have dreamt up such a perfect alibi for herself. That lecherous bastard was completely taken in.'

'But won't she be in danger of her life from now on, Elsa – from that mobster?'

'She seemed to think the risk was worth it, *Commissario!* By the sound of it, she was quite right.'

Nothing remains a secret for very long in Italy, Beppe mused.

Great Aunt Elsa left him to devour his beef stew with a parting wink.

'See you this evening, *Commissario. Buon appetito e…in bocca al lupo!'*

* * *

An anxious wait as darkness fell and there seemed to be no sign of his saviour on the horizon. The rucksack on his back contained only his laptop and mobile phone. The only sound he could hear was that of a Vespa scooter buzzing angrily along lower down in the valley. Elsa was busying herself somewhere in the house, until she emerged with a torch in her hand.

'She's on her way, *Commissario.* I can hear her coming.' The sound of the Vespa was now just below the farm house. Beppe realised, with some trepidation, what Asia had meant when she had told him he would need something warm to wear. He was to be perched precariously on the pillion seat of a wobbly machine driven down a windy road – probably at speed.

'What price freedom?' he muttered to himself as Asia swept up the drive to where he was waiting.

'Hop on, Beppe!' she ordered. 'Sorry I'm a bit late. We have to get to the station by nine o'clock. I shall have to go quite fast. Sorry about the discomfort, *amore della mia vita*, [109] but my car might have been recognised by someone in town.

Beppe barely had time to say 'goodbye' to Great Aunt Elsa and do up the strap of the helmet that Asia had placed over his head.

'Put your arms round my waist, *Commissario* – and hold tight,' she ordered, as they sped off down the pitch-black country lane which led onto the main road into Reggio Calabria.

Beppe was almost beginning to enjoy the ride by the time they arrived outside the train station, still in one piece.

'Come on, *Commissario*. We shall have to run. Your salvation depends on catching this train – to some extent...' she said without any other explanation.

Asia took him unfailingly to the right platform and pushed him unceremoniously on to the train. She shoved an envelope into his hands.

'There's a ticket in there to get you to Rome – and a bit of money. Look out for people you know *en route*, Beppe.'

Beppe took a decision on the spur of the moment. He got off the train and hugged Asia, just as the train was about to pull out of the station. He was shouted at by an official and nearly lost his footing as he hurriedly mounted the steps.

Asia gave him a dazzling smile and mouthed the two magic words: *'Ti amo.'*

---

[109] Love of my life

She turned her back on Beppe. He caught a brief glimpse of a pair of shapely legs - which had so recently been tightly wrapped round his body - walking smartly towards the exit, before the insistent warning sound prior to the train doors closing forced him to get inside the train.

* * *

He had to walk through the train towards the front end of the *Freccia Rossa* [110] as it gathered speed along the dedicated track. He sat down on his reserved seat, still clutching the envelope and ticket. There were two €50 notes inside, which he stuffed into the inside pocket of his new jacket. He simply gazed at the ticket in his hand – not being able to grasp the fact that he was safe. He was on his way home. A sudden irrational fear made him look up and down the train carriage – on the lookout for some alien mafioso figure.

His eyes picked out a middle-aged gentleman sitting on his own a few seats down the corridor. He looked familiar. With a shock, he realised the grey-haired man was staring at *him*. Who was he? Why was he looking so intently at him? The man nodded briefly at him and briefly raised his hand – as if he was giving him a papal blessing.

The shock to Beppe's still tensed-up nervous system was pulpable. It was the *Colonnello,* Pasquale Procopio, without his uniform on. He, Beppe, was being chaperoned home by the DIA. He felt the prickly tears of emotion gathering behind his eyelids.

Beppe acknowledged the *colonnello's* presence – mouthing the words *grazie mille* – before he started weeping

---

[110] The 'Red Arrow'. Italy has succeeded in building a high-speed train track from the north to the south of the peninsula. Cf the UK!

tears of utter relief. He must have fallen asleep out of sheer exhaustion. He woke up, feeling sure that his mouth had been open, since he felt parched. He had been vaguely aware of the train stopping in Naples on its way up to Rome. When he looked up as the train pulled away, he noticed that the *Colonnello* was no longer sitting there.

A man who was sitting on the other side of the aisle handed Beppe a half-drunk bottle of mineral water, with a smile on his lips.

'I guess you need a drink, *signore,*' said the man kindly.

Beppe was back in a world he knew – where good people lived who were aware of the needs of those around them.

'Viva l'Italia!' he muttered to himself, doing his utmost not to drift off again.

When the train finally reached *Roma Termini,* Beppe realised he would still have to pull himself together to face the two-hour journey across Italy to Pescara. He had no identity documents on him – and just enough money to stay in some hotel – but not enough to buy a ticket back to Pescara if he opted for a hotel room. He sighed wearily – but was buoyed up by the thought that he was alive. He could always present himself at some police station and attempt the task of persuading some minor cop that he was a *Commissario* who had fallen foul of the mafia. He might be allowed to sleep in a cell.

As he reached the end of the concourse, he spotted two familiar figures. His heart leapt with joy. The Lady *Questore* was there, smiling broadly at him. She was in the company of his trusted friend, *Ispettore* Pippo Cafarelli. They simply ushered him to the police car they had come in all the way from Pescara.

'Now we are going to take you home to Atri, Beppe, and reunite you with your family,' said Mariastella.

Pippo was in the driver's seat – which meant he would be home sooner rather than later. Beppe fell asleep again almost immediately.

It was Mariastella who made the vital phone call to Sonia – waking her up. Mariastella spelt out the good news calmly. She could hear children's voices shouting with joy. It appeared that Veronica and Lorenzo had been sharing their mother's bed.

When Beppe woke up on the other side of Italy, Mariastella informed her second-in-command that he had been talking in his sleep.

'We didn't quite understand what was going on, Beppe,' she said slyly. 'In your dream, you were insisting we take you to see Don Emanuele. You suggested that you had to go to confession to seek absolution for your sins. Can you throw some light on your dream, *caro Commissario?*'

'*Mi prendete in giro, vero?* [111] You just made that story up, didn't you!' was all the *Commissario* deigned to say as they passed the road sign indicating their arrival in Atri.

Mariastella looked at Pippo. Pippo looked at Mariastella and shrugged his shoulders. Not surprisingly, something disturbing must have happened to Beppe. Mariastella was wondering if *Agente* Asia Sposato had anything to do with Beppe's dream. They might never know the truth.

Beppe got out of the car first. Both Mariastella and Pippo followed suit. Beppe hugged them both in turn.

'*Grazie di cuore!*' said Beppe with feeling.

'Don't come back to work until you are ready, Beppe.

'Oh, I'll be fine in a couple of days' time,' Beppe reassured them. 'But I have no documents to my name at the moment.'

---

[111] You two are pulling my leg, aren't you?

'I believe the police in Reggio Calabria rescued your possessions. They have promised to send them to Via Pesaro immediately.'

Beppe walked up to the front door with a sense of wonder. There had been hours when he thought he would never return home again. The house lights were on. He could hear voices from inside the door. Veronica was asking: 'But how long will he be, *mamma?*'

Having no door key, he knocked on the door. He was home – even if he could still not quite believe it.

Beppe had walked up to the entrance door just as the sun was beginning to rise over the distant mountains to the east. When Sonia ran to open the door, Beppe had the impression that the sun had suddenly risen. He was bathed in the warmth of his family's joy and laughter. He hugged his wife and his two children – physically aware of the pressure of Sonia's belly against him.

'Adesso siamo in cinque,' [112] he announced formally – as if to reassert his position as head of his tribe. The family remained hugging, simply because none of them wanted to break the solid nucleus which glued them all together. The other three people present simply clapped their hands together to express the delight and relief that they were all sharing.

When, finally, they pulled themselves apart, it was the turn of Sonia's parents to be hugged. Beppe then turned to Annamaria, who took three steps to cover the distance between them. She hugged him for much longer than mere good manners demanded.

'Strange,' thought Beppe. 'It was almost as if she knew exactly where I was standing.'

---

[112] Now there are five of us.

Finally, the family of 'five' climbed up the stairs to the top floor. There was no hurry to get up the following morning. Beppe and Sonia got into bed together. Instinctively, Beppe began to stroke Sonia's body in an attempt to cancel the memory of the day before.

He was saved from any embarrassment by the arrival of Veronica and Lorenzo, who chose to occupy the middle of the bed, with one parent on each side.

'You decide who you want to sleep next to, Lori,' said Veronica in her sweetest voice; more because she did not want to be the one who would appear to favour one parent above the other - rather than being motivated by an act of kindness towards her younger sibling.

Beppe sighed contentedly. His children did not appear to have suffered any emotional damage. His daughter was as subtly manipulative as ever towards her brother – who did not seem to mind either way.

24: *Unforeseen consequences...*

Cocooned by the sense of comfort generated by their four united bodies, Beppe would have been happy to fall asleep again. But he was besieged by questions from Veronica, who insisted that he should tell them the story of his capture and his final escape. Beppe succeeded in giving a potted version of the salient events of his adventure.

'And finally, I was rescued by the DIA police and driven in the darkness to the railway station – where they had a special train ready to take me back to Rome,' Beppe concluded – pleased that he had avoided telling any lies.

In the end, even Veronica was tired enough to fall asleep until well past their normal breakfast time.

'Something you should know, *papà,*' whispered Lorenzo before Beppe fell asleep. 'Annamaria has begun to see things.'

Nobody seemed to comment on Lorenzo's little revelation. But Beppe recalled the impression he had momentarily had before the family went upstairs.

On waking up after nine o'clock the following morning, Beppe found the upstairs floor deserted. Sonia and Annamaria must have taken the children to school and then gone shopping, he supposed.

Sonia's parents confirmed this when he went downstairs fully dressed. He had had his first long shower and his first shave in several days. He thought guiltily that Asia must have endured his stubbly chin on her soft skin without complaint.

'Did all that really happen?' he asked himself. To his dismay, the answer was a resounding 'yes'.

When the ladies returned, Sonia kissed Beppe warmly and told him that she loved him – but there seemed to be an edge to her affection which had been so whole-hearted the night before. And, inexplicably, Annamaria was wearing sunglasses despite the sky being cloudy.

Sonia, Annamaria and Beppe were upstairs again, sitting round the kitchen table – where all family matters were inevitably discussed.

Beppe remembered the whispered words of Lorenzo just before he had fallen asleep.

'Annamaria?' said Beppe – his voice inflected upwards. Sonia was looking at the screen on her mobile phone.

'A text message and photo from the *Questore,*' she explained. 'She hopes you are feeling stronger this morning, Beppe.'

Annamaria was 'looking' appealingly in Sonia's direction from behind her sunglasses.

'A very strange thing has happened to Annamaria,' explained Sonia. 'She seems to be able to see shadowy figures – and she is aware of what she assumes must be 'light'.

'But that is wonderful, isn't it, Annamaria?'

'It is very disturbing, Beppe. I am so used to my blindness. It is part of my world – and always has been. I'm wearing these sunglasses just so I can pretend to be normally blind, as I was before. Doesn't that sound silly?'

'No, Annamaria. I can well understand how you must be feeling. But how did this come about?'

Sonia answered on Annamaria's behalf.

'Annamaria blames Don Emanuele, Beppe. We all went to visit him the day after you were…the day after your disappearance. I felt so distraught. I wanted to seek comfort from the only man in the world who seems to be able to see into the future.'

'And did he give you the reassurance you were seeking?' asked Beppe.

'Yes, as usual. He seemed to understand that you would be…saved. He also laid his hands on Annamaria – as he does to all sorts of people. It was on the way home that Annamaria's eyes began to itch. Then she realised she could see our silhouettes moving about. I promised we would take her somewhere when you got back, *amore.*'

'Of course, we will. I'll phone Bruno Esposito at the hospital in Pescara immediately. We'll go and talk to him tomorrow.'

Beppe had stood up and walked round to put his arm around Annamaria's shoulders.

'Maybe we should go and talk to Don Emanuele too, while we are down there,' suggested Beppe.

All three of them walked round in a dream until Lorenzo and Veronica returned home unexpectedly at midday. Veronica had managed to persuade her teacher to take her home, after collecting Lorenzo from his nursery school on the way.

'I told her that you had been taken away by the mafia, *papà.* I said we both had to go home at lunchtime to make sure you had not disappeared again.'

'And your teacher believed you, Vero?' asked Sonia teasingly.

'Well, I did have to burst into tears to convince her,' replied their daughter.

The solemn mood was broken. Life had taken on a sense of normality again – a feeling which did not wear off until Annamaria had reluctantly taken her leave to return to her downstairs quarters and Veronica and Lorenzo had been denied access to the parental bed and fallen asleep together in their own bedroom.

Sonia was snuggling up to Beppe. One gets used to the *modus operandi* of ones partner after years of intimacy, reasoned Beppe. Thus, he knew instinctively that Sonia was about to probe more deeply into the events surrounding his rescue. He recalled that, earlier on in the day, she had been very coy about showing him a photo she had received from Mariastella Martellini. What if Sonia had requested a photo of Beppe's 'saviour'? Beppe had not probed into the details of what had transpired between Don Emanuele and 'his' two ladies. That encounter might well have been complex.

He did not have long to wait before Sonia clarified her feelings towards him.

'I suspect, Beppe, that the version of the story you told us in the early hours of this morning was somewhat lacking in detail. *Non mi sbaglio, vero?*' [113]

Beppe sighed. He had known all along that he would be incapable of deceiving Sonia.

'Before you begin your confession, *amore,* let me tell you about the extraordinary way we found out about your rescue, whilst we were with Don Emanuele. It might help to jog your memory as to your more recent escapades.'

Her voice was laden with heavy irony.

'Don Emanuele had a vision – which even he failed to interpret. He told us some quite prosaic details about flying in an aeroplane over India, China, Malasia and coming down to land in Pescara – all in the space of a few minutes. And you will never guess who revealed - in one single word – the key to his dream?'

Beppe, the great detective, thought long and hard about this enigma - the process taking him almost as much as sixty seconds. By a simple process of elimination, he finally replied:

'Veronica!'

---

[113] I'm not mistaken, am I?

Sonia was quite deflated by the accuracy of her partner's reasoning. But she was not yet ready to surrender.

'And what do you think that one word was which our daughter came out with?'

'Asia, obviously!'

Sonia fell silent – taken aback by Beppe's powers of deduction.

'And,' continued Beppe – with every sign of humility in his demeanour – 'Mariastella must have sent you a photo of Asia in reply to your request.'

'Did you make love to this young woman, Beppe? She is very sexy and very beautiful – quite irresistible, I would say. She's the spitting image of that young actress…what's her name? The one who played the older Lina in that book by Elena Ferrante.'

Beppe sensed that his beloved partner was about to burst into tears of anger and pain. He steeled himself before replying.

'Yes, I did make love to her, Sonia. But let me tell you exactly how it happened – before you tear me apart.'

The quiet authority with which Beppe had spoken stemmed any verbal retribution. He prayed that his brain would manage to formulate a convincing argument. His future and that of his family could be hanging in the balance.

'I had spent three days locked up in a bedroom on the top floor of a remote farmhouse, clad in nothing more than a pair of pyjamas. I had been visited by the mafia *boss* who was responsible for murdering that girl in Annamaria's *palazzo*. He took sadistic pleasure in telling me he was going to sell me off to the Spanò clan in Catanzaro, whose path I crossed a couple of months ago – as I am sure you remember. I was desperate because I was missing you and had no way of telling you what had happened to me. My fear that I would never see you again drove me to a state of depression that I have never felt so acutely in my whole life.

Then, suddenly, out the blue, this beautiful young woman appeared in my bedroom and told me she was with the DIA and that she had come to rescue me. Apart from you, *amore mio,* I have never in my life met any woman so full of vitality, humour and passion, all rolled into one. She told me she had one favour to ask of me. She wanted me to be the first man to make love to her – just because she had seen a photo of me which she had acquired from Mariastella in order to be able to identify me.

She told me that she had been raped by the self-same mafia *boss* who had threatened me. He was her uncle and she had been raped by him when she was only fourteen. The trauma has stayed with her for eight long years – leaving her repulsed by the thought of intimacy with another man. She did not beg me to make love to her. She did not for one minute imply that making love to her was a condition of her returning that evening to take me to safety. She just stood there, begging me with her whole being, not to reject her.

So, I did exactly what she asked me to do. And yes, I did enjoy every minute of it, Sonia. I don't know how I would have felt for the rest of my life if I had refused to show her what making love can and should be like.'

There was a silence which lasted for an eternity from the other side of the bed. Sonia moved close to him and whispered:

'That is one of the most moving stories I have ever heard in my life, *amore mio.* I admire and love you even more than I did before. I am happy to have shared your body with someone else. Just this once, mind!'

'I should tell you one more thing, Sonia,' said Beppe with great solemnity.

'Please don't tell me you did it twice, *Commissario!*'

Beppe chuckled at the abrupt change of tack.

'No Sonia. I was going to tell you that I have decided to accept the post of *Questore* in Terramonti – if it is still on offer.'

Sonia, baby and all, flung herself at Beppe, clinging to him with tears of relief and happiness running down her cheeks.

'*Grazie, grazie, grazie,* Beppe! *Ti amo per sempre.* Mind you,' she added, 'you might end up being the first *Questore* in Italy to run into danger as soon as you get up and leave your desk.'

Beppe hugged her tightly and did not let go.

'After what I have lived through these last few days, Sonia, sitting behind a desk for the rest of my life sounds quite enticing!'

25:   *Close encounters with an archbishop – et al…*

'We'll go and see Don Emanuele first, *ragazze,* ' [114] explained Beppe, as he, Sonia and Annamaria were driving down south towards Pescara. To Beppe, a whole century seemed to have elapsed since he had last made this journey. His misadventures in Calabria appeared to have elongated his perception of time to a kind of infinity.

'Our appointment with my friend Bruno at the hospital isn't until 11 o'clock.'

'A shame,' said Annamaria. 'It's the only part of today that I wanted to get over and done with.'

'Have no fears, Annamaria,' Beppe told her. 'Doctor Bruno Esposito is a kind of hospitalised version of Don Emanuele. He will understand exactly how you are feeling.'

'I like your analogy, Beppe,' replied Annamaria tartly, from the rear seat and with her sunglasses firmly in place. 'But I would just like to point out that I feel far from comfortable in the presence of your archbishop!'

Both Beppe and Sonia laughed at Annamaria's typically spirited response.

'You are a gem, Annamaria,' said Sonia. 'You are also one the easiest persons to live with I have ever known. You feel like one of the family already.'

Beppe and Sonia registered an emotionally choked *'grazie mille'* from the back seat.

'Does Don Emanuele know we're coming?' asked Annamaria, after a protracted silence.

'Don Emanuele *always* knows when someone is coming to see him,' replied Beppe. 'With three of us coming at once, he will have felt the vibes well in advance.'

---

[114] Girls

Beppe's reply had done little to reassure their back-seat passenger.

'Mmmm…' was all she said.

* * *

If their spiritual leader had experienced any surprise at their arrival, it certainly did not register on his face. He was smiling broadly at the group of three – as if their arrival had simply enhanced his joy of being alive.

'*His* version of a warm embrace,' considered Beppe, as Don Emanuele led them into the kitchen.

Don Emanuele took one look at the expression on Annamaria's face.

'*O Dio mio!* I see you disapprove of me. Have I done something wrong, Annamaria? Please tell me what the matter is.'

His voice was so soothing and the aura that he gave off had a calming effect on Annamaria. Neither Sonia nor Beppe felt like interrupting the poignant silence which followed. Later on, Annamaria confessed to them that she had felt a tidal wave of love flowing through her body. Not love for any specific person, but simply a sense of well-being.

'No, Don Emanuele. You have done nothing wrong. It is simply that I do not understand what is happening to me.'

Don Emanuele listened without interruption to Annamaria Intimo's account of her reprieve from total blindness. He wore a deeply thoughtful expression on his face – only smiling briefly when Annamaria mentioned tripping over the family dog when she had first taken a few independent steps towards the children.

'You may well smile, Don Emanuele...' began Annamaria.

'How did you *know* I was smiling?' asked Don Emanuele. His voice sounded genuinely curious.

The question took Annamaria by surprise.

'I don't...know...precisely, Don Emanuele,' she stammered. 'Some subtle change in the air, I suppose.'

For once, Don Emanuele did not obey his usual instincts – which involved him kneeling on the stone altar steps in the cathedral and falling into what often seemed like a deep trance.

'What strikes me immediately, Annamaria, is that you have evolved into a remarkable and beautiful human being. You live your life to the full – probably seeing with your inner eyes more than most sighted people do. I certainly did not pray for you to be cured of your blindness last time we met. Strangely enough, it never occurred to me to ask God that you should be healed. Maybe just because you already seemed to be such a 'whole' person.'

'How do you know all that?' asked Annamaria, sharply. 'You've only met me once.'

'Don Emanuele, too, has hidden gifts, Annamaria. You shouldn't be so surprised.'

It had been Sonia who had spoken these words. The Archbishop took up the trialogue once again.

'Don't be concerned, Annamaria. Your ability to see shadows is not of my doing. Besides which, if one is to take the New Testament literally, Jesus would have made a much better job than I did of restoring your sight!'

Even Annamaria had to smile at Don Emanuele's words, which would have bordered on the blasphemous, coming from anyone else's lips. But the Archbishop had not finished talking. His voice had returned to its former solemnity:

'I believe your new-found gift has a purpose, Annamaria. You will be better able to react when there is a further threat to your life. In the near future, if I am not mistaken. Stay near Beppe over the next few days, Annamaria.'

The three visitors left Don Emanuele shortly after that. He had simply accompanied them to the presbytery door, raising his hands in blessing with the words:

'Dio sia con voi, amici miei.' [115]

'Heaven forbid!' said Annamaria when they were seated once again in the car and heading towards the hospital. 'I do hope I haven't been converted!'

She had not put on her sunglasses again - and her eyes appeared to be alight with a sense of the mystery created by *that* archbishop - until she recalled his ominous parting words. If, indeed, another attempt on her life was to be made, would she not be forced to become some kind of believer? A scary prospect!'

But Annamaria Intimo felt fully 'alive' again.

* * *

Beppe's friend, Bruno Esposito, was waiting for the three of them outside the main entrance of the *Santo Spirito* hospital. The 'blind' girl, whom he had never seen before, was being marched along arm in arm with Beppe on her right and Sonia on her left. Bruno had the impression that she was reluctant to be there.

After embracing his friends, Bruno turned to Annamaria. She was not proffering her hand to be shaken. He gently stroked her arm, and spoke to her:

---

[115] God be with you, my friends.

'There is absolutely nothing to be worried about, *signorina*. We have one eye-specialist who is probably the best in Italy – if not in the whole world. She is also a good friend of mine, who will be delighted to meet you. I think she read about you in the local paper. She is naturally very curious to meet you in person after she read about how you identified those two crooks – just by your sense of smell. She told me it would be an honour to make your acquaintance.'

The timbre of his voice and the well-chosen words seemed to reassure Annamaria, who replied:

'I'm going through with this visit to please Beppe and Sonia, Bruno. Even their two children have been exhorting me to come and see you.'

'I am sure you will feel more at ease when you meet my colleague, Silvia.'

Bruno had not given the eye-surgeon's surname, Beppe noticed with curiosity. On being introduced to Silvia, he understood why. He could only look at Sonia with his eyebrow raised in ironic amusement. Sonia too, had read the doctor's surname on her identity tag. One of the best known Abruzzese surnames – De Cecco, [116] - the same surname as the famous pasta manufacturer from the town of Fara San Martino.

The secrecy proved to be pointless when Silvia De Cecco introduced herself to Annamaria after taking her hands in both of hers and introducing herself as Silvia De Cecco.

Annamaria, despite herself, burst into a fit of giggles which she was not at great pains to control.

'How comical!' she told the eye-surgeon. 'I feel better already. And, you really did not need to be so tactful, *Dottore* Bruno. I'm actually quite proud of being blind.'

---

[116] 'Cecco' is almost identical in sound to the word 'cieco' – which means 'blind'.

Bruno Esposito merely added:

'So I see, *Signorina* Intimo. You are not the reserved person that I was expecting to meet. *Brava...bravissima!'*

Silvia De Cecco then dismissed the 'audience' and told them to go and get something to eat and drink.

'Come back in about an hour-and-a-half's time. I am quite sure that Annamaria doesn't want you two gawping at her while we carry out these simple tests – and we shall need to be isolated when we carry out the brain scan. Nothing to worry about, Annamaria,' said Silvia, as she linked an arm under her patient's and led her away, chatting amiably about the moment when she 'identified' the mobster who smelt of sardines.

'Absolutely mind-blowing! The most amusing thing I have come across for ages!' Beppe heard the surgeon saying to Annamaria as she led her off down a corridor – away from the six 'prying' eyes.

* * *

It was nearer two hours later when a thoughtful but relaxed Annamaria was led back into the waiting arms of Sonia and Beppe. Bruno Esposito had been needed elsewhere in the hospital. He knew he could catch up on any developments at any time he wished.

Beppe and Sonia merely looked intensely at the eye surgeon, whose arm was still linked under Annamaria's.

'We shall be writing a full report over the next few days. But I have to confess to being mystified. Ideally, we would have liked to go back to her birth – but Annmaria tells me that her parents tended to accept her blindness as if it was simply part of God's will for her, and so they took virtually no steps to have her analysed. She was born at home with a country midwife present somewhere miles away from any hospital up in the mountains.'

'So, we shall have to wait for your written report?' asked Sonia – who sounded disappointed.

'Well, not entirely, no, Sonia. I can tell you now that the report may not shed any further light on what seems to be happening to Annamaria's sight. The only similar case I have read about happened to a girl in Argentina. But she had just returned home from a visit to Lourdes. You can see where I am going with this, can't you? At a first glance, there appears to be nothing wrong with Annamaria's ophthalmic cortex – which is in itself very odd. I am sure you both know that the images we see of the world outside are actually formed at the back of our heads. Somehow, we are tricked by nature into believing we are looking at a solid world.'

The eye-surgeon was greeted with a blank look in their eyes and a pair of heads being shaken from side to side.

'The human brain is totally unbelievable in its complexity. It's capacity to function simply extends to infinity inside the tight confines of our skulls. Put simply, even Annamaria seeing silhouettes and light should not be possible. I have told Annamaria that I could give her new lenses in her eyes – but that would involve a very delicate operation - with no absolute guarantees at the end.'

'I said 'no' to that, Sonia, Beppe. I would rather continue in my own sweet, dark, little world. *Che sarà, sarà!* I'll let nature decide.'

A silent group walked side by side with arms linked back towards the car.

'Can we please go and see Mariastella?' asked Annamaria. 'I would love to…see her again.'

Beppe looked at Sonia. She alone knew why her *Commissario* husband might wish to delay this encounter. But Beppe knew that breaking the news of his decision to accept the post of *Questore* should be faced without delay.

'Just let me phone my parents,' said Sonia. 'Veronica and Lorenzo will have to suffer the disappointment of being picked up by their grandparents again – life back to normal!'

Annamaria was wondering if she would ever be able to have children of her own. One thing she had been promised by Silvia De Cecco had been a strong indication as to whether her blindness was hereditary – or not. The doctor had been inclined to believe the latter. It was the first time in her relatively short life that Annamaria had given serious thought to this aspect of her 'affliction'.

'After all, all I will need is a man,' she told herself.

26:   *As one Questore to another...*

Beppe's imminent arrival, with his two women in tow, had somehow become common knowledge at the *Questura* in Via Pesaro. Word had spread with lightning speed. Thus, the three were happily subjected to a welcoming committee on their arrival. Mariastella herself, heading the line-up.

The celebrated trio were obliged to be hugged - or had their hands shaken warmly - as they moved down the queue; Beppe followed by Sonia and Annamaria, who felt loved by this succession of men and women, some of whom she 'recognised' by their stature or their voices.

Suddenly, Annamaria found herself in contact with a man who was exactly her height, whose voice she instantly recognised.

'You are the officer I met at the murder scene, aren't you? I recognised you at once. Donato Pavone, isn't it?' whispered Annamaria.

Donato held her arms gently and kissed her cheeks softly.

'I've been longing to do that, *signorina,*' said the voice, 'ever since I first saw you.'

Annamaria told Beppe and Sonia, later on in that long day, that she had felt some electric current running through her body at the brief contact with this man.

The seconds' longer contact had not been remarked upon by anyone other than the two people concerned.

When Beppe, Sonia and Annamaria had set foot on the stairs with the lady *Questore* in the lead, Annamaria spoke out unexpectedly.

'I wonder if I could leave you for thirty minutes or so?' she said. 'I could collect some more fresh clothes while you are discussing your private business.'

'Of course, Annamaria,' said Beppe. I'll ask one of the officers to take you to your apartment.'

'I would like *Agente* Donato Pavone to accompany me,' she replied firmly.

Beppe raised an eyebrow, but did not demure.

'Donato,' said Beppe to his trusted junior officer. 'I have a little job for you...' he told him what it was. Officer Pavone did not give anything away by word or gesture.

'Certainly, *capo*. I need twenty minutes to complete something that needs doing urgently first of all. I'll keep *Signorina* Intimo with me while I finish the task in hand.'

* * *

Beppe, Sonia and Mariastella were soon ensconced on the long sofa in her office.

Without mincing his words, Beppe told Mariastella about his decision.

'I imagine I shall be here for a number of weeks longer while the details are finalised, but...'

Beppe had stopped talking because, instead of looking shattered as he had secretly hoped, the *Questore* was looking relieved.

'I knew you'd be secretly happy to see the back of me, Mariastella,' exclaimed Beppe, trying to make his hurt seem like a jibe.

'Oh, it's not like that at all, Beppe!' Mariastella reassured him. 'It was pure relief. I didn't want to let *you* down. I'm going to resign from this post. My partner and I are adopting two refugee children – a brother and a sister. I want to devote myself to these kids – to compensate for the fact I can't have my own. That is the sole reason why I looked relieved.'

Sonia and Beppe congratulated Mariastella warmly and went on to talk about other matters.

'I want to bring you up-to-date as to what is happening in Reggio Calabria. I've just had a lengthy conversation with *Il Colonnello* Pasquale Precopio…'

Mariastella did not continue, simply because her *Commissario* was frowning – as if he had just had an unpleasant thought.

'You must forgive me, Mariastella. I have to stop Annamaria and Officer Pavone going back into her apartment. It was something that Don Emanuele told us about thirty minutes ago. It may be nothing but I cannot take that risk. Sonia will tell you…'

The Archbishop's parting words had suddenly come to mind. Don Emanuele had said that Annamaria should stay near *him.* But surely that implied also that he should stay near *her.*

Sonia had turned pale as Beppe rushed off.

'Not again!' she said, almost sobbing in despair. She knew what Beppe was about to do and explained as briefly as she could why her husband had rushed off. Mariastella did not hesitate.

'Come on, Sonia. We'll follow close on his heels.'

* * *

'Did you see Officer Pavone and the blind girl leaving?' shouted Beppe as he was passing the reception desk.

'Yes, *capo.* No more than ten minutes ago.'

Beppe was feeling more than a little idiotic as he drove the family car at reckless speed in the direction of *I Tulipani Gialli,* using his horn as if it had been a police car siren.

'You are being paranoid, Beppe Stancato!' his level-headed self was telling him accusingly. 'You're going to have egg all over your face in a few minutes' time. As if any mafia *boss* is going to run the risk of attempting to raid the same place three times in a row!'

In his haste, he realised he had taken a long way round to reach Annamaria's *palazzo*. The police car driven by Officer Pavone was already parked outside the flats. The occupants had already gone inside. Beppe drove the family car up on to the pavement and ran towards the entrance door. He had overlooked the fact that he would be unable to simply push the entrance door to gain admission.

He cursed himself, the saints in heaven – and almost blamed the Archbishop too, for creating the panic in the first place. He banged on the reinforced glass door with one hand and held his finger down on the janitor's bell until the elderly figure came limping up to the door with an alarmed expression on his wrinkled face. To his credit, the janitor recognised *that Commissario,* who had roundly told him off for his lack of security a couple of weeks previously.

'Did you see one of my officers coming in a few minutes ago with that blind girl from apartment twenty-four?'

'No, *Commissario,* I'm sorry. I was busy mending a...'

'Has anyone you didn't know tried to get into apartment twenty-four at any stage?'

'No *Commissario* – apart from one of your uniformed officers who asked me to let him into number twenty-four earlier this morning. I haven't seen him come out. I thought...'

Whatever the janitor thought was cut off by the sound of a gun-shot, echoing down from the floors above.

'O Dio!' said Beppe as he headed for the stairwell. He could not waste time waiting for the lift.'

'Should I call the police?' called out the befuddled janitor to the departing figure.

'No – call the undertaker!' he shouted out as he bound up the steps two at a time to reach the second floor.

The janitor would probably have done as the *Commissario* had suggested - had it not been for the fact that there was someone else banging noisily on the entrance door and ringing his bell as if all hell had broken loose.

Two women pushed passed him as soon as he released the latch – not even deigning to utter a word of explanation.

When Beppe rushed into Annamaria's flat, it took him a good ten seconds to take in the almost comical scene that presented itself to his disbelieving eyes.

At first sight, he saw only Annamaria Intimo, who appeared to be lying on her sofa, looking pale, but very much alive. Beppe needed to take four more steps into the living room before he saw the figure of *Agente* Donato Pavone sitting on the chest of some burly thug, who appeared to be wearing a policeman's uniform. Beppe could barely believe his eyes. It was the mobster who had dragged him off his hotel bed in the middle of the night back in Reggio Calabria. Officer Pavone was pointing a pistol at his captive's temple.

The man was bleeding copiously all over the polished parquet flooring from a bullet wound to his thigh.

'We will call for an ambulance – but only when you tell us who sent you!' Officer Pavone was informing him calmly.

'He smells of onions, Beppe,' said Annamaria Intimo, with a faint smile playing on her lips.

'You can relax, *Agente* Pavone. I know who sent this thug; his name is Gregorio Giuffrè – *vero, signore?* And congratulations, Donato. You have fired the first shot of your career to very good effect.'

It was obvious that the thug had not recognised the man whom he had abducted in distant Reggio Calabria. Beppe did not bother to enlighten him.

A breathless Sonia, accompanied by Mariastella Martellini, smiled radiantly at her unharmed husband and said, sarcastically:

Bravo, Beppe Stancato! Now let that be an end to it!'

The lady *Questore's* mobile phone was ringing at this inopportune moment.

She took one look at her phone and switched it immediately into loud-speaker mode.

'It's *Colonnello* Pasquale Procopio from Reggio Calabrio,' she said with disbelief in her voice, as the senior DIA officer began to speak.

'I think I ought to warn you, Mariastella. We intercepted a call from that mafioso boss we both know so well – Gregorio Giuffrè. If what I hope is correct, we should be able to put him behind bars for years – *l'ergastolo,* [117] if we're lucky. But we learnt that he has sent someone to Pescara to have a second attempt at eliminating Annamaria Intimo. The idiot thought he would get one back at our *Commissario* by killing his wife! He obviously got his wires a bit crossed, it seems. I thought I ought to share this with you as quickly as possible…'

Mariastella laughed down the phone.

'You are roughly five minutes too late, *Colonnello.* But don't worry. We got there just in time.'

'But how did you…?' began Pasquale Procopio.

'I'll get Beppe to phone you back. He can tell you all about our archbishop's gift of prescience. You'll find it fascinating. Right now, we have a bleeding mobster to get to hospital – the prison hospital,' she said aloud for the benefit of

---

[117] Life imprisonment

the man who was still groaning softly from his prone position on Annamaria's parquet flooring.

'Beppe, Sonia, Annamaria,' said the lady *Questore*. This might be the last time I ever have to say this: Go home, Beppe, and be with your whole family. We'll take it from here.'

There was a movement from the sofa as Annamaria stood up. Beppe and Sonia only learnt later on, in the car going back to Atri, that Annamaria had seen the mafioso's silhouette, with a knife raised to stab her. She had stepped backwards and lost her balance as she accidently rolled over the back of the sofa to safety. She had not realised exactly where she had been standing. But her cry had alerted Officer Pavone – checking the bathroom for intruders. He had shot the thug neatly in his left thigh.

'I have to go home with Beppe and Sonia now, Donato,' said Annamaria, who was now standing face to face, close up to her saviour. 'But I shall be back very soon to thank you properly.'

They were the same height. Annamaria's hands were feeling the shape of his face, before she kissed him briefly on the mouth.

Donato Pavone recovered with remarkable aplomb, patted his revolver in its holster and said to his *capo:*

'Thank you for your timely arrival, *capo! Tutto bene ciò che finisce bene* – as they say!' [118]

* * *

Nobody in the car, travelling at a leisurely pace along the country road towards Atri, seemed able to launch into a meaningful conversation after Annamaria had told them how

---

[118] All's well that ends well.

234

she had seen her attacker's shadow. Whatever words anybody spoke, were likely to sound trivial after the momentous sequence of events of that day.

Beppe was idly thinking about whether it would be possible to change his mind about becoming a *questore*. It became obvious to him that such a reversal would no longer be tenable. He sighed nostalgically.

Sonia was still bathing in the joyous feeling of security that Beppe's hazardous passage through the last few nightmare days was over. Then she turned her mind to the pleasant task of deciding what to cook that evening – to celebrate. She had a fairly accurate notion in her head as to the direction Beppe's thoughts might be heading as he drove the three of them home. He would be nursing a nostalgic hope of reprieve by some earthly *deus ex machina.*

'No way out, *Commissario!'* she assured him out loud.

'Ah, *touché, Sonia.* Telepathy at work again!' said Beppe. 'I know, Sonia. The die is cast!'

In the end, it was Annamaria who broke the comfortable silence, which had followed Beppe's announcement, with words that provoked quiet laughter from her audience of two.

'It's just as I feared, Beppe, Sonia. I am now forced into believing in what I can only assume is the supernatural.'

Beppe and Sonia were both wondering what aspect of the 'supernatural' had affected their house guest the most. In light of her sudden *colpo di fulmine* [119] in respect of the *Questura's* newest recruit and her miraculous escape from being stabbed by the *mafioso,* the choice must be bewildering.

They had arrived home and, not unexpectedly, Veronica and Lorenzo were outside the house – anxiously awaiting their arrival. One missing parent had been bad enough – two would

---

[119] 'Love at first sight' Lit: A lightning strike

have meant the end of their little world. Veronica even put her arm round her brother's shoulders as the three adults got out of the car.

Sonia hugged and kissed her children, just as she felt the first little kick inside her belly. She felt a wave of happiness spread through her body. Somehow, the uncertainty in their lives had been resolved at a stroke. She experienced a feeling of security rise up from her stomach and pass through her chest on its way to her head.

'I guess it must be Don Emanuele's neutrinos at work,' she thought fancifully.

27:   *The youngest marriage counsellor in Italy...*

The decision as to what to cook was taken out of Sonia's hands as soon as Beppe suggested another visit to their local *agriturismo, La Quercia,* to celebrate the family's 'return' to unity. The restaurant specialised in a variety of *antipasti* which would arrive on the table in a continuous stream until they could eat no more.

Annamaria was assured that her presence was absolutely vital to their sense of family unity.

'I love *antipasti,'* declared Annamaria. 'It means that nobody has to read out loud all the items on the menu – just for my benefit. I have only ever come across one restaurant which provided their menu in braille.'

Whether out of tact or simply because they could not face so much food, Sonia's parents opted out of the restaurant visit.

'Roberto doesn't want to miss the final episode of this drama on Rai Uno,' was Irene's excuse. 'It's called Blanca...'

Annamaria laughed out loud, to everyone's surprise.

'That's the series about the blind girl who helps the police solve crimes in the *Questura* in Genova, isn't it? My sister's been banging on about that for three weeks. She says I really ought to watch it – that's how brainless my sister is!' said Annamaria – as usual not mincing her words on the subject of her sibling.

Veronica decided to fill the time, before going out to eat, with a new game she had invented for Annamaria's benefit. She had dragooned Lorenzo into joining in – not entirely against his will and better judgement.

'Seeing as how you are able to see our shadow-shapes now, Annamaria, we can play a kind of charades – where we mime actions and you have to guess what we're doing.'

Veronica's inventiveness seemed boundless – as she mimed a person swimming, cooking a pizza, playing tennis, washing the dishes, having a shower and washing her hair - until her actions grew so outlandish that Lorenzo gave up on the game. But only after he had performed a perfect mime of someone conducting an orchestra – which Annamaria could not fathom out.

Annamaria seemed inexplicably happy and stayed talking to Veronica until it was time to dress up for the outing to the *agriturismo*. It was from the horse's mouth that an enthralled Veronica learnt about what had transpired that day. Annamaria had gone into the minutest details of her ordeal far more graphically than she would have dared to do had the younger and far more sensitive Lorenzo been present.

This arrangement suited Veronica well. She could relate what she was hearing to her younger brother before he fell asleep – with her own embellishments added for good measure.

Veronica was intrigued by Annamaria's account of Officer Donato Pavone's timely shooting of the mobster before he could stab her – thereby saving her life.

'You must have fallen in love with him in that precious moment of time, Annamaria. I bet you kissed him before you left him!'

Veronica noticed with great glee that her impudent observation had produced a blush on her friend's cheeks.

'I do think you must not be too hasty about this kiss,' said Veronica, seeing an opportunity to sound adult-like.

'I mean you hardly know him yet – and you do not know what he looks like!'

'Ah, but to me, Vero, it does not matter what he looks like – because I am blind. But he 'feels' the right person for me. That's what matters in my world. And I bet when your mum and dad first met, your mum knew immediately that Beppe was the right man for her.'

'Don't you believe it, Annamaria! My *papà* had to get married at the last moment because I was already in my mum's belly.'

Veronica's probing into personal details was mercifully brought to an end by the arrival of Sonia, telling her daughter to go and get dressed.

'Did you know that Annamaria has a boyfriend now, *mamma?*' asked Veronica.

'Are you letting your imagination run wild again, Vero?' was all Sonia said with feigned severity. 'Leave Annamaria to sort out her own private life.'

'Did *you* see them kissing, *mamma?*' was Veronica's parting shot.

'Go and get ready, Vero. The taxi will be here in ten minutes.'

Round the breakfast table, the following morning, Annamaria broke the morning cereal-eating-coffee-slurping ritual by asking Beppe if she could accompany him to Pescara.

'Of course, you can, Annamaria. I'm sure you have lots to do,' Beppe replied neutrally. His mind was on what lay in store for him that day; telling his team about his momentous decision – and that of the Lady *Questore* to boot.

Lorenzo was smirking. He had been extensively filled-in the previous night by his sister before he had been allowed to fall asleep. He had guessed who Annamaria would prefer to spend her time with that day.

Forza, Annamaria!' [120] said the seven-year-old boy, to everyone's amusement. 'Don't listen to my sister. She can be so *invadente!*' [121]

---

[120] Go for it!

The look on Veronica's face was a picture of fury directed at her younger brother. But she wisely gave way to the predominant mood. The fact that everyone present was laughing sympathetically at her, brought the customary radiant smile back to her face.

But as soon as she went into her classroom that morning, Veronica made a beeline for her teacher.

'What does *invadente* mean, please *Signorina* Molè?'

On hearing the teacher's explanation, Veronica smiled happily.

She liked the idea that she was *invadente*. She felt flattered by her brother's description of her – even though she had to swallow her pride that HE had known a word that she had never heard of.

* * *

Beppe was listening intensely to Mariastella Martellini's account of the entrapment and arrest of the mafioso *boss*, Gregorio Giuffrè – and the part that Asia Sposato had played prior to his encounter with her at the farmhouse.

'This Giuffrè character was invited to a secret mafia clan meeting by Fausto Talarico – where Gregorio Giuffrè was intending to carry out his great *coup*,' Mariastella was explaining to Beppe. 'But the DIA had managed to pass on news of the plot to Fausto Talarico to forewarn him of the attempt on his life. It was all part of a devious plot by the DIA.'

'Sometimes, this ploy is the only way we can get at the local clans – by setting one clan against another in the hope that they will end up murdering each other,' *Colonnello* Procopio

---

[121] A very 'adult' word for 'intrusive'.

told me. The DIA stepped in at the last minute to prevent a wholesale massacre.'

'Any news on Asia Sposato?' asked Beppe as casually as he could.

'Ah, your saviour, Beppe! I have no specific news about that amazing young lady. I understand her part in bringing Gregorio Giuffrè to justice has been handled well. But her report of her being raped when she was fourteen by that despicable apology for a human being means that she could easily become a target for reprisals. I have spoken to her on the phone and promised her a safe place to hide up here if ever she feels her life is at risk.'

'But did you meet Gregorio Giuffrè in person, Mariastella? Your dislike of that monster seems to be so personal.'

Mariastella explained to an astounded *Commissario* about her compulsory visit to the night club in the company of Asia – and the unpleasant experience of having to dance close up with the man who was holding him hostage.

'There seems to be a lot of detail for us to catch up on, Mariastella – when we have time.'

'I agree, Beppe. I am very curious to find out the details of how Asia succeeded in rescuing *you* from the clutches of Giuffrè at the eleventh hour.'

Beppe looked hard at his phone as if the gadget would provide him with an escape route.

'I have to meet the team in twenty minutes time, Mariastella – and break the news about my promotion and your resignation. I'm not looking forward to it!'

'In twenty minutes, Beppe? That gives you ample time to tell me about your rescue! I am sure it must have been an unforgettable experience.'

The intense look on his *capo's* face was irresistible.

'*Va bene,* Mariastella. I will tell *you* exactly what happened. But this is very personal, I should warn you. So far only Sonia knows.'

By the end of his account, Mariastella had stopped smiling. Two tears were trickling down her cheeks.

'I think I love that girl,' she said.

'I know exactly what you mean, Mariastella.'

'I suppose we should talk about your future as a *questore,*' said Mariastella when her flood of emotion was back under control.

'Yes, Maristella. In fact, a thought has occurred to me.'

Maristella was looking at her second-in-command. She knew exactly what was coming next.

'If you are intending to retire in the near future – for the most praise-worthy reasons I have ever heard of for resigning from a post – this must mean that there will be a position here in Pescara for a new *Questore?* The logical conclusion would be...'

Mariastella Martellini was smiling apologetically.

'That was my first thought too, Beppe. But I am sorry to say that the powers that be in Rome had anticipated your request. It seems they have other priorities in mind, *caro Commissario!* You made a very positive impression on the mayor of Terramonti, it appears. I'm sorry to say that he has been pulling some important strings among certain influential people in Rome. Your appointment as *Questore* is dependent on you accepting that specific post.'

Beppe shrugged a shoulder.

'So be it!' he stated resignedly.

* * *

The meeting which Beppe then held with the police force of Via Pesaro was decidedly more emotional than even he had anticipated. The atmosphere of pure shock was, Beppe noted, akin to the reaction provoked by an Italian football team losing three-zero to Bulgaria. Theoretically impossible! Officers Campione and Cardinale were in tears. Pippo Cafarelli had turned as white as a sheet and Officers Gino Martelli and Danilo Simone threatened to resign. Giacomo D'Amico declared he would bring forward his retirement to coincide with Beppe's departure.

Only the massive form of *Agente* Luigi Rocco – nicknamed the Mountain Bear – remained totally impassive, as he rose to his feet amidst the silence and told the assembled officers with a growl that the *Commissario's* promotion was well-deserved. This produced a standing ovation for their leader. Only the new boy, Officer Donato Pavone, had a pensive look on his face, as he fixed his *capo* with a hard look – which said clearly: 'I'm going to ask for a transfer!' Until, he recalled that he would have to take a second person into consideration; after which he joined in with the general applause.

When Beppe went on to explain that they would be deserted by their lady *Questore* as well – and her reasons for doing so – there was a round of normal hand-clapping as they sat down again. Apparently, nothing could match their consternation more than the loss of their very own *Commissario*.

* * *

Beppe would have preferred to head for home rather than face the accusing looks on the part of his closest friend and ally on the Pescara police force – *Ispettore* Pippo Cafarelli -

who collared him as soon as the other officers had drifted away in a state of shock.

'I'm sorry, Pippo,' said Beppe. 'I had no choice in the matter. I made a solemn promise to Sonia that I would accept this post – simply because I could never run the risk of a repeat performance of my disappearance in Calabria. And look on the bright side, Pippo – you are in line for promotion to at least a *vice Commissario* as soon as I have gone.'

'That is no consolation to me whatsoever compared to losing you from our lives, Beppe.'

Further discussion was cut short by an unexpected phone call from none other than Don Emanuele – asking Beppe if he would pay him a brief visit before he returned home to Atri.

'I have some news for you, Beppe – and a token gift that goes with it. It will only take a few minutes, if as I suspect, you will want to return to Atri as soon as possible after your hectic day.'

'How did you know…?' began Beppe pointlessly, before he cut the question short. Don Emanuele always knew everything in advance,

Thus, what the Archbishop said next caught him off guard.

'I have Annamaria with me,' he said. 'She has told me everything. She was brought here by one of your young officers earlier on today – at her own request. Officer Pavone will have to come and pick her up – unless you come round. That will save Donato a second trip. See you in a few minutes, Beppe!'

* * *

Intrigued by Don Emanuele's words, Beppe drove the short distance to the cathedral. He found Annamaria in the company of Eugenia Mancino enjoying what appeared to be an hilarious private joke. Eugenia had been the mayoress of a small town up in the mountains. [122] She had, apparently, become attached to the Archbishop of Pescara. As far as the population of Pescara was concerned, she acted as Don Emanuele's housekeeper.

Beppe did not have time to find out what had kindled the two women's spontaneous friendship, since he was led off to another part of the presbytery by Don Emanuele.

'Congratulations on your up-coming promotion, Beppe. You will be sorely missed by us all here in Pescara. But I am certain we shall never lose contact with each other. The bonds are too strong. But it is another matter – quite trivial by comparison – which led me to ask you round here.'

Was the Archbishop going to suggest that he, Beppe, should make a clean breast of his recent act of infidelity?

The *Commissario* should have known better than to think such thoughts whilst in Don Emanuele's presence.

'No, Beppe. I do not want to hear your confession – simply because I would refuse to give you absolution.'

'Was what I did so wicked, Don Emanuele?' asked Beppe, not entirely jokingly.

'No, Beppe. I would refuse to absolve you, because you have done nothing wrong in the eyes of God. Besides which your 'sin' would pale into nothing compared with my 'sins'. I am sure you understand what I am saying!'

Don Emanuele did not even wait for Beppe to comment before continuing:

'Have you heard that *Il Professore Pisano* [123] and I are going to give a live televised lecture on God and Physics in the

---

[122] See: Death is Buried
[123] Reference to 'The Vanishintheg Physicist'

cathedral next Sunday? In front of a churchful of Pescaresi. It should be quite lively!'

Beppe merely shook his head by way of reply.

'I've been a bit out of touch during the last few days, Don Emanuele,' he added as an afterthought.

'So I understand, *caro* Beppe. I would be honoured if you and your family would be present during the TV interview. So, I'm offering you seven free tickets. One for each family member and two for guests. But you will all have to sit in the front row – to give me moral support!'

'We shall all be there, Don Emanuele – including Annamaria Intimo, I suspect.

'And her new companion – the young officer who drove her to the *Duomo* today, so I am told.'

'Who told you *that,* Don Emanuele?'

'Annamaria did!' answered the Archbishop. *'Un colpo di fulmine,* she said. I gave her our blessing.'

'Ah! That settles the matter, then!' murmured Beppe.

When Beppe did the simple addition in the car, he turned to Annamaria with the words:

'I make that only six tickets. Don Emanuele can't count. At least, he has *one* weakness.'

'I suggest that the seventh ticket might be for the new member of your family – who, don't forget, is already a human being with a soul as far as the Pope is concerned.'

'Ah yes. *Grazie.* Annamaria! How thoughtless of me! I stand corrected.'

* * *

Sitting round the family table that evening, Annamaria Intimo broke the news to her adoptive family that she would be moving back to her flat very soon.

Veronica and Lorenzo were visibly upset.

'I am sure I shall be back to visit you soon,' Annamaria promised them. 'You have all changed my life completely over the last few weeks. I shall be eternally grateful to you all – but especially to you two wonderful children, who have made me laugh again. So many amazing things have happened – just because of all of you. I am sure you have worked out by now that I shall have someone who will be keeping me company in the future.'

'I tried to tell you to take things slowly, Annamaria,' piped up Veronica, seizing her last chance to fulfil her role as counsellor.

'*Forza,* Annamaria!' interjected Lorenzo. 'Don't listen to my sister. She is so…'

'*INVADENTE'* Lorenzo and Veronica had called out in perfect harmony - even if the word meant something slightly different in each case.

'We have loved having you with us, Annamaria,' said Sonia. 'You will always be welcome here.'

'And I might have a special 'Blanca' job for you, Annamaria – as soon as I begin working in Terramonti. It's just an idea at the moment.'

Annmaria's face glowed with pleasure at the thought that she could help Beppe in his new post as *Questore.*

'Meanwhile,' said Beppe, 'we shall all be together again this coming Sunday – including your *fidanzato,* [124] Annamaria. We are all going to church in Pescara.'

'CHURCH?' said Veronica and Lorenzo disparagingly.

---

[124] Boyfriend : fiancé

'With one big difference,' said Beppe. 'You two will both have the opportunity to appear 'live' on television!'

'It is so wonderful to have you back with us, *papà!* stated Veronica – with no apparent connection to what they had just been talking about.

'We were all so scared when you disappeared!' added Lorenzo.

28:   *How not to be bored in church...*

The cathedral was not simply packed full of people; it was seething with living souls of every age from a nearly eight-year-old boy called Lorenzo to a number of ninety-year-olds in wheelchairs squeezed into the aisle spaces, surreptitiously adjusting their hearing aids. Babes-in-arms had been discouraged – simply because their protests at being enclosed between the walls of a church would have interfered with the microphones. The sense of expectancy was more like that of a horde of escapees from the ancient land of Egypt – awaiting the dawning of a New Age.

The two vacant 'thrones' were set on the top steps where the altar stood – for once empty of the usual Sunday accoutrements.

The all-seeing eye of the television camera was focused on the two thrones – awaiting the arrival of the god-like form of Don Emanuele in the shining armour of his pristine white alb and the modestly-clad figure of a less well-known celebrity who some remembered as a jovial man in his early fifties who looked more like everybody's notion of a favourite uncle. This was, of course, *il Professore* Donato Pisano - the now renowned physicist who had been 'banned' from the Montenegro Physics laboratory, buried underground in the mountains above L'Aquila, because of his heretical belief that neutrinos could travel faster than the speed of light. [125]

When the two figures emerged from the sacristy and went to sit down on the thrones, a silence settled on the gathered crowd. The only human being who appeared to be moving about naturally was the cameraman, peering through the view-finder on his apparatus.

---

[125] See: The Vanishing Physicist

A hitherto invisible young man had appeared as if by magic where the lectern stood. He tapped the microphone and announced himself as Andrea Massi – the scientific-cum-religious journalist belonging to the local TV station TV-Tavo.

'We tossed a coin a few minutes ago,' he began, 'to decide which of these two distinguished members of our local community we should listen to first. It seemed like the only way to let our invisible deity have a say in the matter.'

The quiet laughter which rippled round the cathedral broke the ice, but the subdued and respectable laughter turned into delighted applause when the two celebrities spoke simultaneously with well-rehearsed unity:

'We are gathered together today to hear the word of God in two totally different languages.'

'I shall be speaking to you first in non-mathematical terms to try to explain to you why I do not disbelieve in God,' stated the notable physicist.

'And I shall be speaking to you in non-ecclesiastical language to try to explain to you all why we should actively believe in God and the Holy Spirit,' declared Don Emanuele, solemnly.

A united front was sealed by a handshake before Donato Pisano began speaking.

A nearly ten-year-old girl called Veronica in the front row was already looking forward to the next day at school when she could tell everybody that her *papà* was going to be an *Inquisitore* – even though she was sure that the word she had learnt in a history lesson had referred to some rather nasty people in the Middle Ages. An anomaly which would need to be cleared up when she got home.

Lorenzo was listening intently to the speakers – only wishing he had understood the word *nonno-ecleeziastico* – something to do with grandads? He leant over to whisper in his father's ear, but saw only a raised forefinger demanding his silence. The physicist's next words held Lorenzo transfixed – in a way which few of his teachers had ever managed to achieve.

'Just imagine, if you will, that you are a neutrino – my favourite particle of all time! You are virtually without any mass. You are more like a stream of invisible water rushing by. Can you imagine that?'

The physicist paused and looked at his audience. Most of them were shaking their heads. One or two were nodding as wisely as they dared.

'You are so absolutely tiny that you can pass through anything solid without colliding with almost any other particle in your path. And those other tiny particles are HUGE compared with neutrinos. Yet even an 'enormous' atom would have to be multiplied twenty million times before you could see it with your naked eye. That is the miraculous universe we are lucky enough to live in.'

Donato paused again while his 'congregation' were busy trying to visualise an atom.

'How long do you think it would take you to count up to twenty million if you began at number one and carried on counting one number every second? It is impossible, of course, because by the time you reached a few thousand, it would take increasingly more than one second even to say the number out loud.'

A few of the 'audience' raised a tentative hand – especially some of the bolder *Liceo Scientifica* teenagers – and had the courage to venture a guess.

'About seven days?' was the highest bidder.

'Well, I am sorry to tell you that counting up to twenty million would take you two-hundred-and-forty days – without a single break for lunch – or sleeping.'

There was a stunned silence as many of those present tried to grapple with the notion of the word 'tiny' when applied to a neutrino.

'And when I tell you that millions of these neutrinos are passing through your body every second, you must start wondering what our mysterious universe is really like. Depending on who you are, you may well believe that these tiny particles are more like little spirits travelling through your body at the speed of light.

If you are a 'nutty professor' like me, you will believe that my neutrinos can and do travel faster than the speed of light when they feel like it.

If God exists – as I feel must be the case – then he is a spirit, not a 'he' or a 'she'. I have to consider the absolute miracle of our world...of our Universe. It is a simple, proven fact that absolutely everything that exists is made up of the same tiny particles as we humans. Snakes, spiders, cats, dogs, the food we eat, houses, trees and helicopters – are all made up of the same basic elements. That in itself is a miracle! The millions of different objects and people that we see depend on the same few quarks being assembled together into myriads of different combinations. The only difference between you and the Gran Sasso mountains is that they are changing more slowly than you are.'

The silence was absolute. Nobody in the cathedral seemed to be breathing.

'I could – and often do – go on for hours on end,' said Donato Pisano. 'But now I am going to allow Don Emanuele to speak. A few years ago, I told him what I have just told you about neutrinos. Don Emanuele has never, as far as I know, doubted that God exists. Now I want you to listen to his interpretation of what neutrinos might be.

'This holy man – your archbishop – has become a real crackpot physicist – even worse than me! He believes that the elusive 'god particle' which scientists preach about is in point of fact the neutrino – not the Higg's Boson. So, I am going to stop talking now and allow him to tell you about *his* conclusions as to the meaning of life. Don Emanuele?'

The prospect of listening to the Archbishop saying *anything* that was more unbelievable than what they had just heard guaranteed a universal silence from the several hundred people present. It was the Sermon on the Mount all over again – except that nobody was feeling hungry, thought Sonia.

'When I was a child,' began Don Emanuele, 'I thought, just like the child I was, that God was some white-coated priest up in the clouds. As I grew older, I began, in my adolescent way, to poor scorn on what I was being told from the pulpit. Many aspects of life in the back streets of Naples, led me to believe in Satan rather than in God – before I realised in my muddled teenage way that the one could not exist without the other. My time spent as an army chaplain during the first invasion of Iraq made me believe in the essential underlying goodness of ordinary people.

So...all things considered, I came to the conclusion that some kind of Holy Spirit must exist. But it was not until I met Donato Pisano a few years ago that I began to realise that God can and frequently does manifest...'

The Archbishop had paused in the middle of his sentence.

253

'This is why talking about God becomes impossible. I almost said: *'God manifests himself...* But, as my dear friend Donato has already pointed out, God is not a human being. I often get asked by my dearest parishioners why God sent a man down to save the world in the shape of Jesus. I reply that God has often sent women down to save the world too – often in the shape of the mothers of our children.'

Some of the more sensitive beings in the congregation had felt deeply moved by their Archbishop's words – to the point of feeling that prickly sensation of gathering tears.

But Don Emanuele pulled them back from the brink of emotion.

'As I was saying, my friend the physicist showed me a way forward with his neutrinos. It took me many months to see that, neutrinos, which are absolutely everywhere around us – must be there for a purpose. Only *Professore* Pisano had dared to proclaim that his neutrinos were capable of travelling faster than the speed of light. All hell broke loose. Donato Pisano was kidnapped – by the American secret services, who wanted to abduct him and smuggle him over to the other side of the Atlantic because of his beliefs.

But that is another story, which involves our own *Commissario* from the Pescara police headquarters – who is present here today with his wife and three children – although one of them is still inside Sonia's body.

As I was saying, Donato put me on the right track. Why, I thought, should there be two aspects of creation that were limited to travelling at the speed of light? Firstly, light itself, and secondly Donato's neutrinos.

What if neutrinos provide some sort of media through which God can communicate with human beings – if we have ears to hear with and a bit of faith to believe with?

There…I have declared myself to be worse than any over-imaginative, crazy physicist. But, thank you, *Professore* Donato Pisano. You may be the first person to shed some true light on the manner in which God – I hope not Satan too – succeeds in contacting us. It could be the link between the supernatural and the physical world – which must be far more closely entwined than we humans have ever realised.

I am going to share a recent event in my life with all of you today – inside our cathedral, and beyond, as soon as this meeting goes 'live'.

You may not yet be aware that our *Commissario,* Beppe Stancato, was recently saved from death at the hands of the Calabrian mafia by a remarkable young police woman from Reggio Calabria. Beppe's beautiful wife and children had come to seek consolation from me. They were accompanied by another remarkable lady called Annamaria – who is also present with us today. She is unique because she is almost totally blind – and yet succeeded in identifying the killers of Laura Ianni – a tragic drama with which you are all too familiar.

I was allowed a glimpse into the future and was able to reassure Sonia – the *Commissario's* wife – that her husband would be returned to her – thanks to this police woman whose name is Asia.

I hope I am not pushing the boundaries of Physics too far when I tell you that I was able to predict a future event – Beppe's rescue – by my vision of this girl, Asia – which was not so much a vision of her face, but rather a very large map!

Such mysteries can only happen if something – neutrinos or the Holy Spirit – can travel faster than the speed of light, thereby reversing our perception of time.

I now await cries of protest from the media – or howls of outrage from official Vatican sources. I can at least be sure that I shall finally meet *Il Papa Francesco* in the near future. Amen!'

The 'amen' had been the sign to the TV presenter, Andrea Massi, that Don Emanuele had said all he wanted to say.

There was no burst of applause – just an astounded silence.

'And now, we are going to allow two questions from the younger generation – in fact, from the *Commissario's* own two children, Veronica and Lorenzo. After that, the official TV programme will be terminated – and the TV cameras switched off. But I understand that our two brilliant guests are willing to stay behind a bit longer if your curiosity has not yet been satisfied.

And now – I present to you all, Veronica and Lorenzo Stancato...'

The *Commissario* himself had organised this addition to the TV broadcast. Having promised that his two children would be 'live on television', he had not dared to disappoint them.

Veronica rose to the occasion first, delighted to be in the limelight – if only because she knew that at least half of her classmates would be watching.

'Don Emanuele – do you believe in ghosts?'

'Children and dogs,' thought the *Commissario*. Never let either of them loose in front of a television camera. Veronica's question had not been the one they had discussed beforehand. At least, her inoffensive charm would allow her to get away with it, thought Beppe, on hearing another ripple of laughter that spread through the congregation.

Don Emanuele also rose to the occasion.

'Yes, Veronica, I do believe in ghosts – because I have met one. It was while I was an army chaplain in Iraq. I was eating my supper in the barracks. A young Italian soldier whom I knew as Giovanni was sitting opposite me in silence. I sensed he did not feel like talking, or eating, so I merely smiled at him when I got up to go to my quarters. It was only when I stopped and asked another officer as to why Giovanni was looking so sad. 'Maybe he has lost a friend to this ghastly war?'

'There must be some mistake, padre,' said the senior officer sadly. 'I have just sent news of Giovanni Scarpa's death to his parents. His body is in the morgue.'

A shocked silence had once again settled in the Cathedral. Veronica had begun to sob quietly and had to be comforted by her mother. Her moment of glory had evaporated.

'I am sorry, Veronica. You asked me a very important question – and I gave you a very truthful answer. But you do not need to feel ashamed at all. Maybe your brother's question is going to be just as intriguing as yours?'

Lorenzo shook his head. He obviously elicited sympathy in equal measure to his sister. Lots of the women were smiling at this serious-looking boy, shy but determined to put on a brave face for the cameras.

'No, Don Emanuele. I'm sorry. I was going to ask the *professore* a question – not you.'

Donato Pisano's smile was so radiant that Lorenzo did not hesitate. Beppe was shocked because neither was his son's astute question the same one which they had rehearsed in the car beforehand. Lorenzo displayed a kind of innocent maturity which belied his age.

'Do you think, *Professore,* that Don Emanuele's idea about neutrinos is true? That they are God's way of talking to us?'

It was the younger members of the 'audience' who practically gave Lorenzo a standing ovation. His question had a beguiling innocence about it which succeeded in summing up everybody's desire to give credence to the Archbishop's earlier mind-blowing revelation.

'Se solamente fosse vero!' [126] had been the predominant thought in the minds of most of the listeners.

Donato Pisano chose his closing words carefully – mindful of the fact that the TV cameras were still recording.

'Yes, I do, Lorenzo. But it might be several decades before the rest of the world begins to catch on.'

* * *

Once the TV crew had switched off the cameras, the charged atmosphere in the cathedral deflated like a burst balloon. Andrea Massi was asked when the broadcast would be aired by one member of the congregation.

'It was a live broadcast, *signore,*' he explained. 'But it will certainly be repeated later on this week.'

After a few banal questions had been attempted by the usual kind of people in mass gatherings who simply liked the sound of their own voices, the congregation began to disperse.

Don Emanuele and Donato Pisano spent a few minutes talking to Veronica and Lorenzo and congratulating them on their courage at standing up in public and asking such 'adult' questions – which went some way to reinstalling Veronica's self-esteem. Andrea Massi came over to the group and thanked them all for their spectacular contributions – before he slid off

---

[126] If only it were true.

258

with the television crew. Annamaria embraced the Stancato family lovingly before she was taken away by a very respectful officer Donato Pavone with the promise she would meet up with them all in the near future. Beppe and his most recent recruit held a brief but private conversation which ended in a mutual handshake.

The drive home back to Atri was quiet. Beppe and Sonia went to great pains to reassure their children that their contributions had been spectacular. The children's first exposure to the public at large had been more traumatic than they had imagined. Lorenzo found out what 'ecclesiastical' meant and Veronica learnt that her *papà* was to be appointed as a *Questore* – not an Inquisitor.

'Although I suspect I shall be behaving in Inquisitor mode during the early days of my appointment,' Beppe had ventured to say.

'But why did you kids change the two questions we had prepared?' asked Sonia out of genuine curiosity.

'I don't know, *mamma,*' replied Veronica. 'It just came out all of a sudden.'

'It just seemed a more important question than the one I made up before,' said Lorenzo.

'Maybe it was just those neutrinos at work,' suggested Beppe.

Nobody in the car either agreed or disagreed.

The family relapsed into a thoughtful silence.

For reasons that nobody could put a finger on, the children once again arrived unbidden in the parental bed that night – thereby delaying a return to marital intimacy by another twenty-four hours.

29: *The new Questore leaves his mark…*

Commissario Stancato became *Questore* Stancato very quietly one day during a ceremony attended by a handful of officials from Rome and his new-found friend, Alonzo di Domenico, the mayor of Terramonti. He had made it a condition of his appointment that the first few weeks would, of necessity, be spent in Pescara and Terramonti – aware that he held all the trump cards.

'I am humanly incapable of simply turning my back on my past life,' he had explained to some snooty official from Rome.

His first task as the new *Questore* was carried out with aplomb and ingenuity on Beppe's part – with the gleeful cooperation of the mayor. Beppe had outlined his devious plot over a 'return' lunch at *La Buona Forchetta* to celebrate his appointment. The simple food went some way to compensating Beppe for what he still considered to be a rash decision.

As soon as the appointment had been officially ratified, Beppe had summonsed a sharp young officer into his top floor quarters. His name was Mario Acrina.'

'*Congratulazioni, Signor Questore.* I have been praying this would happen ever since that morning I woke you up to remind you of your interview. Now, at last, our police headquarters has a chance of becoming functional once again.'

That day now seemed to Beppe to belong to another eon altogether. In point of fact, less than three weeks had elapsed.

'I thank you, *Agente* Acrina for your vote of confidence in me. I am sorry to have to single you out at such an early stage of our acquaintance, but you are in the unenviable position of being the only officer here whom I am sure I can trust. In fact, let us spell it out, you are the only officer I know.'

'*Sono a disposizione, capo!*' [127]

'Even if this involves grassing up a couple of your fellow officers, Mario?' asked Beppe with an intense look on his face.

Agente Acrina remained unrattled.

'If they are the couple of characters whom I suspect you are referring to, it will be a pleasure, *Commissario.* I can't wait!'

Mario Acrino corrected his slip-of-the-tongue immediately. The mistaken title had not even registered with Beppe.

'I'm sorry, *signore...dottore.* [128] A slip of the tongue. You act and talk like a policeman. I think you will shake up the state of lethargy that has existed in this *Questura* for far too long.'

'To be honest, *agente* Mario – I feel much more like a policeman than a *questore.* I am not intending to take on the role of being an aloof public official any time soon.'

Agente Acrina simply replied: *'Meno male, Signor Questore!'* [129]

'I have a list of names of every police officer posted here. Would you be able to identify the individuals we are talking about? I only know them as Officer G and Officer L. Does that ring any bells, with you *Agente* Mario?' asked Beppe hopefully.

Mario Acrina was looking smug.

'Spot on, *signore!* How on earth did you find out so soon? You have only just set foot in this *Questura.'*

'I have my sources, *Agente* Acrina. But he was very cautious about revealing their identity. He only gave me the first letter of their surnames.'

---

[127] I am at your disposal, chief.
[128] Agente Acrina is not certain as to which of the two correct titles to use.
[129] Just as well...

'Their names are Alessandro Gualtieri and Adamo Lombardi. Nobody has either dared nor summoned up the energy to denounce them. So, they are becoming increasingly self-confident in their own immunity. Last week, I gather, they took away a young lady's ID card, until she had agreed to have her apartment redecorated. She was too scared of looking stupid and being dismissed as a hysterical young woman to report them. They have become very adept at intimidation, it seems – always accompanied by an unctuous smile.'

'I have arranged a meeting of every single officer this afternoon at 15.00 hours. Could you give me a nod if both officers are present, Mario? Just so there is no confusion.'

'Of course, I will, *capo*. You will quickly identify them. They inevitably show off in public – simply because nobody of any rank has ever dared to pull them up. They have set themselves up as the team's comedians.'

'I shall take great pleasure in demolishing them! Thank you for your help, *Agente* Mario.'

'*Il piacere è mio, dottore.*' [130]

* * *

There were twenty-one officers – of whom only three were women – waiting with a bored air of *déjà vu* on their faces as Beppe stepped into the room, declining to mount the dais which he assumed he was supposed to stand on. He had forced himself to wear an informal suit on his first official day as *Questore,* but had refused Sonia's suggestion that he wear a tie. 'One metre of self-strangulation!' he had objected.

---

[130] The pleasure is mine. A questore is not technically a police officer. Thus 'dottore' or 'signore' is the correct polite or informal form of address.

The new *Questore* had the impression that the gathered officers had no idea as to why they had been convened – and therefore they had no reason to acknowledge his arrival.

Beppe had caught the eye of his one-and-only ally in the camp – *Agente* Mario Acrina – who had simply nodded, as arranged. Beppe had no difficulty in identifying the two rogue officers. It had to be the couple of cocky young males who were exchanging cynical smirks in the back row.

'I gather that one of you must be in charge – presumably enjoying the rank of *Commissario,*' stated Beppe in a voice laden with heavy sarcasm. 'Maybe you would care to make yourself known? I am the new *Questore* – Signor Giuseppe Stancato – from Calabria.'

The two back-row wise-guys pretended to stifle a snigger at the new arrival's surname. [131] A nondescript uniformed officer announced himself – reluctantly, Beppe thought - to be *Commissario* Bernadini, who made as if to stand up but immediately sat down again.

Beppe was beginning to enjoy himself in this new situation. Was it simply the challenge of being faced with a crew who gave the impression that police work was a mere side-line activity? There were perhaps a couple of faces which showed resentment – but the others didn't seem hostile, just weary of the meaningless routine.

'Well, now you know who I am. So you can all go about your usual business. I shall make a point of meeting you all individually, or in pairs if you prefer. Thank you for attending. *Potete andare.* [132] With the exception of...' Beppe pretended to be searching names from a list. 'Officers Gualtieri and Lombardi.'

---

[131] The 'weary one'
[132] You can go.

Beppe was looking round the assembled officers as if he had no idea of the identity of the two named individuals. The two male officers in question were looking at each other, wary of this newcomer.

'I have a special mission for you two,' said Beppe with feigned charm. 'My sources tell me that you two are very good at dealing with members of the public. I have reports of a couple of strangers – a man and a woman – who have just arrived in Terramonti. Would you be so good as to pay them the usual official visit? Make sure they are not Russian spies – you are familiar with the routine. Right now, please. You know what to do. Give them a bit of the official going-over as new-comers to Terramonti. Check their documents. Nothing too severe. I understand that the woman is blind.'

He handed them a piece of paper with the address on. All sweetness and light, he added:

'*Grazie mille, ragazzi.* Let me know how you get on. Come to my office tomorrow at eleven o'clock.'

He left the two officers smirking at each other.

'He isn't going to give us any trouble,' said Alessandro Gualtieri airily to his mate. 'Come on, let's go.'

Beppe Stancato had very acute hearing. *Agente* Acrina, who was passing close by, raised a thumb in Beppe's direction.

* * *

'They really thought they had it easy, *Commissario,*' announced *Agente* Donato Pavone, who was accompanied by a smiling and relaxed-looking Annamaria Intimo.

'They found the leaky water pipe under the kitchen sink, just as you predicted, Beppe,' said Annamaria. 'Not difficult, since water was seeping out at a steady rate of knots from the loosened joint. They automatically assumed we were an easy target. I did my blind woman act beautifully – making coffee for them. I fumbled with the *moka* pot and deliberately missed the cups while I poured the coffee onto the tabletop. We must have both looked really dumb. Donato was practically falling over himself with gratitude at their every word. We were very convincing.'

'I actually wanted to punch that Lombardi bloke on the nose,' added Donato.

Beppe, Donato Pavone and Annamaria were sitting at Beppe's vast mahogany desk in his new office. It was nine o'clock in the morning.

'And did they offer to get the plumbing seen to at a special price?' asked Beppe.

'Yes, *capo,*' replied Donato. 'You can listen to the voice recorder now if you like. We got everything they said from the moment they walked through the door. Annamaria was brilliant. She kept moving closer to whichever of the two was speaking – as if she was deaf. The expression on their faces clearly indicated a degree of lust. At one point, Lombardi gave Gualtieri a knowing wink – implying that they should pay a return visit when I was not around.'

Beppe switched on the recording device and listened with a malicious smile on his face as the two officers condemned themselves to their just fate.

'Listen to how the tone of their voices change when we suggested we could find our own plumbers,' said Annamaria.

'Don't bother with anybody else, signori. Our plumbers are family members. And it could be your way of saying 'thank you' to us for not confiscating your documents.'

'Don't worry, Annamaria,' Donato could be heard saying in an obsequious voice. 'We'll go along with their kind offer.'

'*Bravi ragazzi!* Your first successful operation as members of the Terramonti police force.'

'Do you think there will be any trouble with my transfer to Terramonti, *capo?*' asked Donato.

'Or with my role as 'special investigator?' asked Annamaria, anxiously.

'None at all, I can assure you. Nobody argues with a *Questore!* Especially not one who is wielding his *scopa nuova,* [133] as I am.' I'll see you back here just before eleven o'clock. I'm sure you will manage to find something to do. Terramonti has a very pretty *centro storico.* '

'We are going to look for a small house to buy,' Annamaria informed her future *capo.* '

'A real case of love at first sight,' thought Beppe as the couple headed for the door. It was amazing how Donato Pavone's former veneer of shyness had been replaced by a quiet self-assurance. A quality which the then *Commissario* had suspected was lurking beneath the surface all along.

* * *

Agenti Lombardi and Gualtieri swaggered into the *Questore's* office – ten minutes late – like a couple of back-street teenage hoodlums who knew that nobody was likely to challenge them.

Beppe had mentally prepared the scenario which would follow as if he had been a film director with a clear image in his mind as to how this bit of live theatre should be enacted. He was

---

[133] New broom – as in the English idiomatic saying.

relishing the prospect of reducing these egotistical youths to the status of earth worms.

They entered, without an apology for their lateness, with a superior smirk on their faces. Beppe was fixing them both with his notorious, unblinking stare. He had put two chairs out. Lombardi pushed his younger colleague forwards as they both sat down on the chairs with their thighs insultingly wide apart.

'I do not recall inviting you to sit down,' stated Beppe with an edge of menace in his voice, which the two men had never encountered from anyone in charge of the *Questura* since their appointment.

Lombardi's first reaction was to look round at his 'audience' with a defiant look on his face. He had not really taken much notice of who was already in the room. He noticed with surprise that there were three of his uniformed 'colleagues' – *Agente* Mario Acrina, who was a bit of an arse-licker, another male officer and a female officer – whom he had always tried to flirt with. The fourth figure was a very striking-looking brunette. *Porco mondo!* It was that blind woman!

The smirk on his face had vanished.

'Stand up! To attention!'

It was the new *Questore* who had spoken without raising his voice – with an authority which Lombardi had never encountered in the short period he had been there.

'You will remain standing until I have finished with you two fake policemen. Then you will really need to sit down, I can assure you both.'

The two officers had turned pale. They looked exactly like two naughty adolescents caught out by their head teacher bullying in the playground.

'Now, I would invite you to look again at the young lady standing over there. Do you recognise her?'

267

'Yes, *Signor Questore*. She's the one you sent us round to interview, yesterday.'

It had been Officer Gualtieri who had replied with a degree of respect in his voice. He had seen the writing on the wall.

'Annamaria,' said Beppe. 'Do you recognise these two officers?'

'Yes, I do. They were the ones who came to our apartment yesterday.'

'That's nonsense!' shouted Officer Lombardi. 'She's completely blind. She can't identify us!'

'*Agente* Pavone, would you be so kind as to accompany Annamaria over here so she can identify these two gentlemen?'

Annamaria came up close to the two men. She drew in her breath.

'Yes, these are the two who came to that apartment yesterday. They smell of a particular brand of cheap cigarettes – and of corruption!'

'Thank you Annamaria. Now, *Agenti* Gualtieri and Lombardi… please take a closer look at the police officer who is next to Annamaria? Any comment you would like to make?'

It was the younger officer, Gualtieri, who first identified *Agente* Pavone as the other man who had been present when they had attempted to take advantage of that 'innocent' couple.

'Keep your mouth shut, Alessandro!' muttered Adamo Lombardi to his mate – who was in point of fact his cousin.

'Now, gentlemen, please be seated. There is something I would like you to listen to.'

The look of fear on their faces on hearing the ensuing recorded conversation of the day before was blatantly obvious.

'*Siamo spacciati!* [134]stated Officer Gualtieri to his partner in crime.

'When will you decide what will happen to us, *Signor Questore?*'

Officer Lombardi had realised belatedly that he would have to show some signs of respect for their new leader.

'Please give me some credit, ex-officer Lombardi. You are dismissed from the police force for a period of two years. I shall review your case after that period. We shall then decide if you are worthy of being reconsidered for this post. You will have to show evidence of the fact that you have made an effort to recompense financially all those whom you have conned in this town. Right now, you may phone your mother and ask her to bring you a change of civilian clothes to your cell downstairs. The uniform, which you are unfit to wear, will be kept in a safe place. You will not wear it again until I decide otherwise.'

As for you, young Alessandro, I have arranged for you to be transferred to a police station in Reggio Calabria for a period of one year. You will be in an area controlled by *La 'ndrangheta.* I trust you will learn the true significance of being a police officer during this period of exile. You will be expected down in Reggio Calabria a week today. I shall give you the details later on. Don't worry, *Agente* Gualtieri – we shall pay for your railway ticket.'

'You two have been let off lightly. You will thank our new *Questore* for the totally fair treatment that he has meted out to you. You don't really deserve such leniency.'

Beppe Stancato was standing there with his mouth open in astonishment. It had been ordinary *Agente* Mario Acrina who had uttered those totally unrehearsed words.

'I couldn't have put it better myself,' said Beppe with a wry smile. 'Now, officers, please escort these two miscreants – one to a cell until his mum turns up with some clothing, and the

---

[134] We've had it!

other off the premises altogether. *Agente* Acrina, I have asked your *Commissario* to reassemble the whole team – minus these two – at 15.00 hours today. He will invite you to tell everybody exactly what has just taken place in my office. I shall join you at quarter past three. You should be there too, Annamaria and Donato. I will personally introduce you to your future colleagues.'

'*Agli ordini, Signor Questore!* stated Officer Acrina with a broad grin on his face.

* * *

Beppe Stancato – who was quite sure he had not acted like a proper *Questore* on this, the first day of his new career – walked into the meeting room as soon as he heard that *Agente* Acrina had come to the end of his narrative, which had been delivered to a disbelieving group of police officers.

Beppe was completely taken aback when all the officers – bar the two who were not there – had risen to their feet and began applauding the man who had just stepped through the door. Approximately forty eyes were turned on him. They kept up the respectful clapping for half a minute – until Beppe held up two hands, as if in surrender.

'*Bravo, Signor Questore!*' called out the voice of a uniformed police woman. They all sat down again, waiting for Beppe to speak.

'I thank you for your favourable appraisal,' said Beppe. 'I am sure that we will become a very successful bunch of *sbirri.*'

At long last, two or three of those present managed a smile at his irreverent last words.

'The only aspect of life here that I would like to mention is that you may look forward to there being a greater proportion of lady officers over the next few months. The number three – at present – will swell to four immediately. May I introduce you to Annamaria Intimo who will fulfil a special role amongst you. She is – almost – blind, but she was an indispensable witness in the case of the recent mafia killing in Pescara. I am certain you know the case I am referring to. Annamaria has talents which are unique. It is now a legend among the police team in Pescara that Annamaria's special gifts enabled her to detect the killers - thanks exclusively to her sense of smell. The mafia clan involved, unwisely sent a mobster who worked in a sardine canning plant in Calabria to do his dirty work. I beg of you to give her a warm welcome. Her *fidanzato, Agente* Donato Pavone, is here with her. He has rashly put in for a transfer from Pescara to the *Questura* here in Terramonti. It seems he did not want to let me out of his sight.'

This time, the subdued laughter was a bit more audible.

'I shall be in Pescara for the next few days – just to say my farewells. But I am genuinely looking forward to working with you all. I am a policeman at heart – not a senior administrator. You should all be very aware of this shortcoming of mine.'

'That suits us well, *Signor Questore!*' It was the present *Commissario* who had spoken – smiling for the first time in ages, so Officer Mario Acrina had informed Beppe, before he, Beppe, headed out of the building for his drive back home to Atri.

'Quite a good day at the office, *amore,*' Beppe told Sonia as they kissed and embraced as if nothing had changed in their lives.

30:   *Plus ça change...?*

The first big change that took place was the addition to the Stancato family of a baby girl, whose name was decided after a fiery dispute between Veronica and Lorenzo as to whose right it was to choose the new name. Veronica had wanted to call her baby sister Asia. Lorenzo pointed out that this was not a suitable first name. He had wanted to call her Francesca.

'That's just because it's the name of the girl you fancy in your class, Lori,' Veronica had teased her brother.

Beppe had intervened, placing an arm round each child.

'As it was your mother who did all the hard work, shall we let her have first choice of name?'

'Why don't we call her Elena?' Sonia suggested. 'I think Elena is a lovely name. 'Elena Stancato sounds just right to me,' And so, the argument was settled amicably enough.

The second change was far more radical. After a suitable period of time following Elena's birth, Beppe and Sonia were united together in intimate love – unhindered by the swelling which was to become their new daughter. It was at that moment of time, when they both felt properly reunited, that the subject of moving house was born.

'We always wanted to live in the country, didn't we, *amore?*' said Sonia. 'And it would make a lot of sense to live somewhere less than forty kilometres away from where you work.'

The idea was tentatively mentioned round the breakfast table the following morning. As luck would have it, Veronica had suffered a minor conflict the day before with her new teacher. Thus, she was more amenable to the notion of moving than she might otherwise have been. The family discussed the idea with Sonia's parents, who were entirely supportive.

'We often drive to Terramonti,' Irena said, 'when we go and visit your brother, Francesco. It will be *due piccioni con una fava!*' [135]

The mayor of Terramonti, Alonzo di Domenico, was delighted when Beppe informed him of his family's intention of looking for a suitable house to live, in or near the town.

'The schools are really first-rate here – especially the *Liceo Scientifico,* for when your kids get a bit older. And it just so happens that my brother-in-law is an estate agent in Terramonti. He is really charming and thorough – and not at all like your run-of-the-mill *agenti immobiliari.*'

And so it was that, after seeing only five houses, the Stancato family were shown a house which they all fell in love with immediately. It would have been quite beyond their financial resources had it not been for Beppe's salary as a *Questore.* It had already become apparent to Beppe that his new position would take him up to retirement age - if not beyond.

The house, which had modest 'grounds' – rather than just a garden – was only four kilometres into the Abruzzese countryside.

'There are more trees visible here than houses,' Sonia had said delightedly.

'Can I have a pony?' was Veronica's first question on completion of the signing of the contract.

'I could take up archery,' proclaimed Lorenzo. Apparently, he had fallen in love with Robin Hood and nurtured a hidden longing to learn how to use a bow and arrow.

Sonia's long-standing desire to cultivate a herb garden could finally come to fruition.

---

[135] Two birds with one stone

Their only 'extravagant' act was to purchase two brand new cars. A family-sized FIAT 500X and a modest Alfa Romeo sport's car for the new *Questore.*

Beppe simply enjoyed running round the garden and up into the open hills. He even found he had time at his disposal to learn how to play chess properly. He had frequent 'coffee-break' games going with *Agente* Mario Acrino – who, initially, would beat Beppe soundly.

'Chess helps you to trap fraudsters and money-launderers,' the young officer claimed. 'It's pure strategy.'

The Stancato family made regular visits to the coast where Beppe's boat, *L'Angelo Custode,* was moored. Only shopping became part of a necessary routine – but their nearest out-of-town supermarket was only a short car ride away.

Veronica and Lorenzo had a short daily walk to the spot where the yellow *scuolabus* picked up the children and teenagers who lived in the outlying districts of Terramonti. They were both as satisfied with school life as children ever can be.

Elena turned out to be a happy, normal child – spoilt by her two siblings who vied with each other for her attention.

Only Beppe's mother protested regularly that her son had moved even further away from her than when they lived in faraway Pescara.

'I don't know why you didn't just go and live on Mars, Beppe!' she stated bitterly on one occasion.

But the real joy arose from Sonia and Beppe's ability to invite their many friends to stay with them. Mariastella Martellini and her Spanish pilot *fidanzato* were among their earliest guests.

'I have to tell you, Beppe and Sonia, that we have Asia living with us for now. She has had to escape from Reggio

Calabria with great reluctance after her rescue of you, Beppe. The local clans have cottoned on to the fact that she was working for the DIA. Her life may be in danger until the clans lose interest in her existence.'

'Why didn't you bring her with you today, Mariastella?' asked Sonia challengingly.

'Well, in light of...you know,' she finished lamely.

'Asia Sposato saved my husband's life. I want to hug her – not plunge a knife into her back,' said Sonia, with all the fire of her early womanhood rekindled.

Beppe simply stood up and kissed Sonia on the mouth – a gesture that he would never normally do in public.

'I am relieved to hear you speak in that way, Sonia,' stated the lady *questore,* 'because Asia has expressed a wish to join the police force of Terramonti – as soon as I told her about your new appointment, Beppe.'

'Has she found a man yet?' asked Beppe.

'No, I don't think so,' replied Mariastella.

Beppe did not need to glance once in Sonia's direction before he spoke. Doing so would have amounted to an insult to Sonia's integrity.

'We desperately need more ladies on the team, Mariastella. Send her to me as soon as she is ready. There are so many eligible bachelors amongst them – especially one I can think of, who would leap over every hurdle to have a *fidanzata* like her!'

And so, as they say, it came to pass.

Another visitor who was welcomed by the whole family was Annamaria Intimo – now engaged to be married. She sometimes liked to be there on her own - when there were no 'special cases' for her to work on.

One warm, sunny day she arrived by taxi during the afternoon. She thought she knew the geography of the grounds well enough to risk a solitary after-dinner walk.'

'But it will be dark soon, Annamaria,' said Veronica kindly.

'The darkness does not bother me, Vero! I'll only walk to the top of the slope, and back.'

But the sun was already sinking and there was no sign of Annamaria.

'We must go and look for her, *papà,*' pleaded Veronica.

Beppe, Veronica and Lorenzo set off up the hill. Lorenzo spotted Annamaria kneeling on the grass, motionless – as if she was praying. She heard the footsteps of the approaching family behind her. She stood up to face them. Veronica noticed she had tears on her cheeks and ran towards her to comfort her. Beppe had realised that, since she had turned ten, Veronica had become far more *simpatica* towards the human race in general.

'*Che cos'hai,* Annamaria? *What's the matter?*'

She had learnt this phrase during her English lessons at school and felt proud of her achievement.

''Nothing at all, Vero. I was just admiring the beauty of the sunset.'

* * *

Several peaceful months elapsed before the new *Questore* encountered his first real challenge. It would help him overcome his sense of guilt that his life was becoming a sinecure – an overpaid sinecure. His overall opinion, which he kept to himself, was simply that the position of *commissario* deserved to be remunerated a great deal more generously than it was under the present system.

He became very adept at giving advice to those below him in rank – almost without getting up from behind his desk. But he was never entirely satisfied unless he was mingling with 'his' team of officers – who now numbered six women. On that front, some slow progress had been made. But he was pleasantly surprised to learn – by accidently overhearing one of the team talking to a fellow officer – that he was referred to in the ranks as *Commissario Numero Due*.

'Who initiated that nickname?' he asked an officer called *Ispettore* Mario Acrina.

'If I remember correctly, it was my *fidanzata, Agente* Asia Sposato, *dottore.*'

'That does not surprise me at all,' replied Beppe.

Some weeks later, during a conversation with *Colonnello* Pasquale Precopio, Beppe learnt with some satisfaction that the young woman, Flora Nisticò, whom they had known as Laura Ianni, had been reunited with her family in Calabria before she was laid to rest in the family tomb. Gregorio Giuffrè was tried and sentenced to life imprisonment for the murder of Flora Nisticò, the attempted murder of Fausto Talarico and Annamaria Intimo – plus the rape of a girl of fourteen, whose name was withheld.

Beppe sighed nostalgically as he replayed in his mind the details of his final investigation as a mere *commissario*.

FINE

Author's notes:

1: I have made much play in this novel of the ability of a blind person to take an active part in the work of crime detection. Although I fondly imagined that I had come up with a very original idea, I was 'disturbed' to discover that the Italian state television, RAI, has run two series of an outstandingly good production called simply, Blanca, about a young blind woman who assists the police in Genova – acted by an Italian actress called Maria Chiara Gianetta. There was even an episode in the second series where Blanca falls off a boat into the sea – which I watched literally only days after I had written about Annamaria Intimo doing the same thing.

The only real-life case of a police force employing a blind person because of their special form of awareness is a police force in Belgium. But I suspect that there must be other similar cases somewhere on this planet.

2: The unusual expression in Italian, *In bocca al lupo,* meaning 'Best of luck' is literally translated as 'In the mouth of the wolf'. The traditional reply is *Crepi!* – which means something like 'Drop dead, wolf.' The more humane and newer version of the correct reply is *Viva il lupo!* – 'Long live the wolf!'

I have not yet come across any Italian who has been able to furnish me with an explanation of the origins of this oft-used expression. I have always suspected that it must be something to do with Romulus and Remus – the supposed founders of the city of Rome – being fed and nurtured by a wolf as abandoned children.

3: The role played by Officer Asia Sposato – who rescues Beppe from the hands of the *'ndrangheta* - is inspired by the character in the film version of Elena Ferrante's mind-blowing novel, *L'amica geniale* – 'My Brilliant Friend'.

In an attempt to bring the character of Asia Sposato to life, I found myself comparing her in appearance and behaviour to the strikingly beautiful young actress who so ably played the role of the 'young adult' Lina in the Rai production of Elena Ferranti's novel. The young actress's name is Ludovica Nasti – whose identity the characters in my novel can never quite recall. The 'fully adult' Lina's role was then taken over by Margherita Mazzucco in the sequel novels by Elena Ferrante.

4:      Miracles, ghosts, the Holy Spirit and neutrinos? Well, all I know is that life, the brain, quantum physics, the universe and everything, is still largely unexplained. I avoided the trap of attempting to 'prove' the existence of the supernatural during the course of this novel. That is a matter for each individual reader to interpret as they wish.

What I *have* done deliberately is to make a prominent feature of the contribution that Beppe's children make to the Stancato family's life. Many outstanding dramas that have influenced me on Italian television set great store by the presence of kids – most notably perhaps, a series which was called 'The Mafia only kills in the Summer' *La mafia uccide solo d'estate,* and a drama called simply *Sorelle* – 'Sisters'.

R.W. March 2024

Copyright © : Richard Walmsley 2024
(nonno-riccardo-publications)

All rights reserved

This book is copyright. Subject to statutory exception and to provisions of relevant collective agreements, no part of this publication may be reproduced, stored in a retrieval system, or transmitted in any form or by any means, without the prior consent of the author.

In this work of fiction, the characters, events and places are either the product of the author's imagination or they are used entirely fictitiously. The moral rights of the author have been asserted. Any resemblance to actual persons, living or dead, is purely coincidental – and used without malice or intent to represent factual reality in any form.

About the author

Richard Walmsley's novels reflect his dedication to and love of that extraordinary part of Europe called Italy – especially to the regions of Puglia and Abruzzo, where the novels are set.

Richard Walmsley lived, loved and taught English to the students of the Università del Salento – in Lecce. He also formed a strong attachment to Abruzzo – one of the most unspoilt regions of Europe.

He continues to decry and utterly reject the devastating political, cultural and economic alienation of the not very United Kingdom from its former European partners, whose history and culture we have shared for centuries. On a personal level, he feels cut off from his many friends and companions in Italy and France – due to an increasing number of travel restrictions. 'Una follia totale! Utter madness, in Richard's opinion.

He believes that our ties with Europe must survive the political catastrophe known as Brexit – the biggest example of political self-harm ever committed in the name of democracy.

He hopes that his novels – and short stories – will revive and sustain that feeling of oneness with Europe and its remarkable citizens. He wishes to thank all those who have enjoyed his novels so far – and especially those who have helped and encouraged him to keep on writing.

Printed in Great Britain
by Amazon